Winx Club™

Dragon's Flame

4

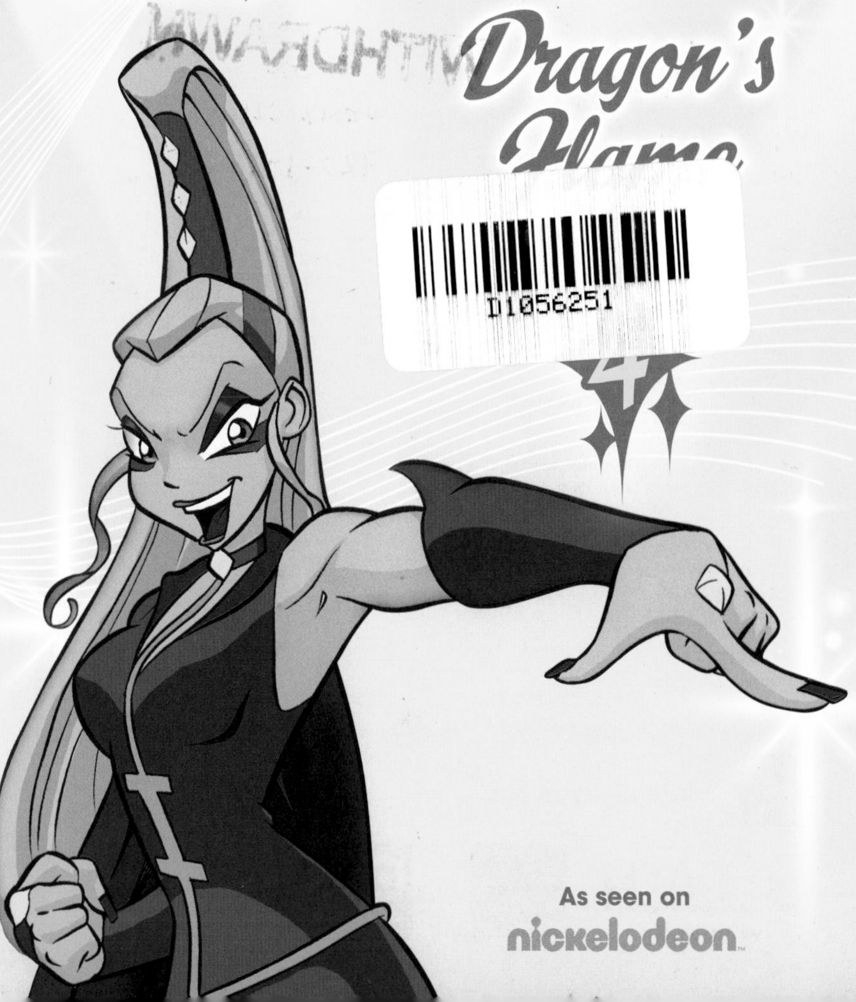

As seen on nickelodeon

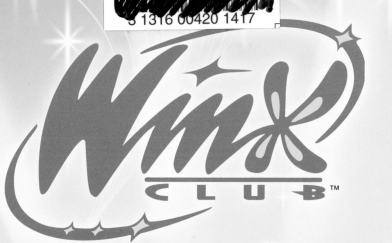

WITHDRAWN
WINX CLUB
420-1417

Winx Club
Volume 4

Winx Club ©2003–2012 Rainbow S.r.l. All Rights Reserved. Series
created by Iginio Straffi www.winxclub.com

Designer • Fawn Lau
Letterer • John Hunt
Editor • Amy Yu

The stories, characters and incidents mentioned in this
publication are entirely fictional.

No portion of this book may be reproduced without
written permission from the copyright holders.

Printed in China

Published by VIZ Media, LLC
P.O. Box 77010
San Francisco, CA 94107

10 9 8 7 6 5 4 3 2 1
First printing, November 2012

www.vizkids.com   www.viz.com

RATED
A
FOR
ALL AGES

PARENTAL ADVISORY
WINX CLUB is rated A and
is suitable for readers of
all ages.
ratings.viz.com

Table of Contents
Volume 4

Dragon's Flame
✦ 6 ✦

Magic Battle
✦ 51 ✦

WITHDRAWN
FRANKLIN PARK LIBRARY
FRANKLIN PARK, IL

Meet the Winx Club

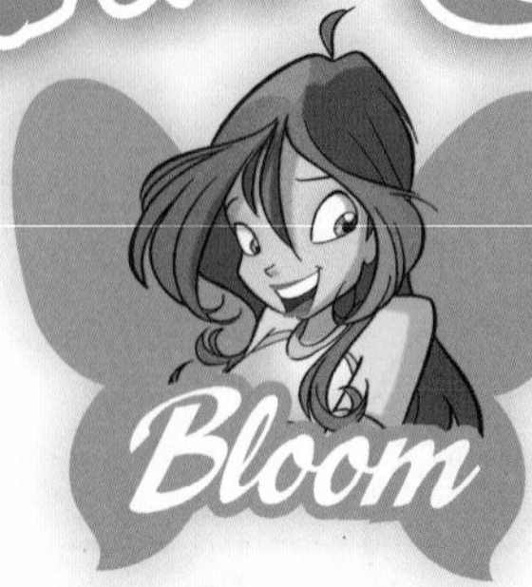
Bloom

Raised on Earth, **BLOOM** had no idea she had magical fairy powers until a chance encounter with Stella. Intelligent and loyal, she is the heart and soul of the Winx Club.

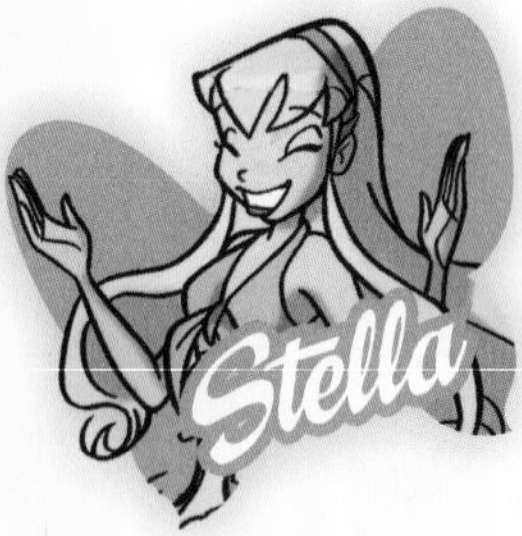
Stella

A princess from Solaria, **STELLA** draws her fairy power from sunlight. Optimistic and carefree, she introduces Bloom to the world of Magix.

Self-confident and a perfectionist, **TECNA** has a vast knowledge of science, which enables her to create devices that can get her and her friends out of trouble.

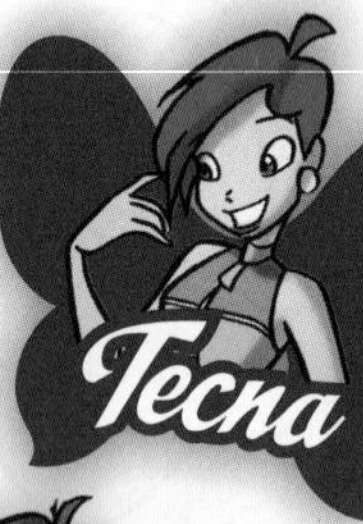
Tecna

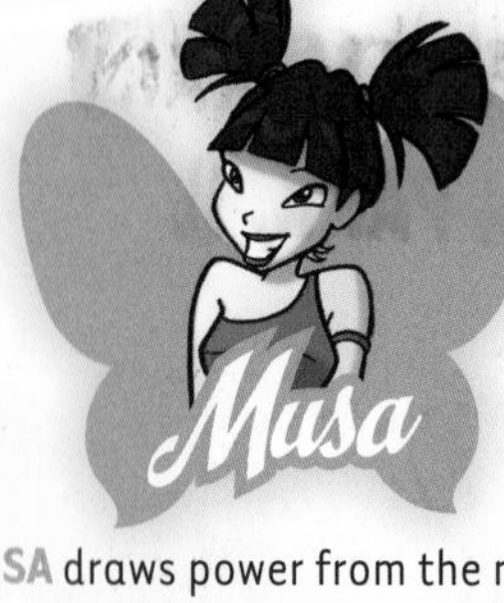
Musa

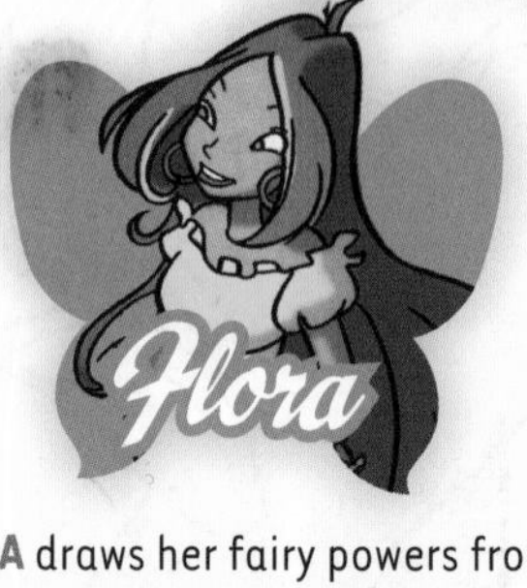
Flora

MUSA draws power from the music she plays. She has a natural talent for investigating, and she's got a keen eye for details.

FLORA draws her fairy powers from flowers, plants and nature in general. Sweet and thoughtful, she tends to be the peacemaker in the group.

Their Friends

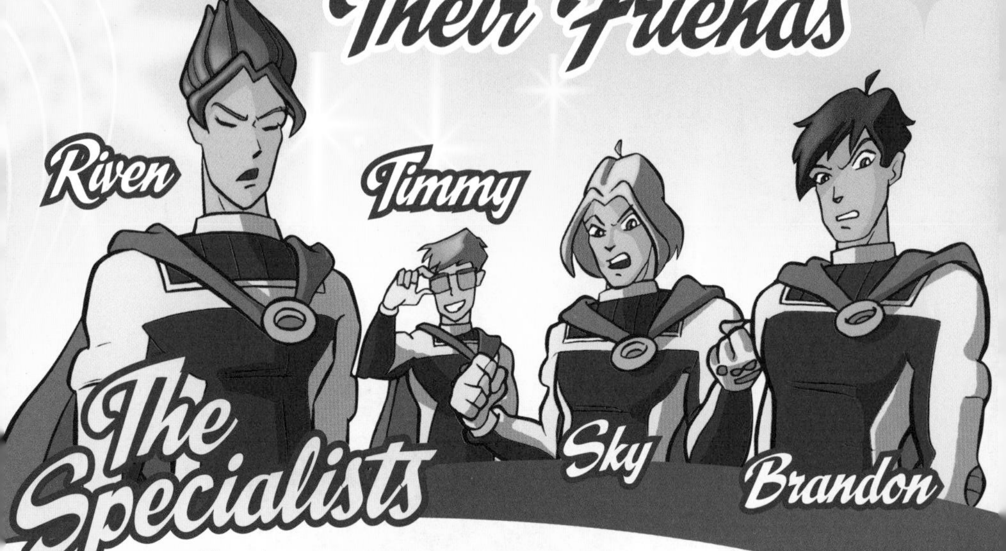
Riven
Timmy
Sky
Brandon

The Specialists

These boys from Red Fountain School are friends with the Winx Club girls and sometimes team up with them to fight trolls and other magical monsters.

Their Foes

THE TRIX are an evil trio of witches from Cloudtower Academy who battle the Winx Club regularly. With leader Icy's freezing powers, Stormy's weather-controlling powers, and Darcy's powers of darkness, these girls love to wreak havoc!

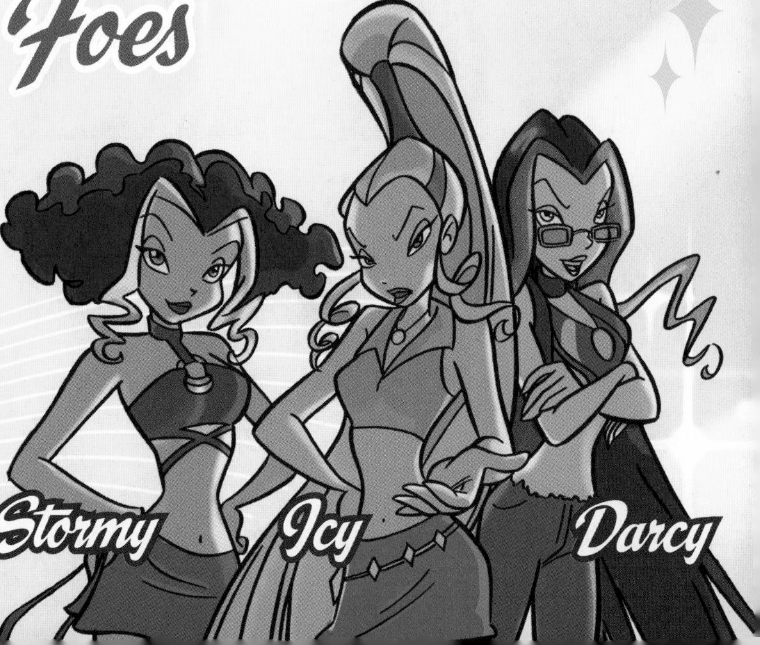
Stormy
Icy
Darcy

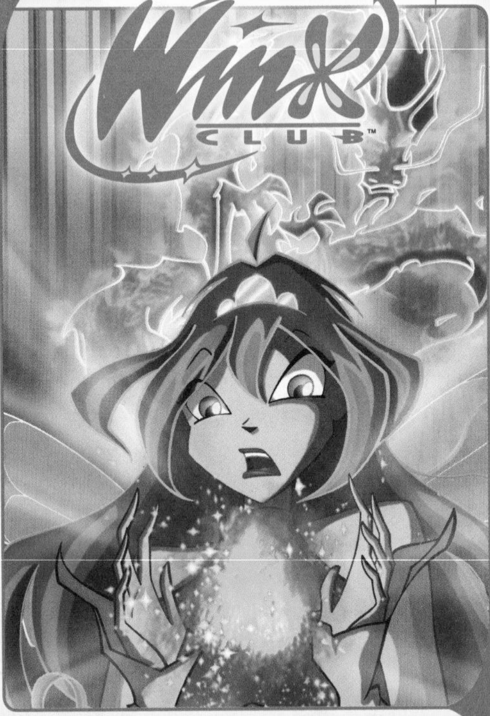
Winx
CLUB

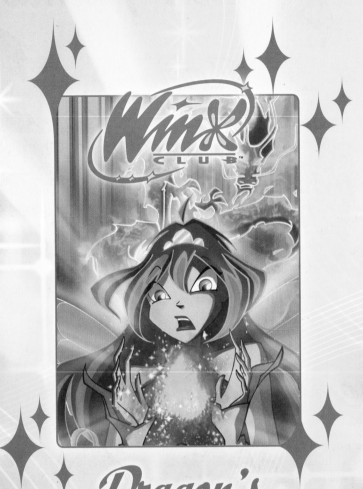

Dragon's Flame

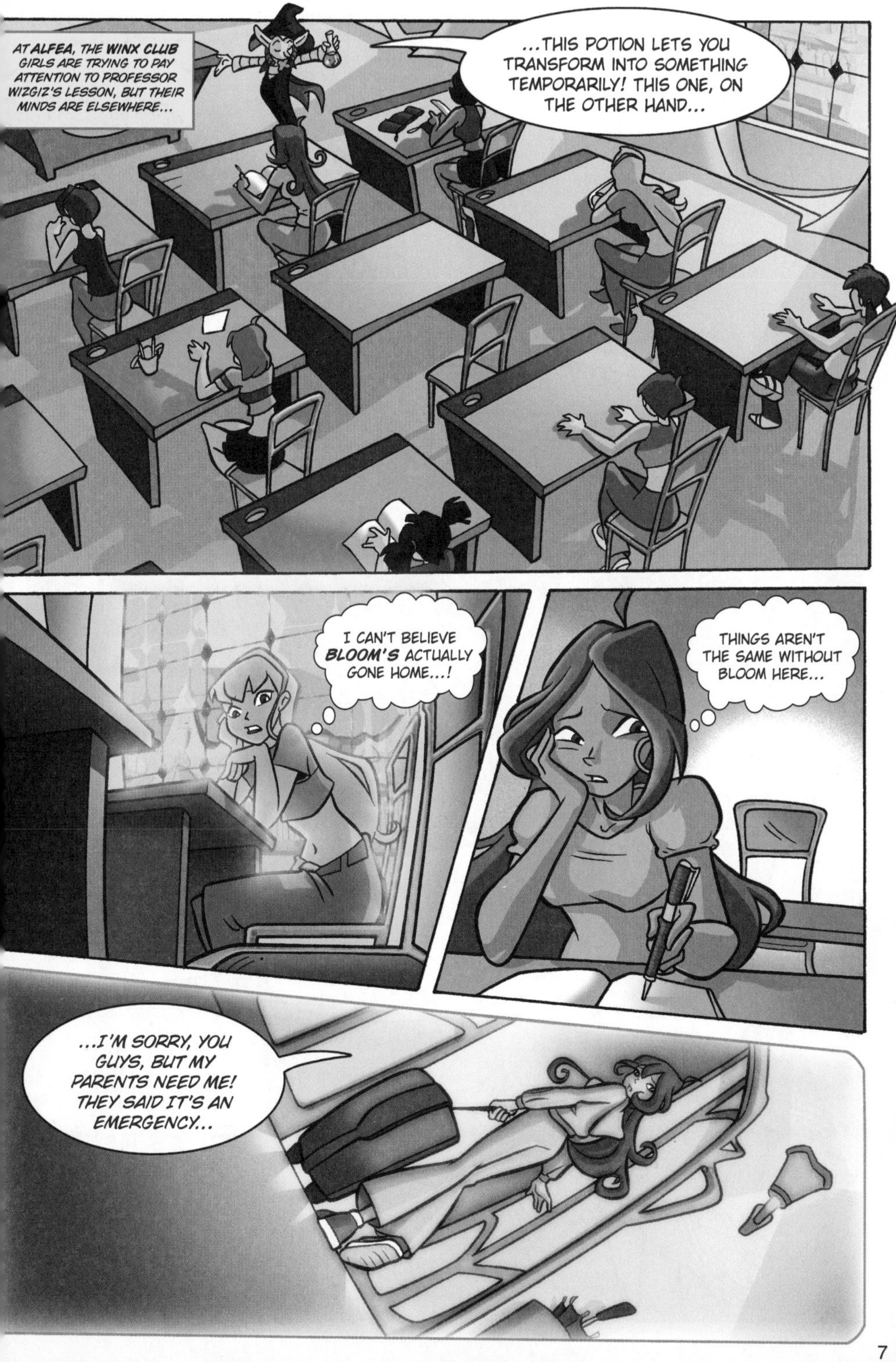
AT ALFEA, THE WINX CLUB GIRLS ARE TRYING TO PAY ATTENTION TO PROFESSOR WIZGIZ'S LESSON, BUT THEIR MINDS ARE ELSEWHERE...
...THIS POTION LETS YOU TRANSFORM INTO SOMETHING TEMPORARILY! THIS ONE, ON THE OTHER HAND...
I CAN'T BELIEVE BLOOM'S ACTUALLY GONE HOME...!
THINGS AREN'T THE SAME WITHOUT BLOOM HERE...
...I'M SORRY, YOU GUYS, BUT MY PARENTS NEED ME! THEY SAID IT'S AN EMERGENCY...

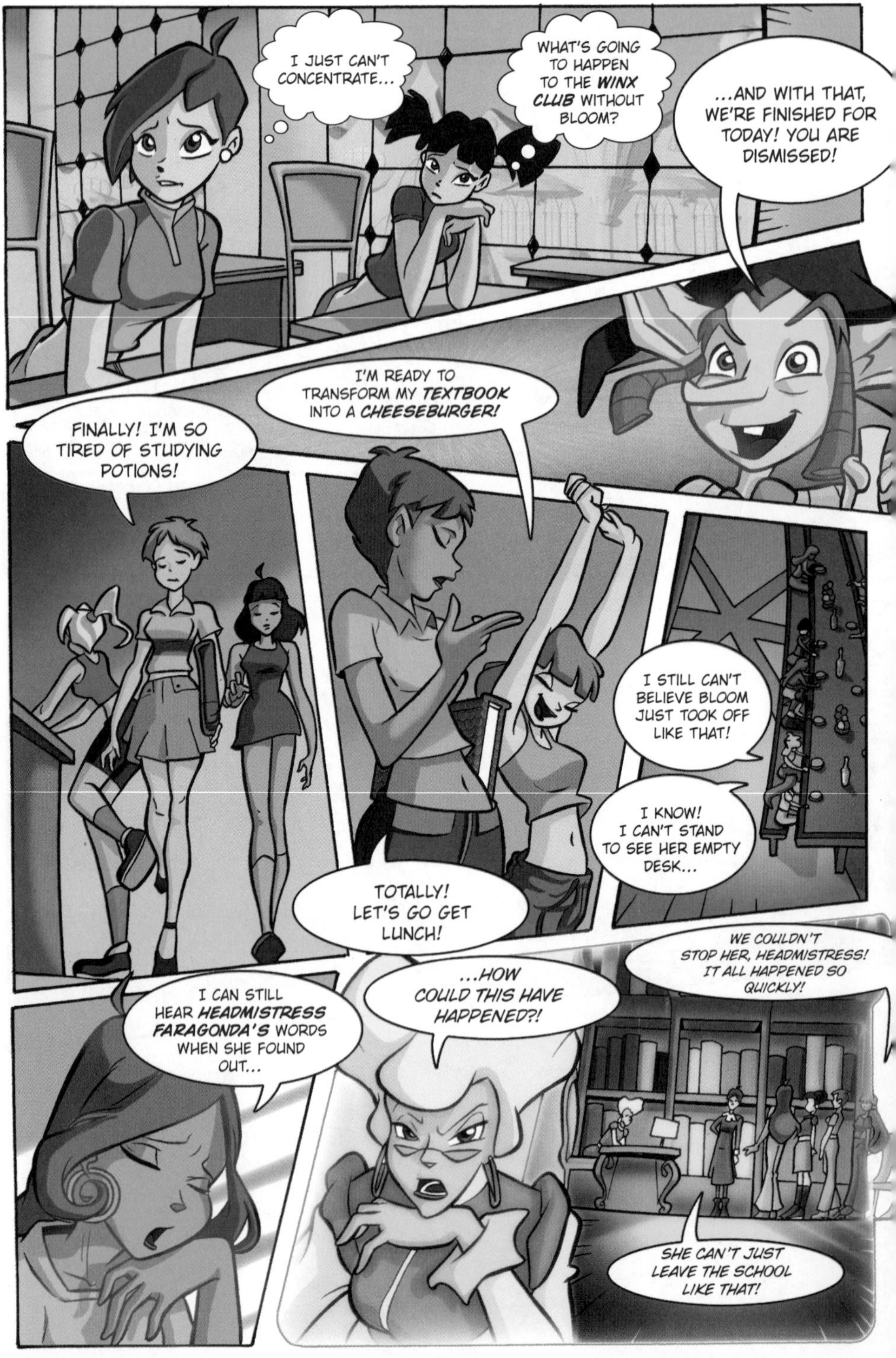
I JUST CAN'T CONCENTRATE...
WHAT'S GOING TO HAPPEN TO THE WINX CLUB WITHOUT BLOOM?
...AND WITH THAT, WE'RE FINISHED FOR TODAY! YOU ARE DISMISSED!
FINALLY! I'M SO TIRED OF STUDYING POTIONS!
I'M READY TO TRANSFORM MY TEXTBOOK INTO A CHEESEBURGER!
TOTALLY! LET'S GO GET LUNCH!
I STILL CAN'T BELIEVE BLOOM JUST TOOK OFF LIKE THAT!
I KNOW! I CAN'T STAND TO SEE HER EMPTY DESK...
I CAN STILL HEAR HEADMISTRESS FARAGONDA'S WORDS WHEN SHE FOUND OUT...
...HOW COULD THIS HAVE HAPPENED?!
WE COULDN'T STOP HER, HEADMISTRESS! IT ALL HAPPENED SO QUICKLY!
SHE CAN'T JUST LEAVE THE SCHOOL LIKE THAT!

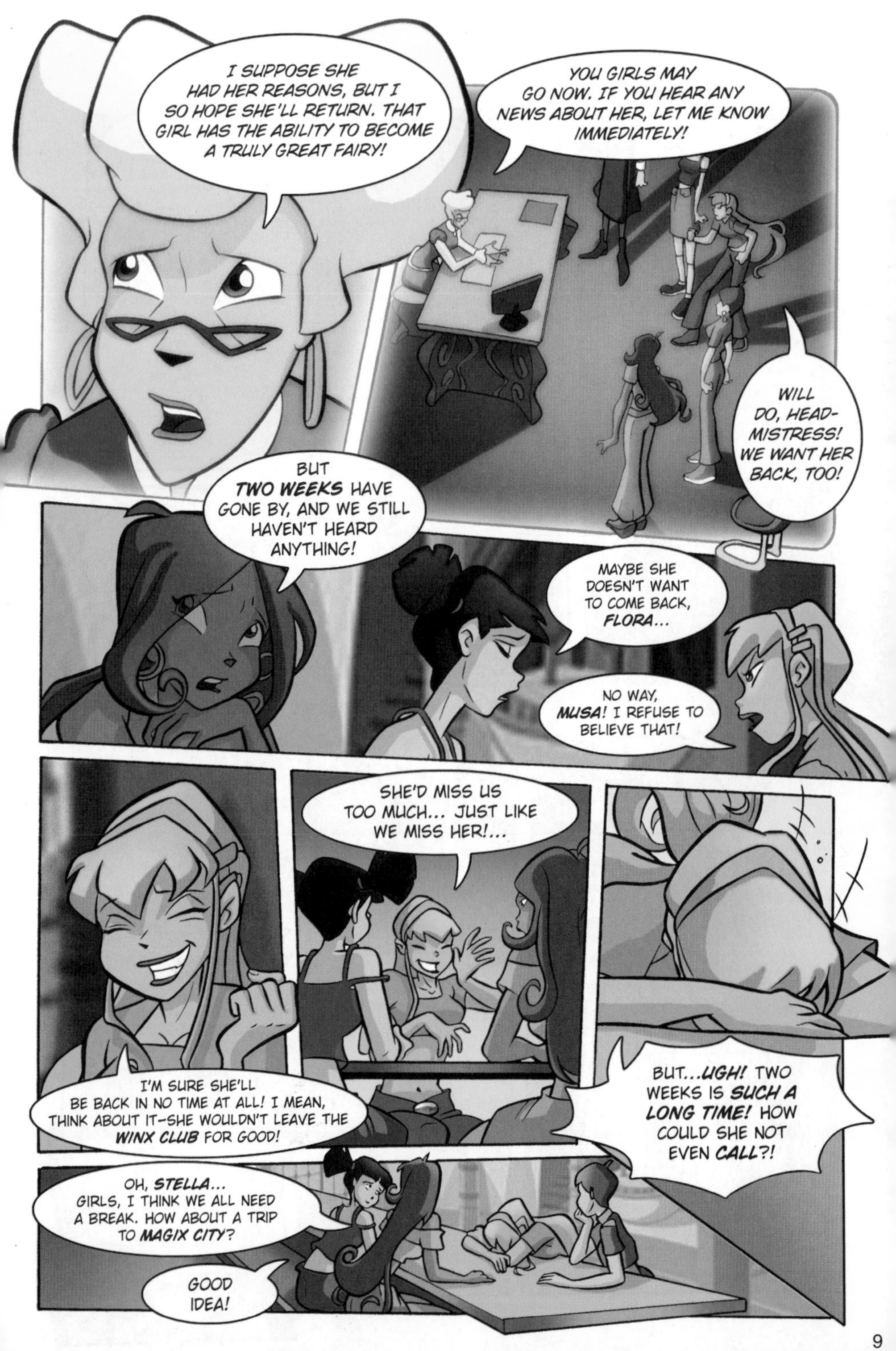
I SUPPOSE SHE HAD HER REASONS, BUT I SO HOPE SHE'LL RETURN. THAT GIRL HAS THE ABILITY TO BECOME A TRULY GREAT FAIRY!
YOU GIRLS MAY GO NOW. IF YOU HEAR ANY NEWS ABOUT HER, LET ME KNOW IMMEDIATELY!
WILL DO, HEAD-MISTRESS! WE WANT HER BACK, TOO!
BUT **TWO WEEKS** HAVE GONE BY, AND WE STILL HAVEN'T HEARD ANYTHING!
MAYBE SHE DOESN'T WANT TO COME BACK, **FLORA**...
NO WAY, **MUSA**! I REFUSE TO BELIEVE THAT!
SHE'D MISS US TOO MUCH... JUST LIKE WE MISS HER!...
I'M SURE SHE'LL BE BACK IN NO TIME AT ALL! I MEAN, THINK ABOUT IT—SHE WOULDN'T LEAVE THE **WINX CLUB** FOR GOOD!
BUT...**UGH!** TWO WEEKS IS **SUCH A LONG TIME!** HOW COULD SHE NOT EVEN **CALL**?!
OH, **STELLA**... GIRLS, I THINK WE ALL NEED A BREAK. HOW ABOUT A TRIP TO **MAGIX CITY**?
GOOD IDEA!

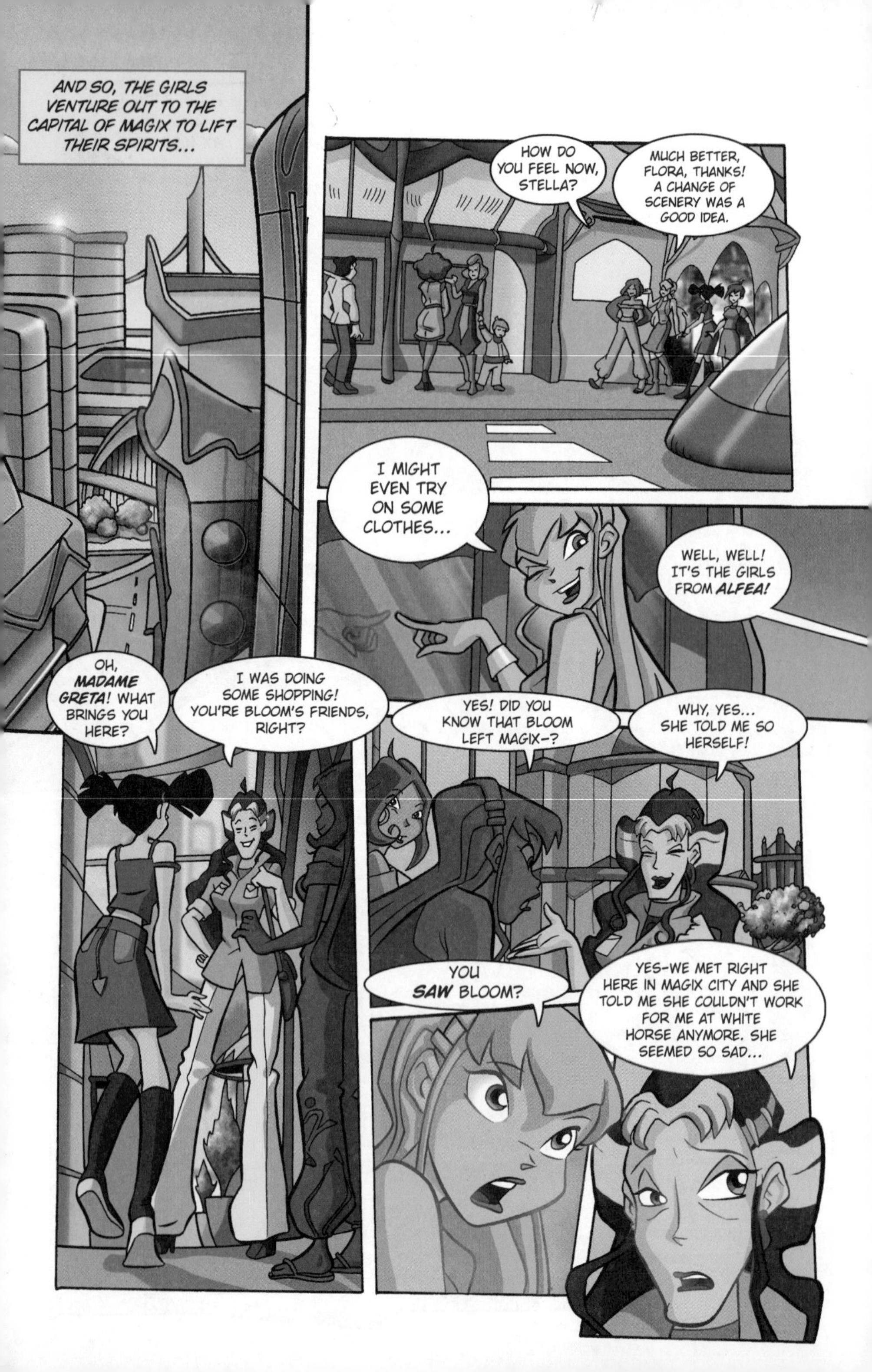
AND SO, THE GIRLS VENTURE OUT TO THE CAPITAL OF MAGIX TO LIFT THEIR SPIRITS...
HOW DO YOU FEEL NOW, STELLA?
MUCH BETTER, FLORA, THANKS! A CHANGE OF SCENERY WAS A GOOD IDEA.
I MIGHT EVEN TRY ON SOME CLOTHES...
WELL, WELL! IT'S THE GIRLS FROM ALFEA!
OH, MADAME GRETA! WHAT BRINGS YOU HERE?
I WAS DOING SOME SHOPPING! YOU'RE BLOOM'S FRIENDS, RIGHT?
YES! DID YOU KNOW THAT BLOOM LEFT MAGIX-?
WHY, YES... SHE TOLD ME SO HERSELF!
YOU SAW BLOOM?
YES-WE MET RIGHT HERE IN MAGIX CITY AND SHE TOLD ME SHE COULDN'T WORK FOR ME AT WHITE HORSE ANYMORE. SHE SEEMED SO SAD...

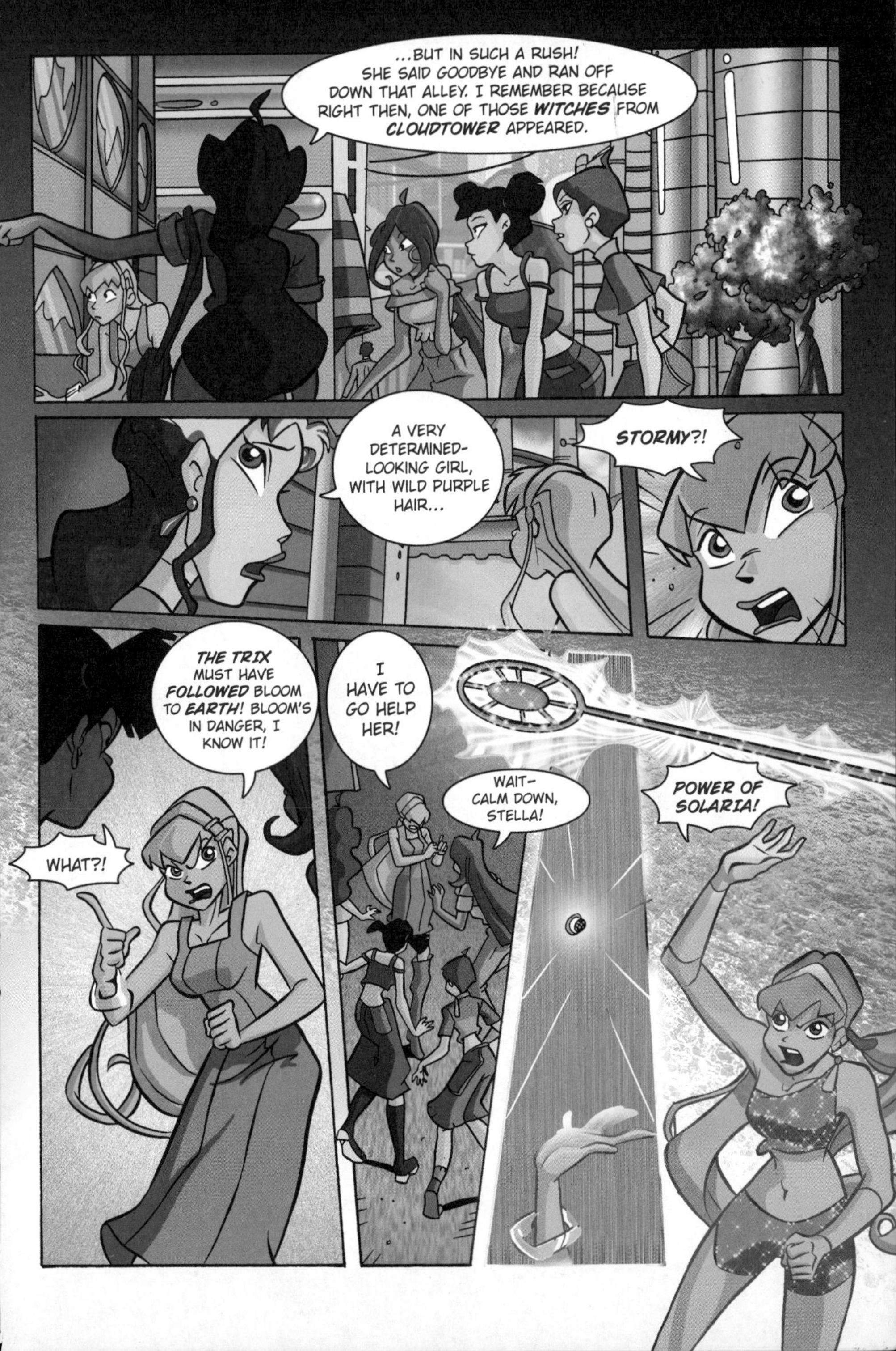
...BUT IN SUCH A RUSH! SHE SAID GOODBYE AND RAN OFF DOWN THAT ALLEY. I REMEMBER BECAUSE RIGHT THEN, ONE OF THOSE WITCHES FROM CLOUDTOWER APPEARED.
A VERY DETERMINED-LOOKING GIRL, WITH WILD PURPLE HAIR...
STORMY?!
WHAT?!
THE TRIX MUST HAVE FOLLOWED BLOOM TO EARTH! BLOOM'S IN DANGER, I KNOW IT!
I HAVE TO GO HELP HER!
WAIT-CALM DOWN, STELLA!
POWER OF SOLARIA!

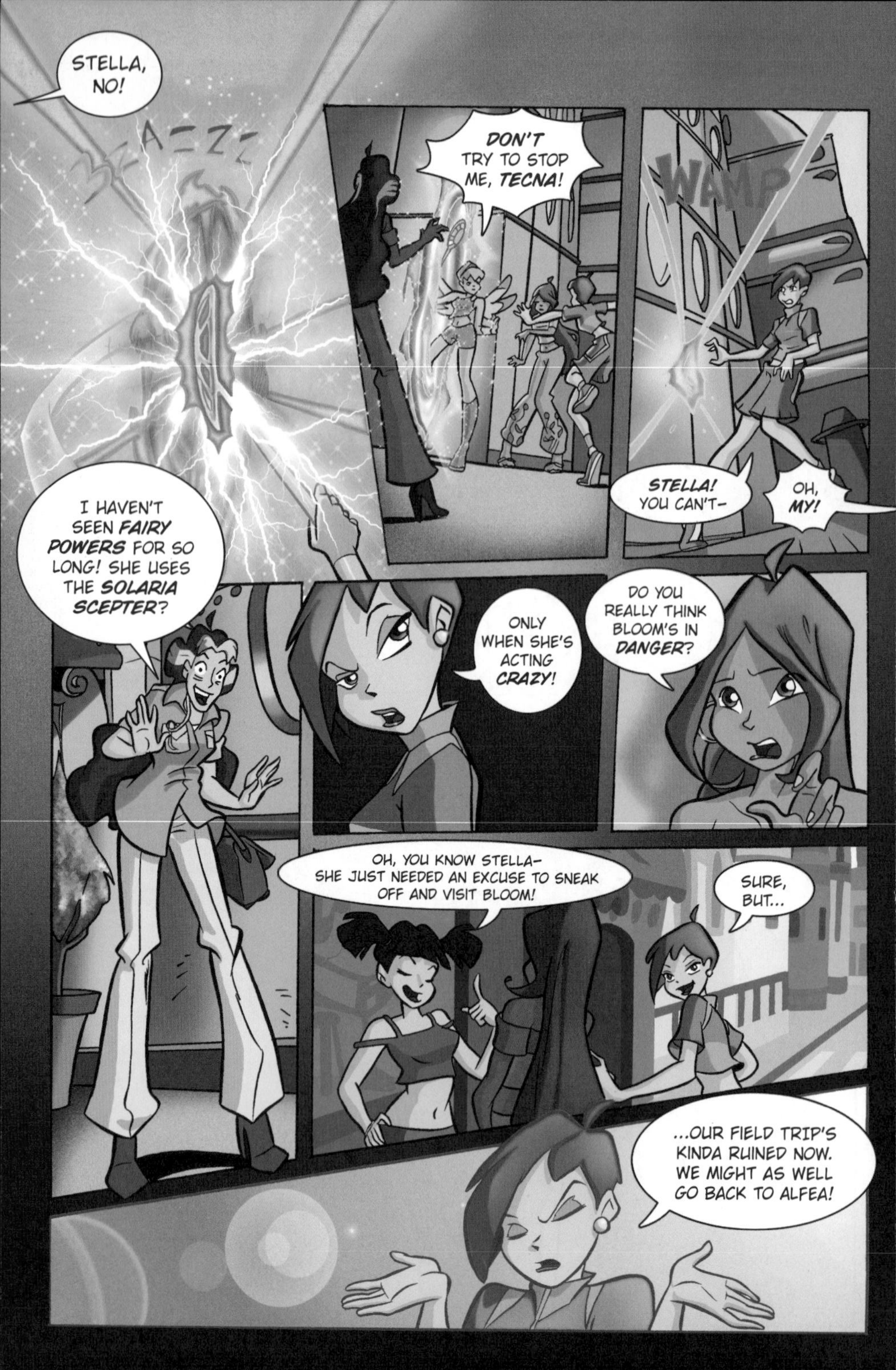
STELLA, NO!
BZZAZZZ
DON'T TRY TO STOP ME, TECNA!
WAMP
STELLA! YOU CAN'T-
OH, MY!
I HAVEN'T SEEN FAIRY POWERS FOR SO LONG! SHE USES THE SOLARIA SCEPTER?
ONLY WHEN SHE'S ACTING CRAZY!
DO YOU REALLY THINK BLOOM'S IN DANGER?
OH, YOU KNOW STELLA- SHE JUST NEEDED AN EXCUSE TO SNEAK OFF AND VISIT BLOOM!
SURE, BUT...
...OUR FIELD TRIP'S KINDA RUINED NOW. WE MIGHT AS WELL GO BACK TO ALFEA!

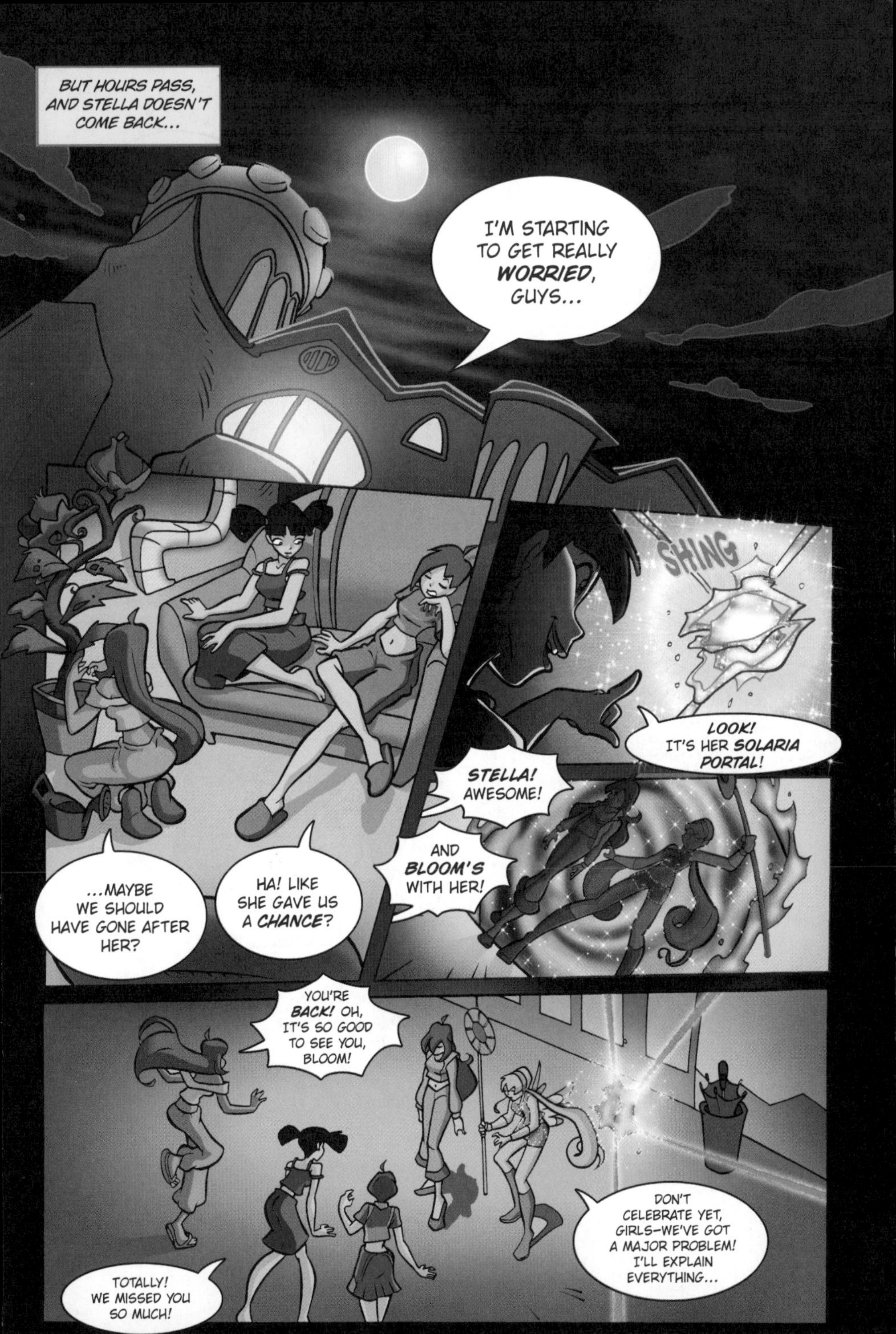
BUT HOURS PASS, AND STELLA DOESN'T COME BACK...
I'M STARTING TO GET REALLY WORRIED, GUYS...
...MAYBE WE SHOULD HAVE GONE AFTER HER?
HA! LIKE SHE GAVE US A CHANCE?
SHING
LOOK! IT'S HER SOLARIA PORTAL!
STELLA! AWESOME!
AND BLOOM'S WITH HER!
YOU'RE BACK! OH, IT'S SO GOOD TO SEE YOU, BLOOM!
TOTALLY! WE MISSED YOU SO MUCH!
DON'T CELEBRATE YET, GIRLS—WE'VE GOT A MAJOR PROBLEM! I'LL EXPLAIN EVERYTHING...

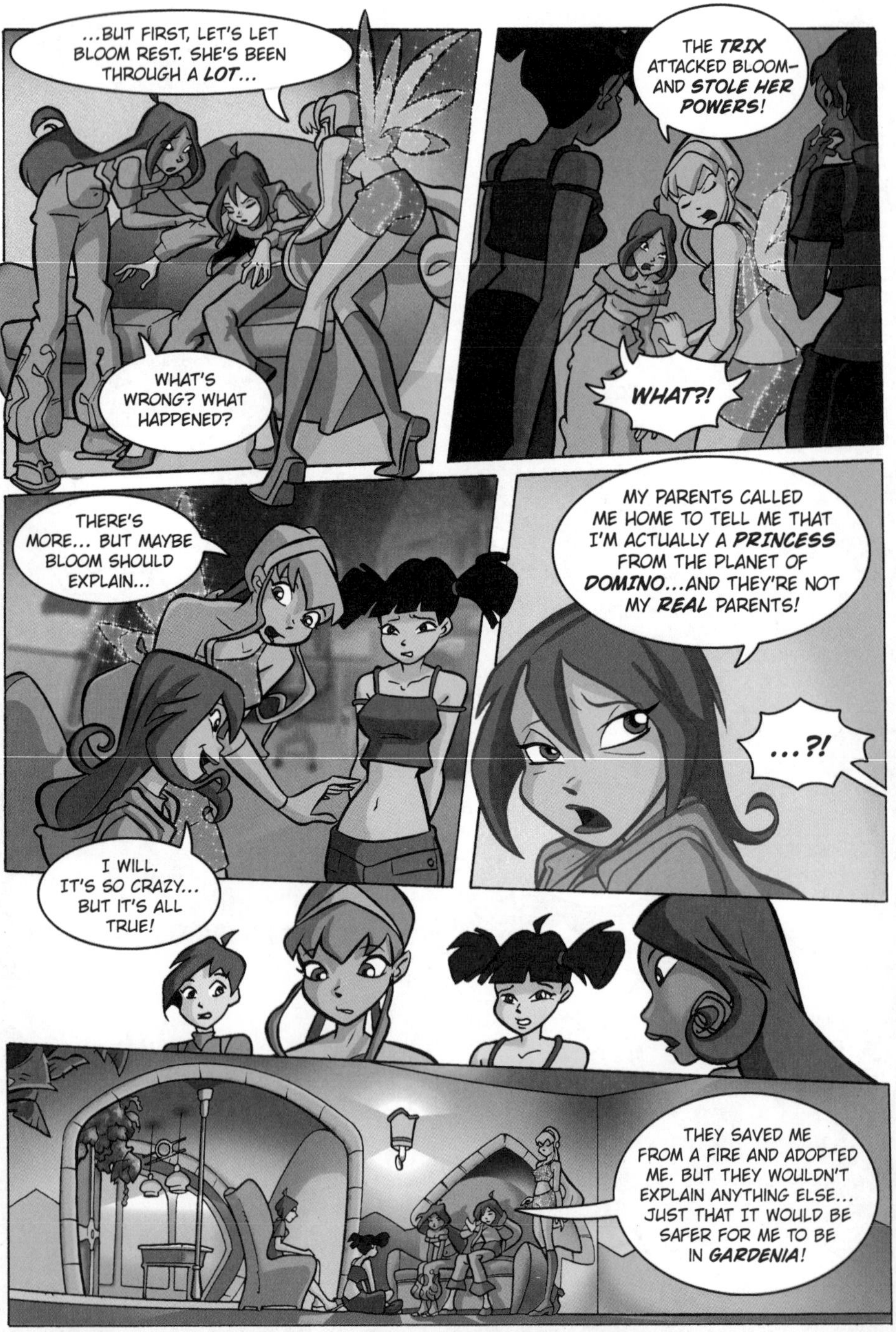
...BUT FIRST, LET'S LET BLOOM REST. SHE'S BEEN THROUGH A LOT...
WHAT'S WRONG? WHAT HAPPENED?
THE TRIX ATTACKED BLOOM– AND STOLE HER POWERS!
WHAT?!
THERE'S MORE... BUT MAYBE BLOOM SHOULD EXPLAIN...
I WILL. IT'S SO CRAZY... BUT IT'S ALL TRUE!
MY PARENTS CALLED ME HOME TO TELL ME THAT I'M ACTUALLY A PRINCESS FROM THE PLANET OF DOMINO...AND THEY'RE NOT MY REAL PARENTS!
...?!
THEY SAVED ME FROM A FIRE AND ADOPTED ME. BUT THEY WOULDN'T EXPLAIN ANYTHING ELSE... JUST THAT IT WOULD BE SAFER FOR ME TO BE IN GARDENIA!

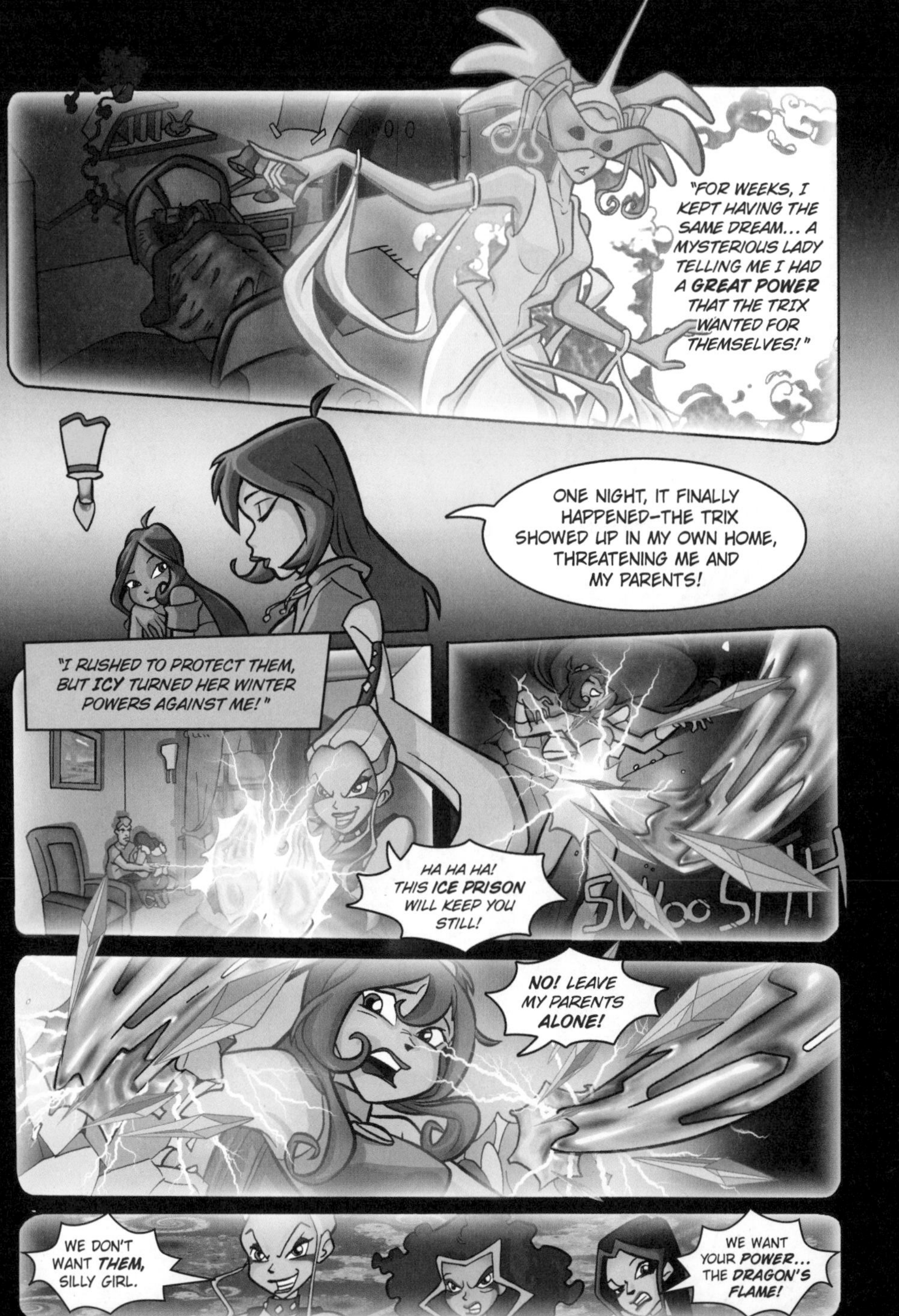

"FOR WEEKS, I KEPT HAVING THE SAME DREAM... A MYSTERIOUS LADY TELLING ME I HAD A **GREAT POWER** THAT THE TRIX WANTED FOR THEMSELVES!"
ONE NIGHT, IT FINALLY HAPPENED–THE TRIX SHOWED UP IN MY OWN HOME, THREATENING ME AND MY PARENTS!
"I RUSHED TO PROTECT THEM, BUT **ICY** TURNED HER WINTER POWERS AGAINST ME!"
HA HA HA! THIS **ICE PRISON** WILL KEEP YOU STILL!
SWOOSHH
NO! LEAVE MY PARENTS **ALONE!**
WE DON'T WANT **THEM,** SILLY GIRL.
WE WANT YOUR **POWER...** THE **DRAGON'S FLAME!**

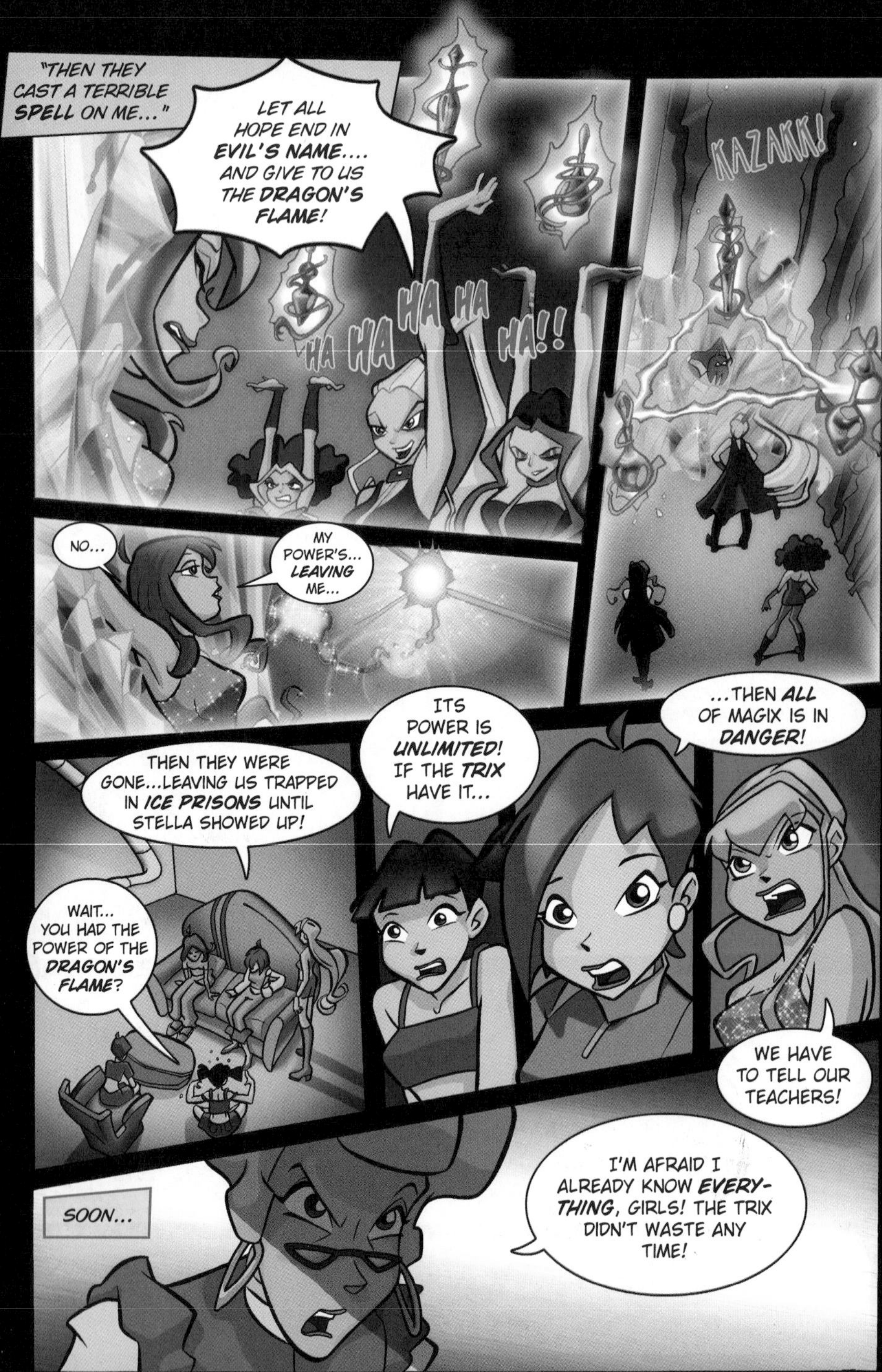
"THEN THEY CAST A TERRIBLE SPELL ON ME..."
LET ALL HOPE END IN EVIL'S NAME.... AND GIVE TO US THE DRAGON'S FLAME!
HA HA HA HA HA!!
KAZAKK!
NO...
MY POWER'S... LEAVING ME...
THEN THEY WERE GONE...LEAVING US TRAPPED IN ICE PRISONS UNTIL STELLA SHOWED UP!
WAIT... YOU HAD THE POWER OF THE DRAGON'S FLAME?
ITS POWER IS UNLIMITED! IF THE TRIX HAVE IT...
...THEN ALL OF MAGIX IS IN DANGER!
WE HAVE TO TELL OUR TEACHERS!
SOON...
I'M AFRAID I ALREADY KNOW EVERYTHING, GIRLS! THE TRIX DIDN'T WASTE ANY TIME!

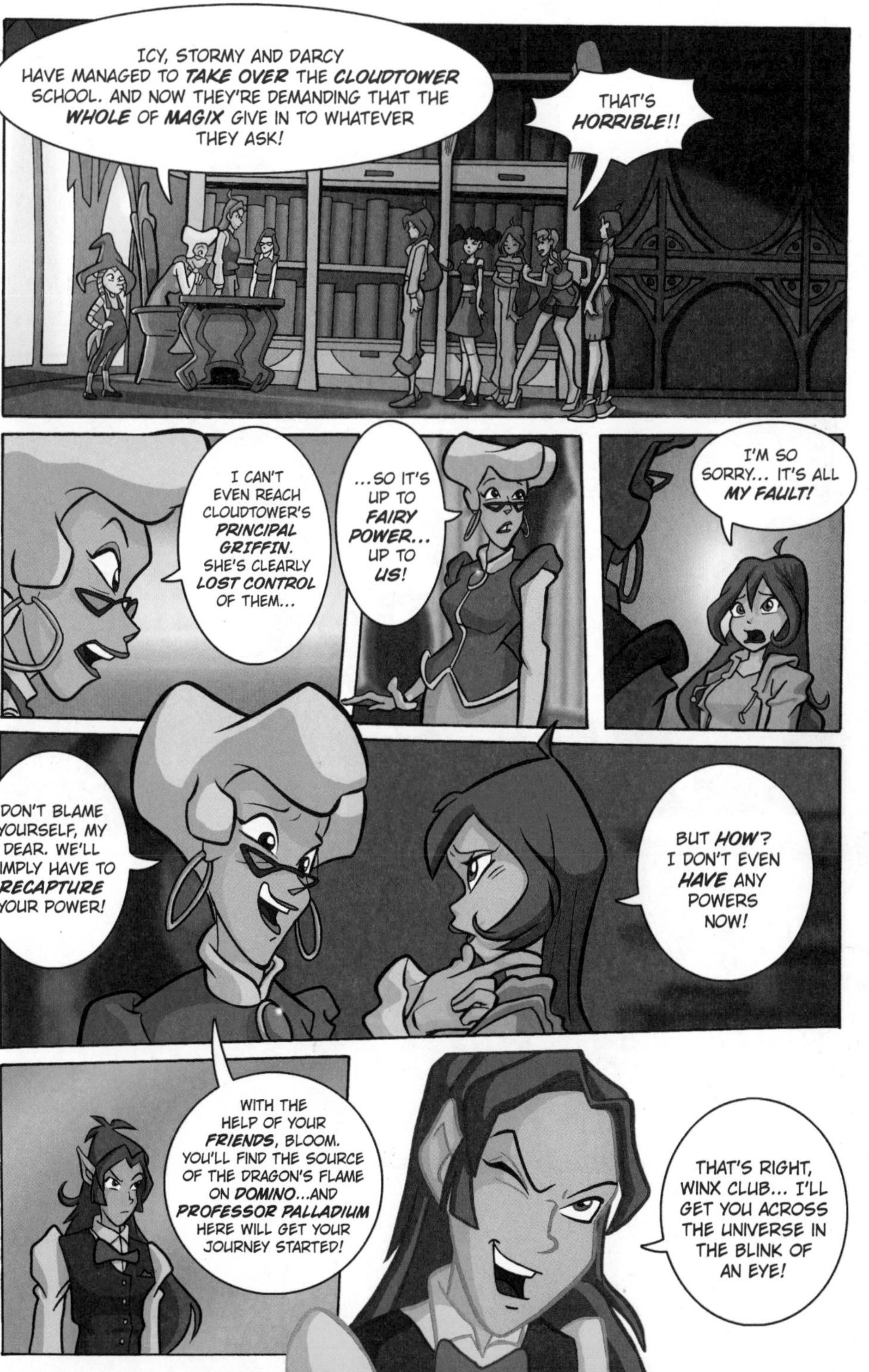
ICY, STORMY AND DARCY HAVE MANAGED TO TAKE OVER THE CLOUDTOWER SCHOOL. AND NOW THEY'RE DEMANDING THAT THE WHOLE OF MAGIX GIVE IN TO WHATEVER THEY ASK!
THAT'S HORRIBLE!!
I CAN'T EVEN REACH CLOUDTOWER'S PRINCIPAL GRIFFIN. SHE'S CLEARLY LOST CONTROL OF THEM...
...SO IT'S UP TO FAIRY POWER... UP TO US!
I'M SO SORRY... IT'S ALL MY FAULT!
DON'T BLAME YOURSELF, MY DEAR. WE'LL SIMPLY HAVE TO RECAPTURE YOUR POWER!
BUT HOW? I DON'T EVEN HAVE ANY POWERS NOW!
WITH THE HELP OF YOUR FRIENDS, BLOOM. YOU'LL FIND THE SOURCE OF THE DRAGON'S FLAME ON DOMINO...AND PROFESSOR PALLADIUM HERE WILL GET YOUR JOURNEY STARTED!
THAT'S RIGHT, WINX CLUB... I'LL GET YOU ACROSS THE UNIVERSE IN THE BLINK OF AN EYE!

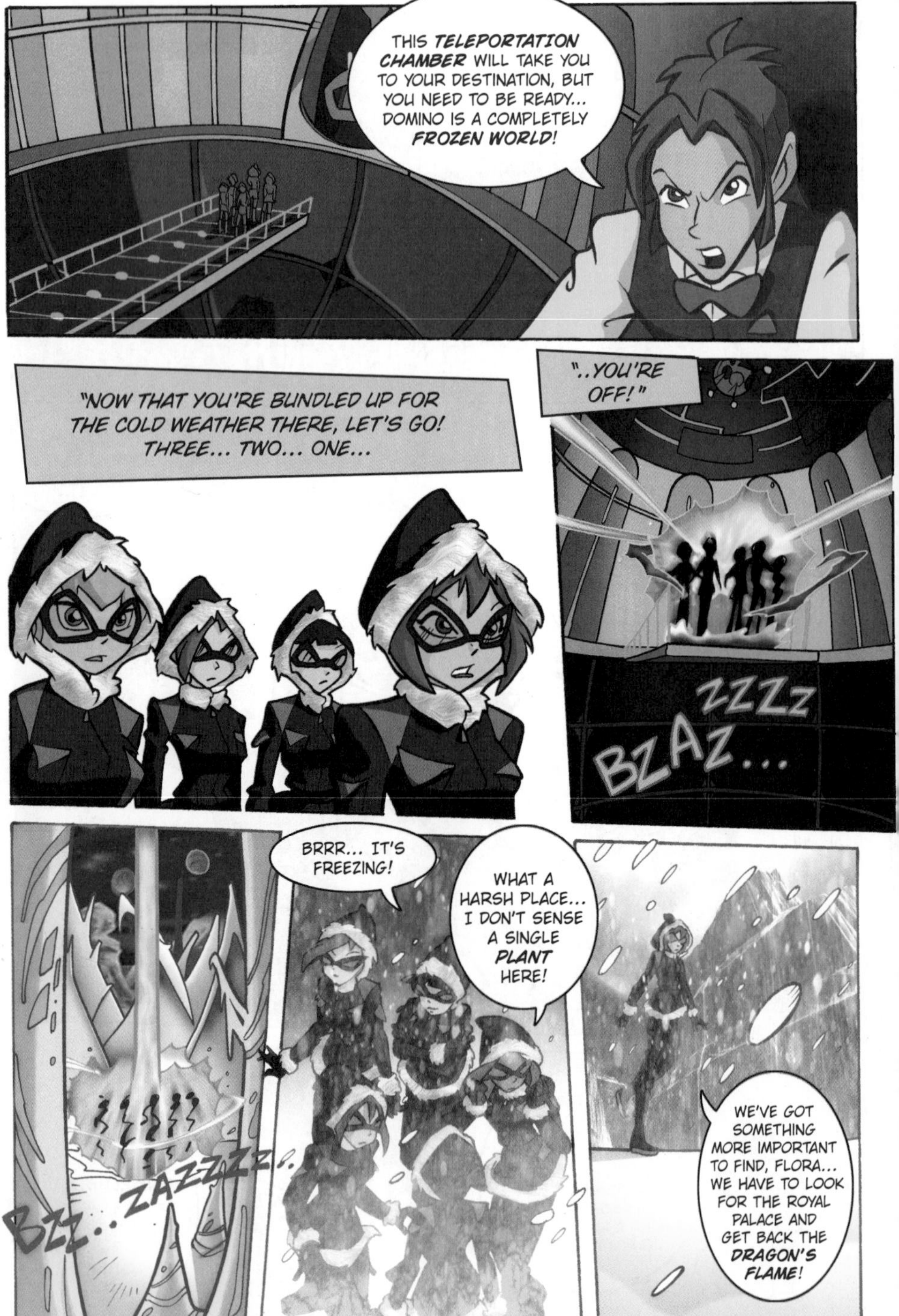
THIS TELEPORTATION CHAMBER WILL TAKE YOU TO YOUR DESTINATION, BUT YOU NEED TO BE READY... DOMINO IS A COMPLETELY FROZEN WORLD!
"NOW THAT YOU'RE BUNDLED UP FOR THE COLD WEATHER THERE, LET'S GO! THREE... TWO... ONE...
"..YOU'RE OFF!"
ZZZz
BZAZ...
BZZ...ZAZZZZZ...
BRRR... IT'S FREEZING!
WHAT A HARSH PLACE... I DON'T SENSE A SINGLE PLANT HERE!
WE'VE GOT SOMETHING MORE IMPORTANT TO FIND, FLORA... WE HAVE TO LOOK FOR THE ROYAL PALACE AND GET BACK THE DRAGON'S FLAME!

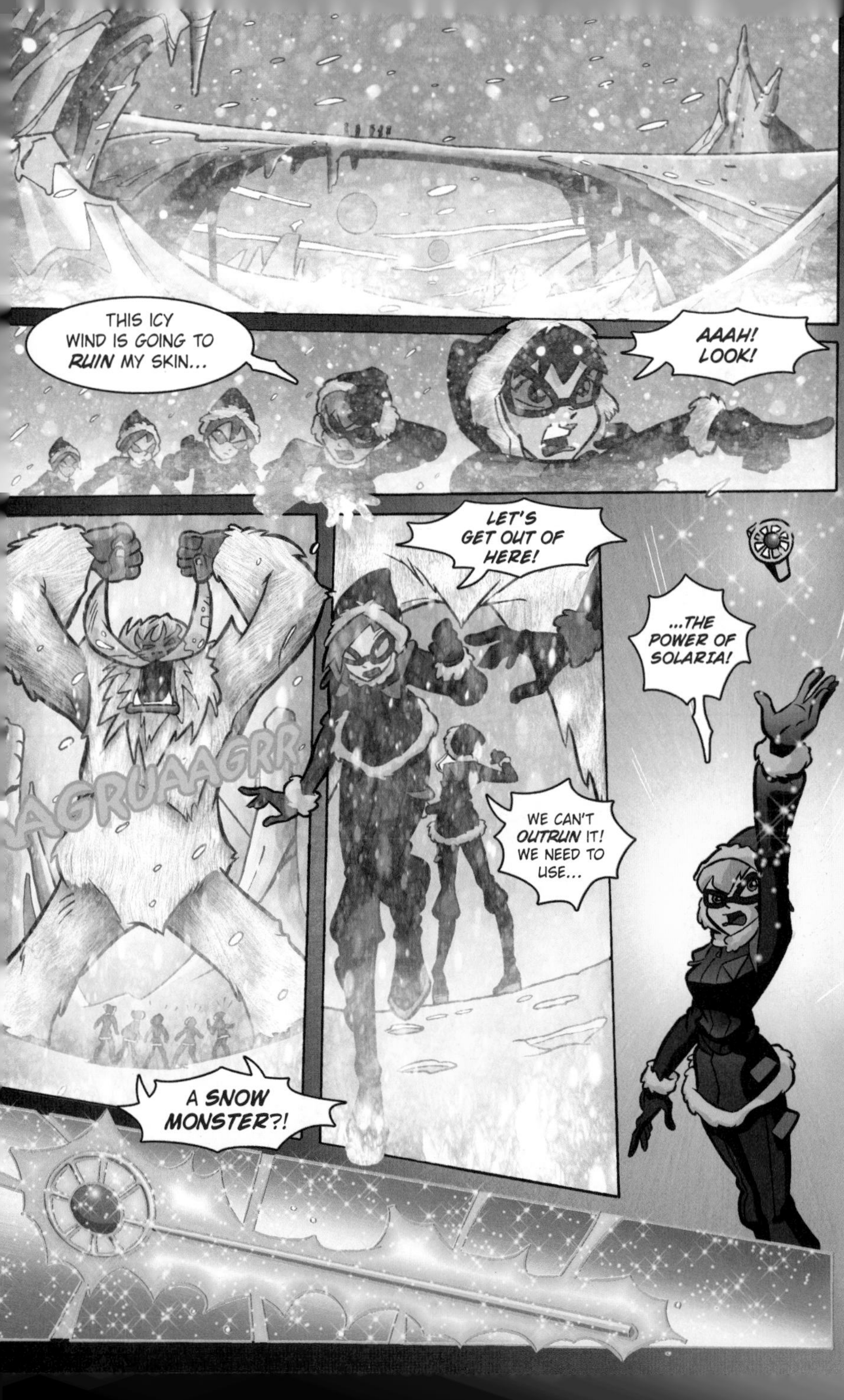
THIS ICY
WIND IS GOING TO
RUIN MY SKIN...
AAAH!
LOOK!
AGRUAAGRR
A SNOW
MONSTER?!
LET'S
GET OUT OF
HERE!
WE CAN'T
OUTRUN IT!
WE NEED TO
USE...
...THE
POWER OF
SOLARIA!

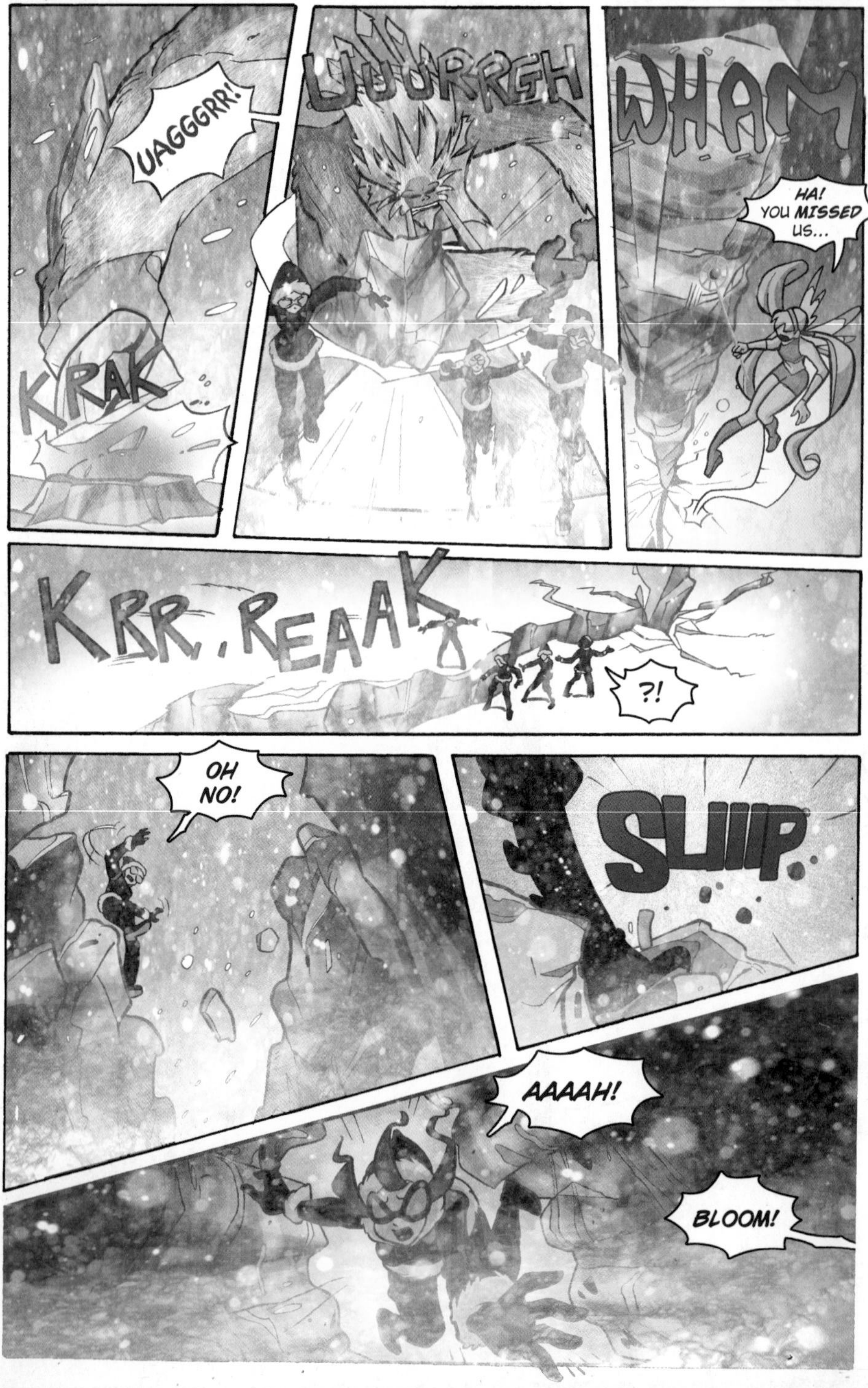
UAGGGRR!
KRAK
UUURRGH
WHAM
HA! YOU MISSED US...
KRR, REAAK
?!
OH NO!
SLIIP
AAAAH!
BLOOM!

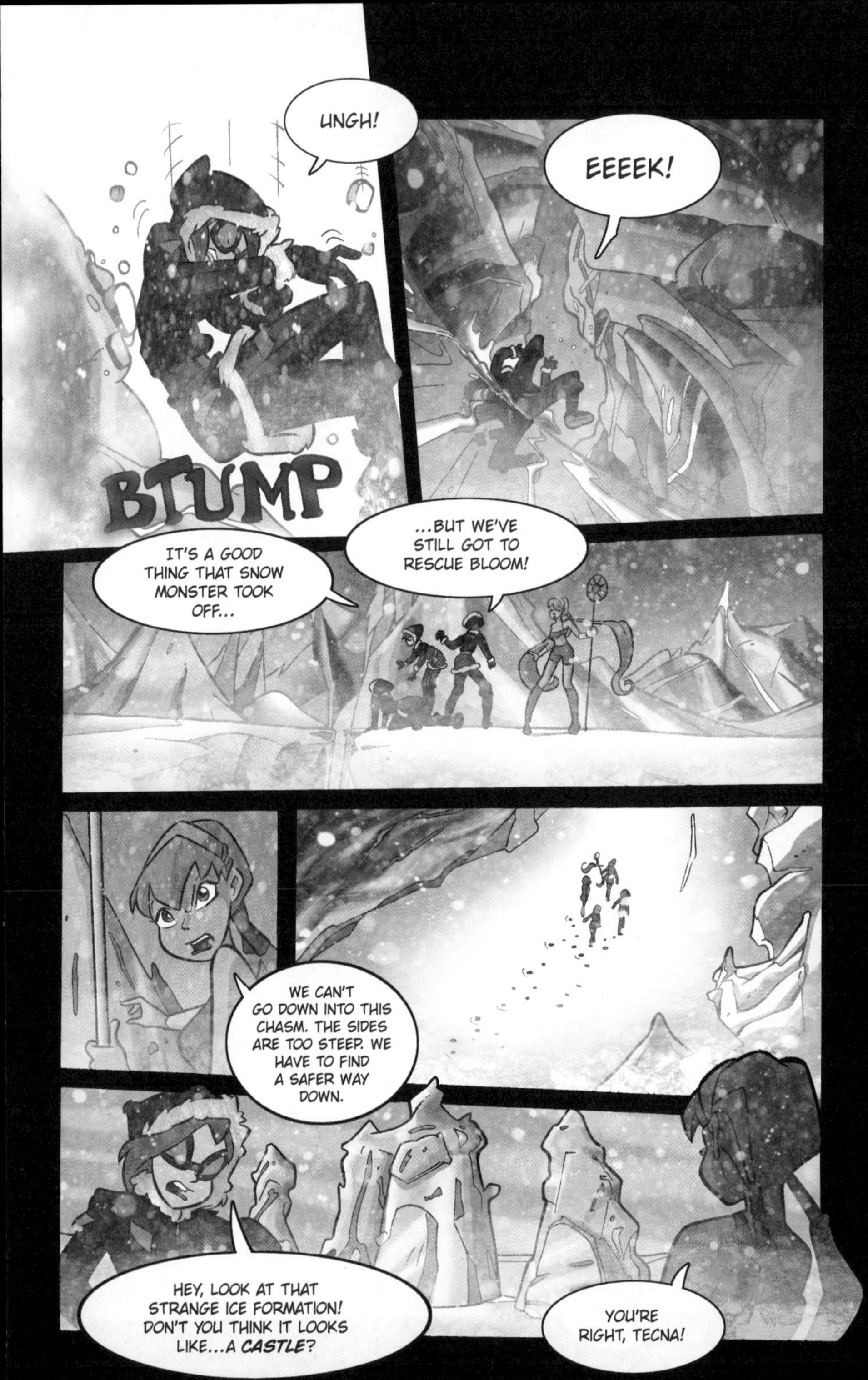
UNGH!
BTUMP
EEEEK!
IT'S A GOOD THING THAT SNOW MONSTER TOOK OFF...
...BUT WE'VE STILL GOT TO RESCUE BLOOM!
WE CAN'T GO DOWN INTO THIS CHASM. THE SIDES ARE TOO STEEP. WE HAVE TO FIND A SAFER WAY DOWN.
HEY, LOOK AT THAT STRANGE ICE FORMATION! DON'T YOU THINK IT LOOKS LIKE...A *CASTLE*?
YOU'RE RIGHT, TECNA!

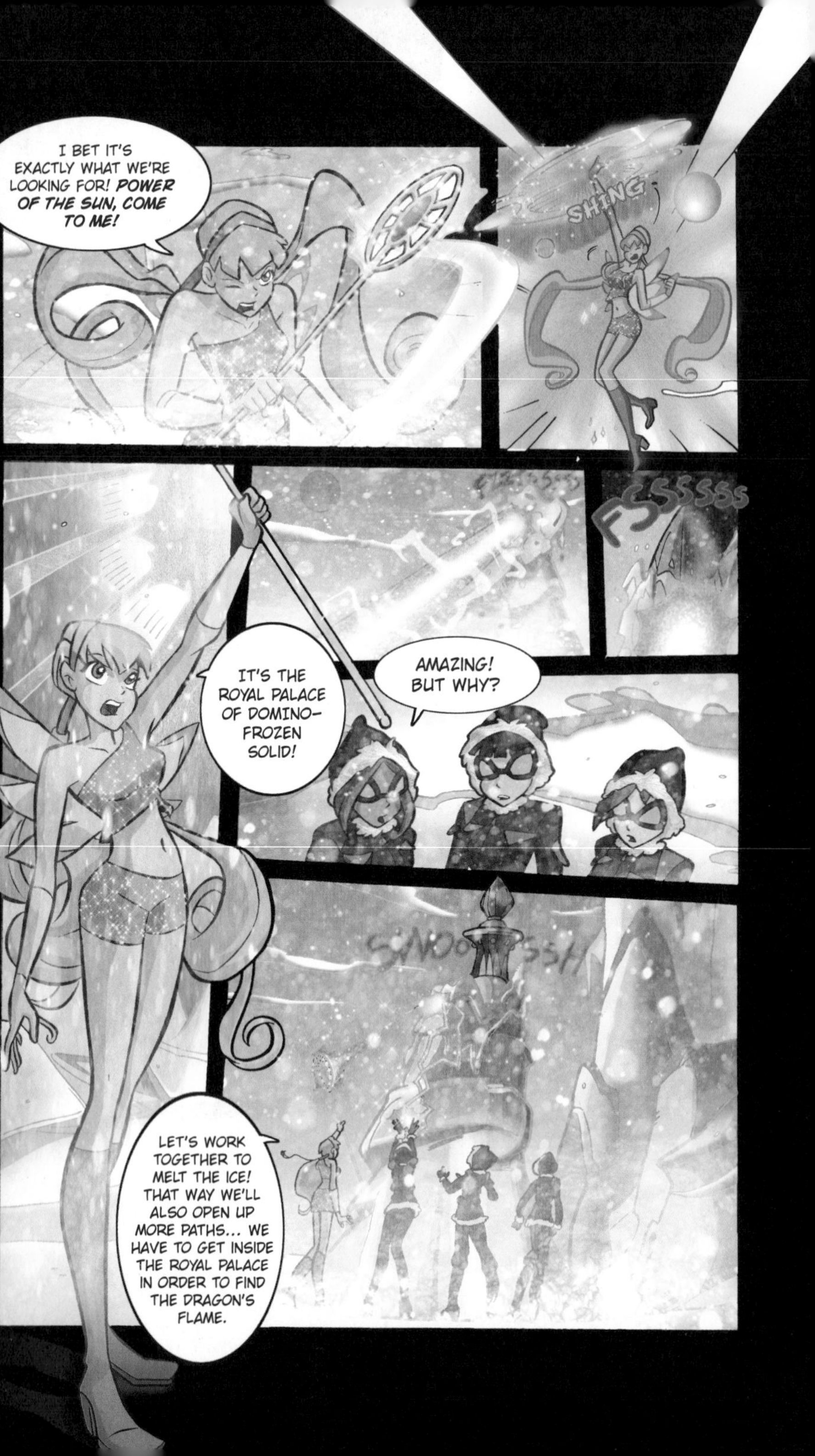

I BET IT'S EXACTLY WHAT WE'RE LOOKING FOR! *POWER OF THE SUN, COME TO ME!*
SHING
FSSSSSS
IT'S THE ROYAL PALACE OF DOMINO— FROZEN SOLID!
AMAZING! BUT WHY?
LET'S WORK TOGETHER TO MELT THE ICE! THAT WAY WE'LL ALSO OPEN UP MORE PATHS... WE HAVE TO GET INSIDE THE ROYAL PALACE IN ORDER TO FIND THE DRAGON'S FLAME.

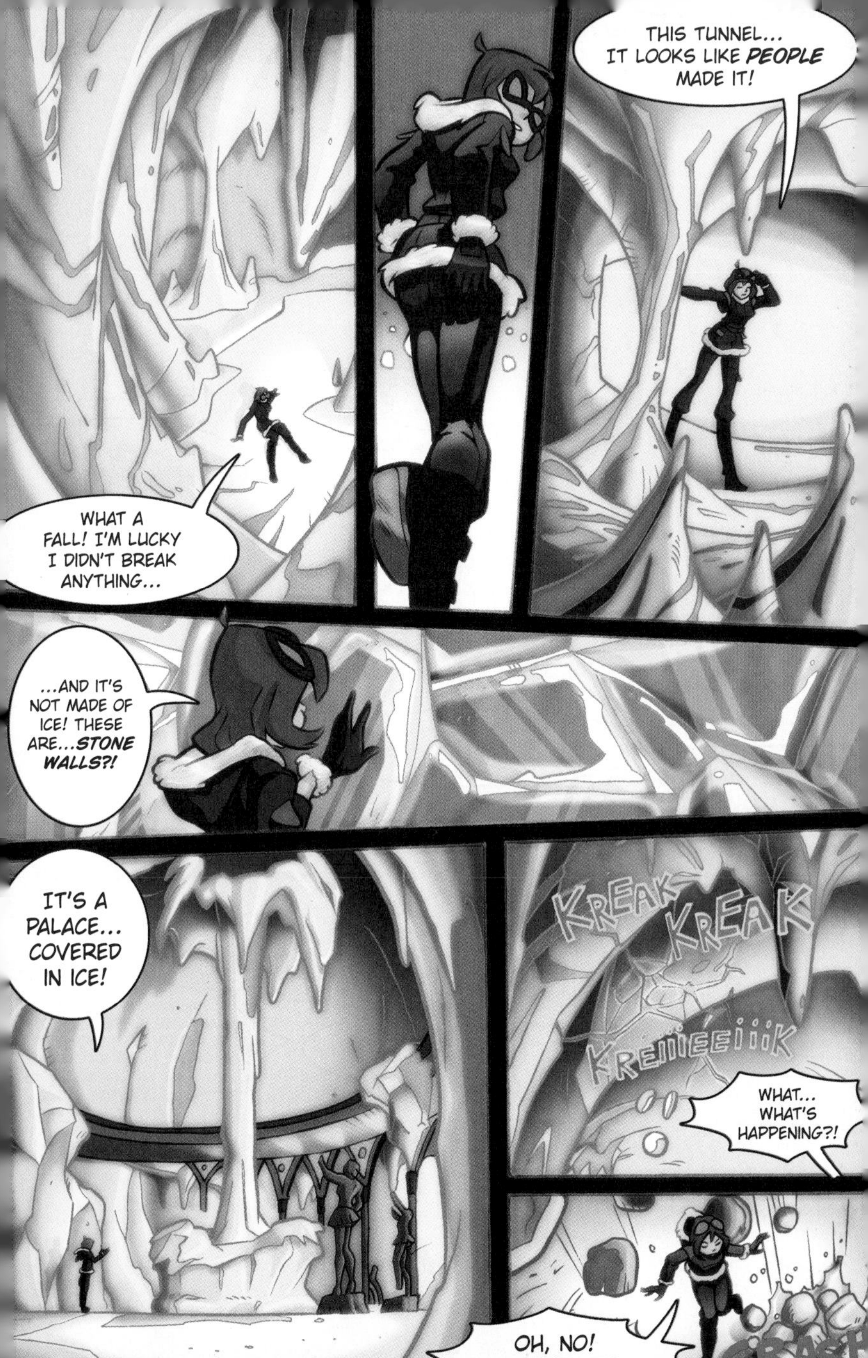
WHAT A FALL! I'M LUCKY I DIDN'T BREAK ANYTHING...
THIS TUNNEL... IT LOOKS LIKE PEOPLE MADE IT!
...AND IT'S NOT MADE OF ICE! THESE ARE...STONE WALLS?!
IT'S A PALACE... COVERED IN ICE!
KREAK KREAK
KREIIIEEIIIK
WHAT... WHAT'S HAPPENING?!
OH, NO! A CAVE-IN!
CRASH

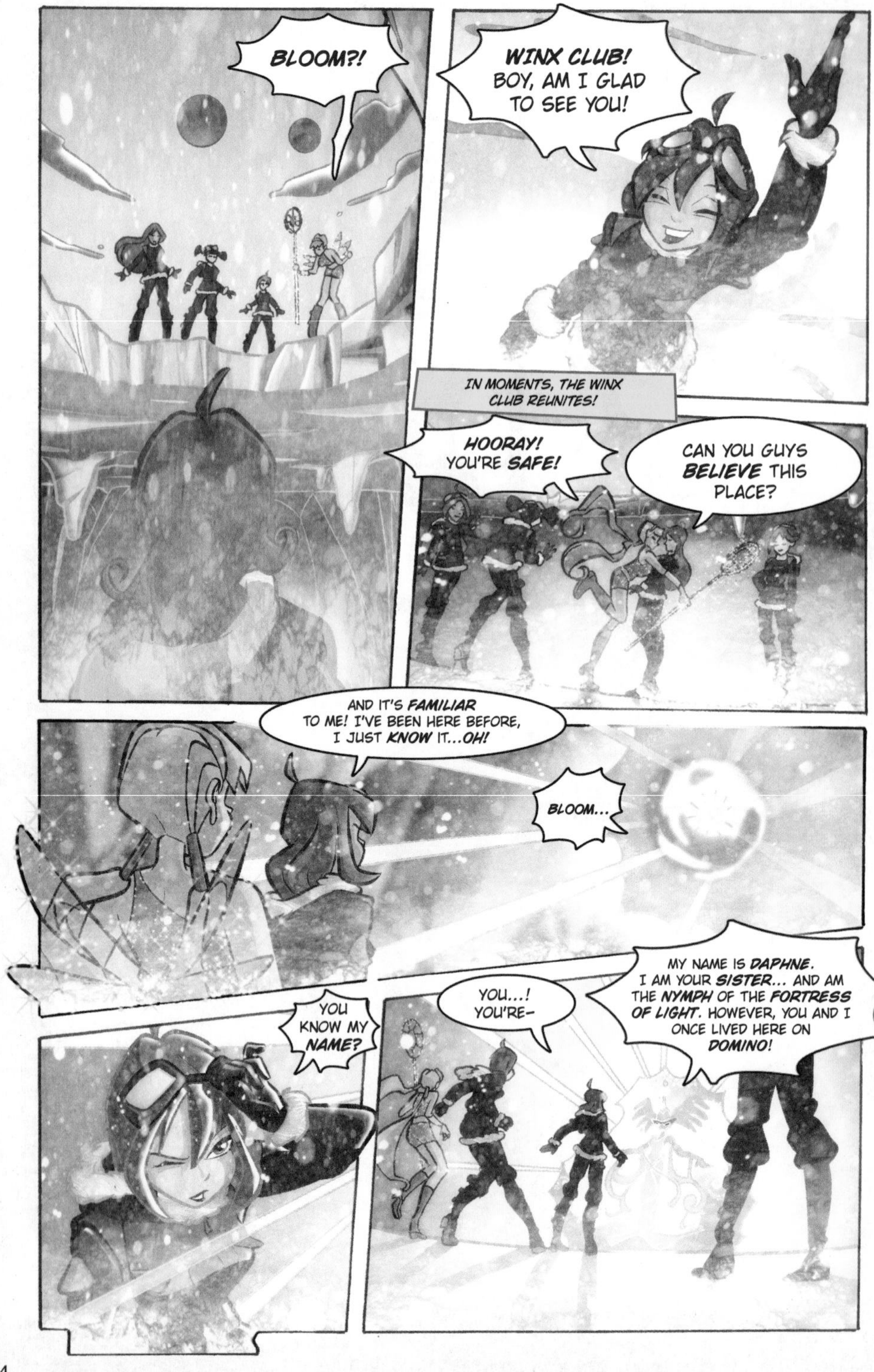
BLOOM?!
WINX CLUB! BOY, AM I GLAD TO SEE YOU!
IN MOMENTS, THE WINX CLUB REUNITES!
HOORAY! YOU'RE SAFE!
CAN YOU GUYS BELIEVE THIS PLACE?
AND IT'S FAMILIAR TO ME! I'VE BEEN HERE BEFORE, I JUST KNOW IT...OH!
BLOOM...
YOU KNOW MY NAME?
YOU...! YOU'RE-
MY NAME IS DAPHNE. I AM YOUR SISTER... AND AM THE NYMPH OF THE FORTRESS OF LIGHT. HOWEVER, YOU AND I ONCE LIVED HERE ON DOMINO!

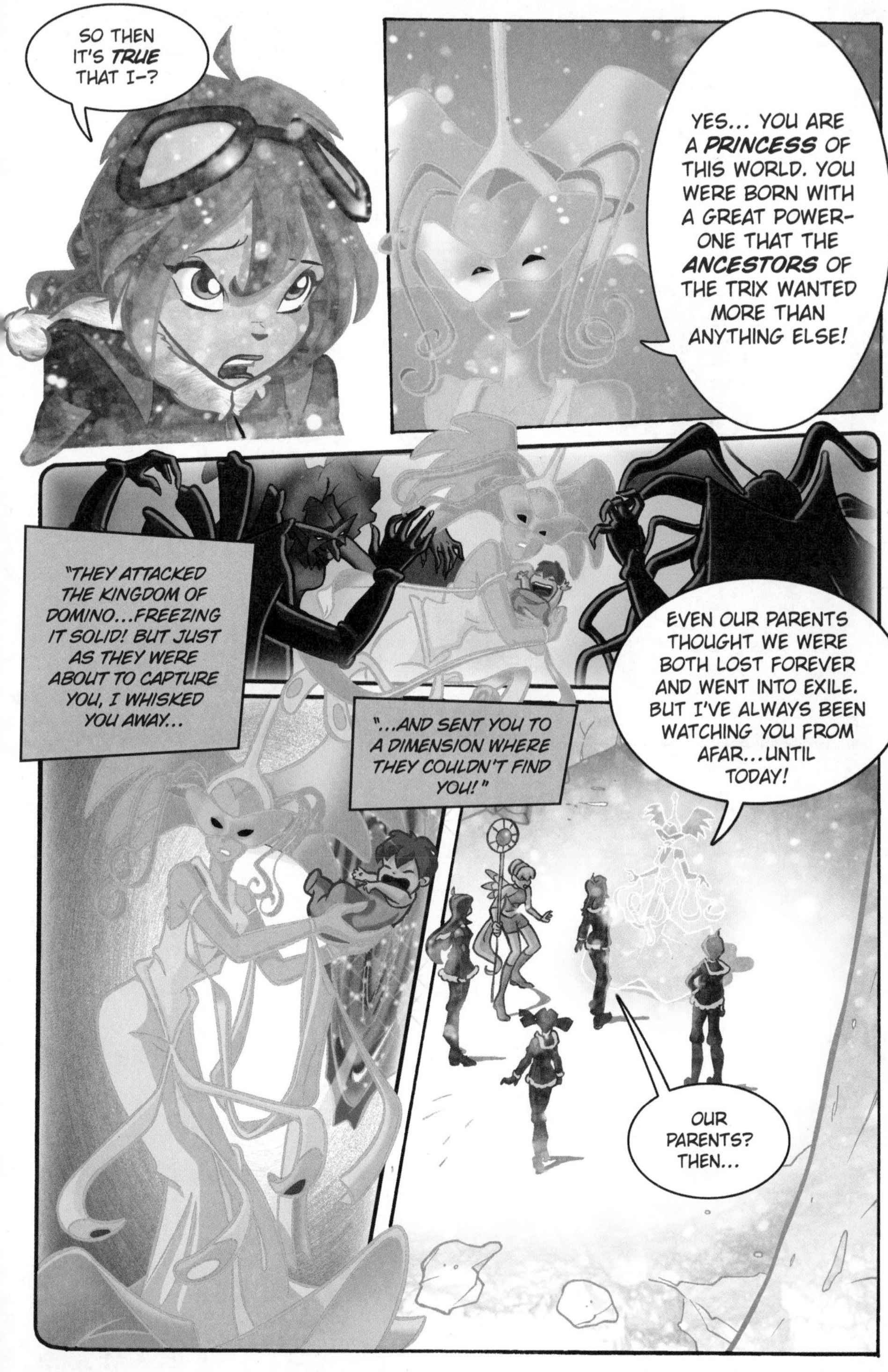
SO THEN IT'S **TRUE** THAT I-?
YES... YOU ARE A **PRINCESS** OF THIS WORLD. YOU WERE BORN WITH A GREAT POWER- ONE THAT THE **ANCESTORS** OF THE TRIX WANTED MORE THAN ANYTHING ELSE!
"THEY ATTACKED THE KINGDOM OF DOMINO...FREEZING IT SOLID! BUT JUST AS THEY WERE ABOUT TO CAPTURE YOU, I WHISKED YOU AWAY...
"...AND SENT YOU TO A DIMENSION WHERE THEY COULDN'T FIND YOU!"
EVEN OUR PARENTS THOUGHT WE WERE BOTH LOST FOREVER AND WENT INTO EXILE. BUT I'VE ALWAYS BEEN WATCHING YOU FROM AFAR...UNTIL TODAY!
OUR PARENTS? THEN...

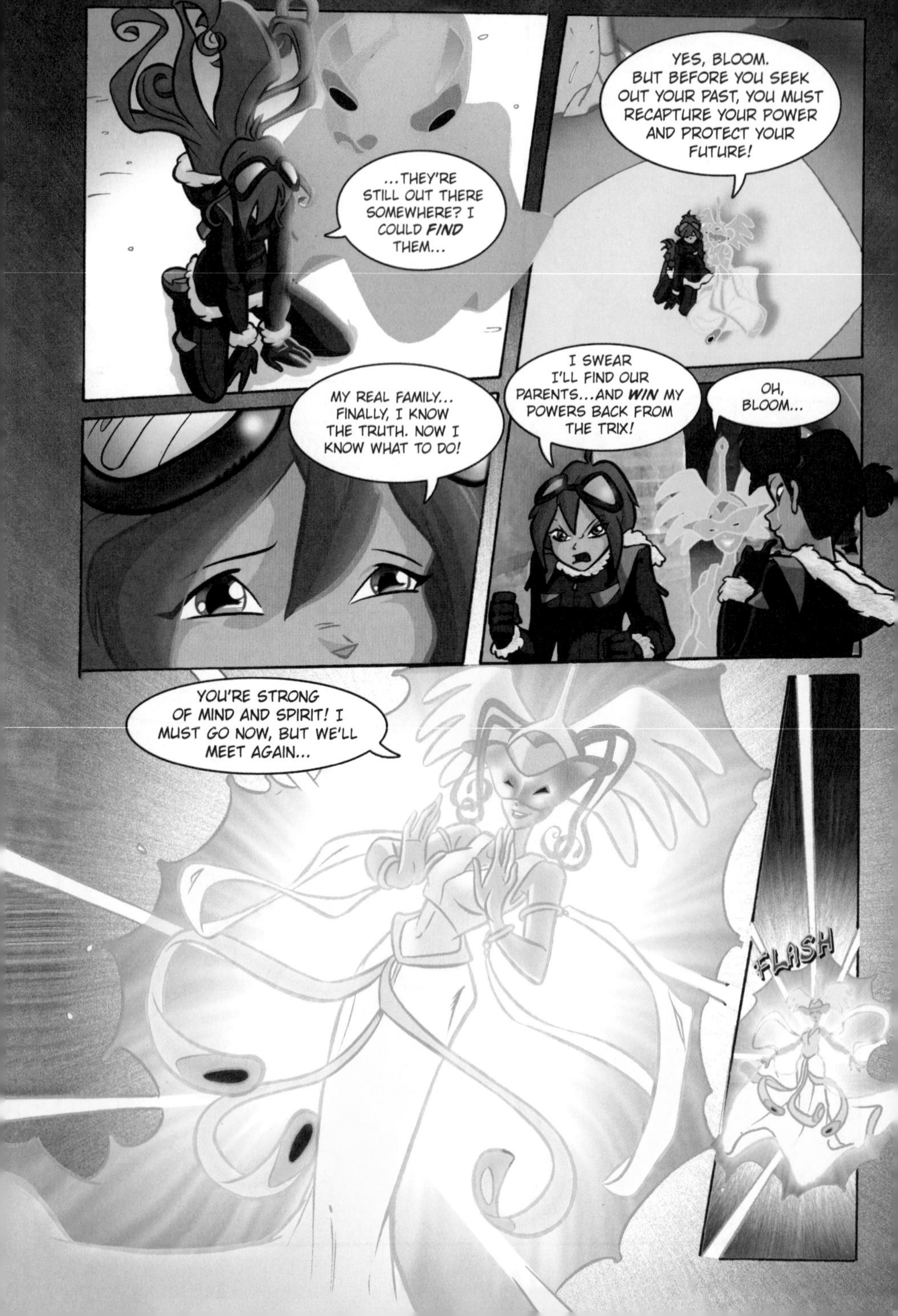
...THEY'RE STILL OUT THERE SOMEWHERE? I COULD FIND THEM...
YES, BLOOM. BUT BEFORE YOU SEEK OUT YOUR PAST, YOU MUST RECAPTURE YOUR POWER AND PROTECT YOUR FUTURE!
MY REAL FAMILY... FINALLY, I KNOW THE TRUTH. NOW I KNOW WHAT TO DO!
I SWEAR I'LL FIND OUR PARENTS...AND WIN MY POWERS BACK FROM THE TRIX!
OH, BLOOM...
YOU'RE STRONG OF MIND AND SPIRIT! I MUST GO NOW, BUT WE'LL MEET AGAIN...
FLASH

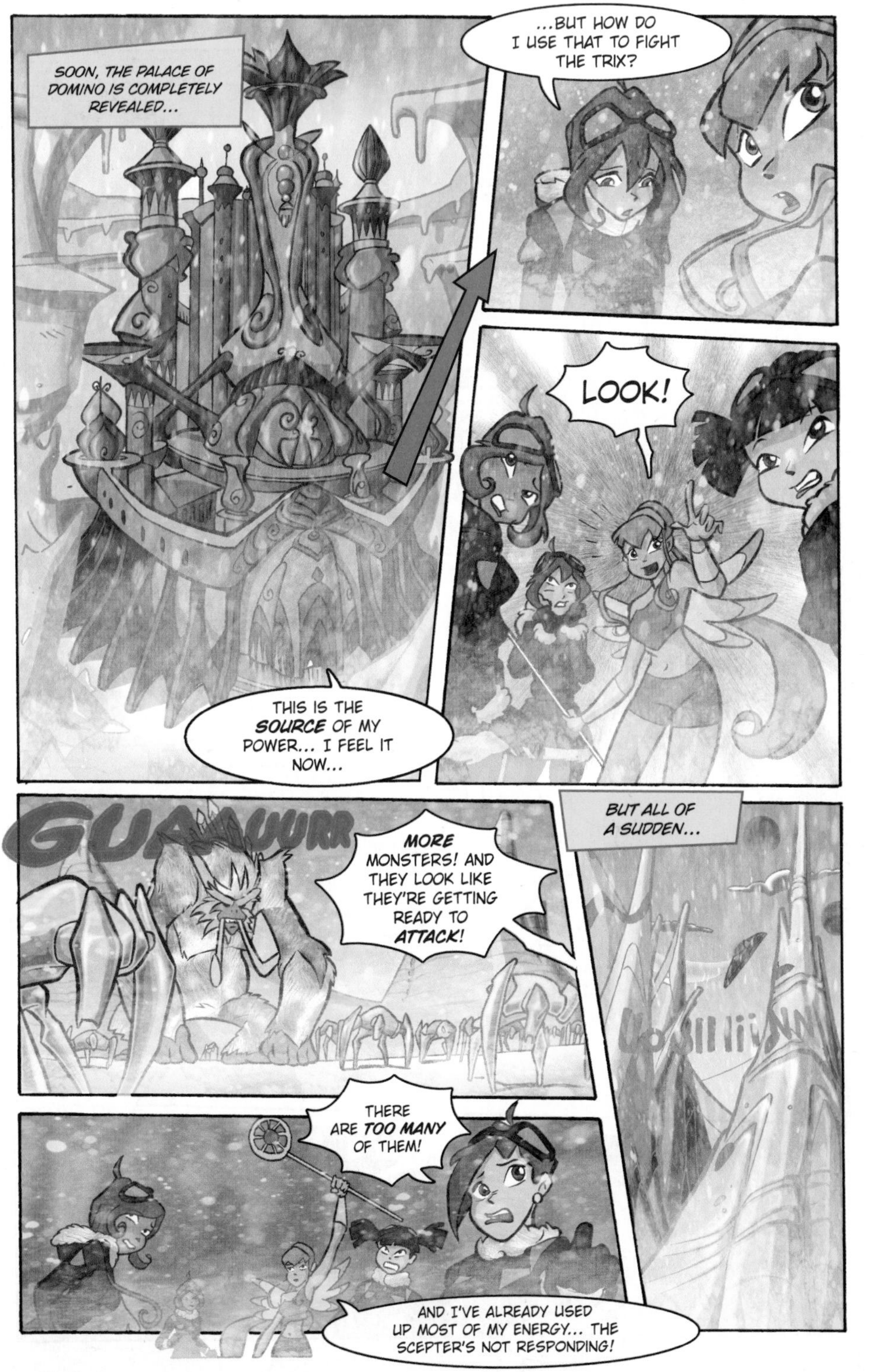
SOON, THE PALACE OF DOMINO IS COMPLETELY REVEALED...
...BUT HOW DO I USE THAT TO FIGHT THE TRIX?
LOOK!
THIS IS THE *SOURCE* OF MY POWER... I FEEL IT NOW...
GUAAUURR
MORE MONSTERS! AND THEY LOOK LIKE THEY'RE GETTING READY TO *ATTACK*!
BUT ALL OF A SUDDEN...
THERE ARE *TOO MANY* OF THEM!
AND I'VE ALREADY USED UP MOST OF MY ENERGY... THE SCEPTER'S NOT RESPONDING!

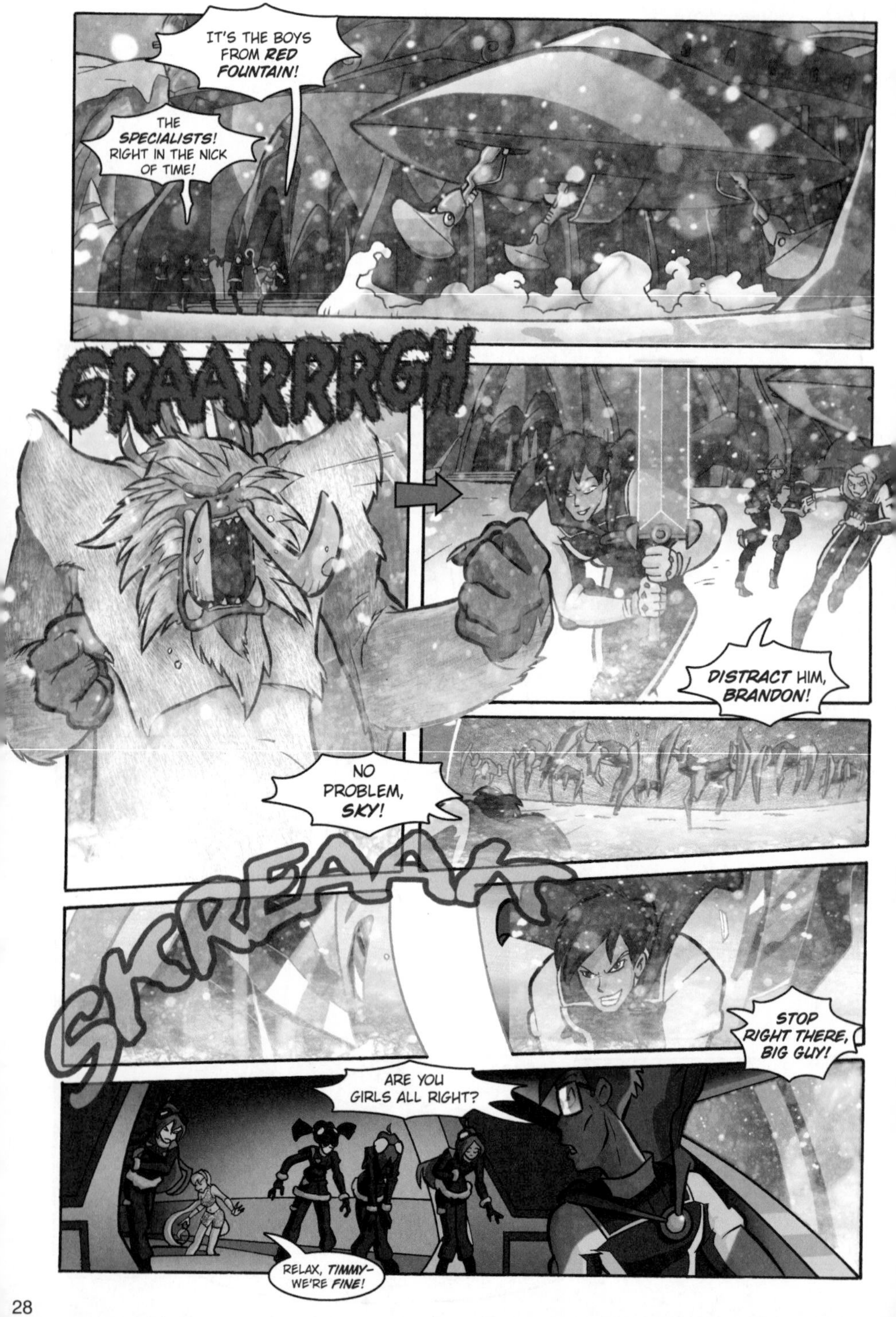
IT'S THE BOYS FROM RED FOUNTAIN!
THE SPECIALISTS! RIGHT IN THE NICK OF TIME!
GRAARRRGH
DISTRACT HIM, BRANDON!
NO PROBLEM, SKY!
SKREAAAK
STOP RIGHT THERE, BIG GUY!
ARE YOU GIRLS ALL RIGHT?
RELAX, TIMMY– WE'RE FINE!

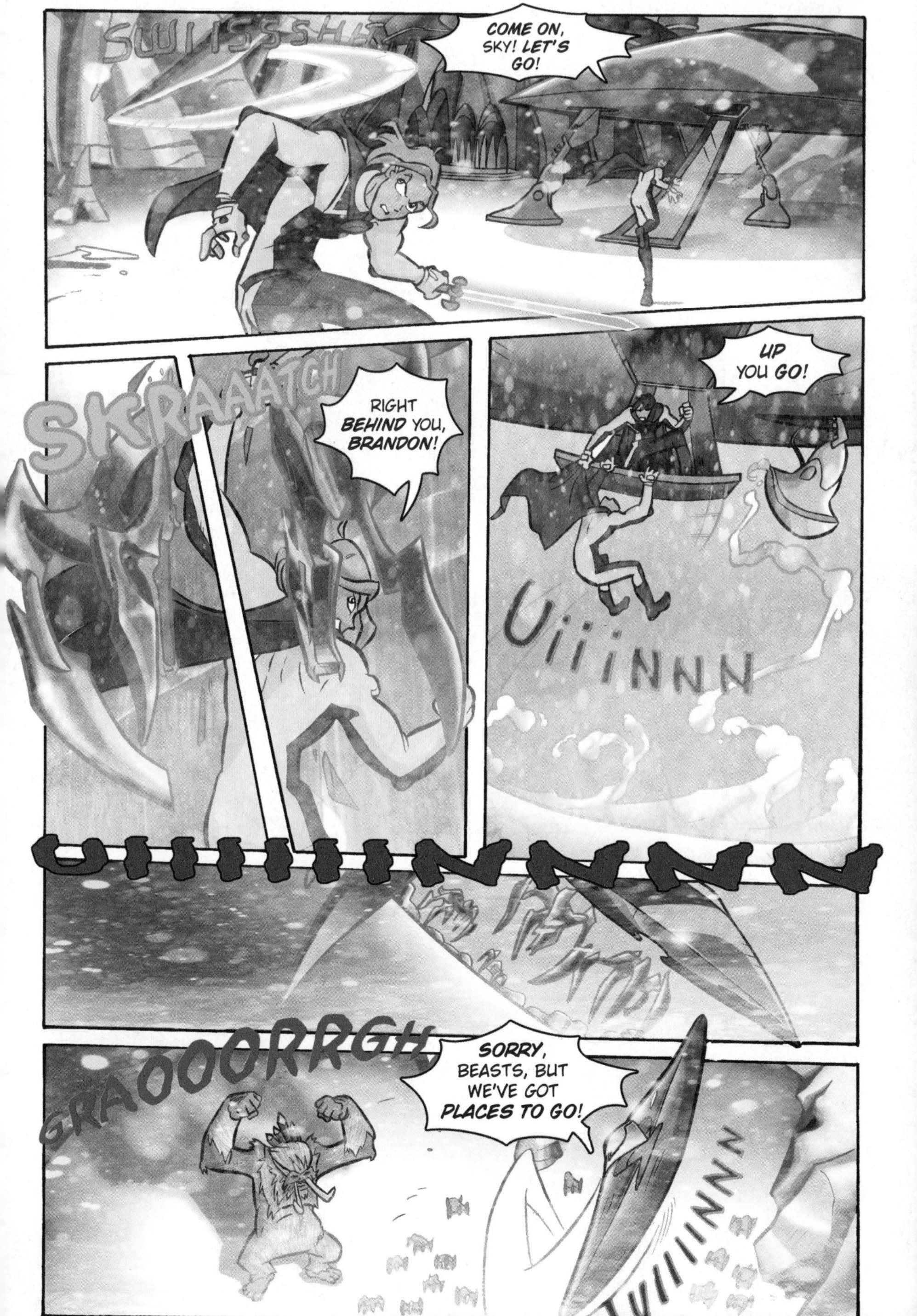
SWIISSSHH
COME ON, SKY! LET'S GO!
SKRAAAATCH
RIGHT BEHIND YOU, BRANDON!
UP YOU GO!
UiiiNNN
UIIIIIIINNNNN
GRAOOOORRGH
SORRY, BEASTS, BUT WE'VE GOT PLACES TO GO!
TUIIIINNN

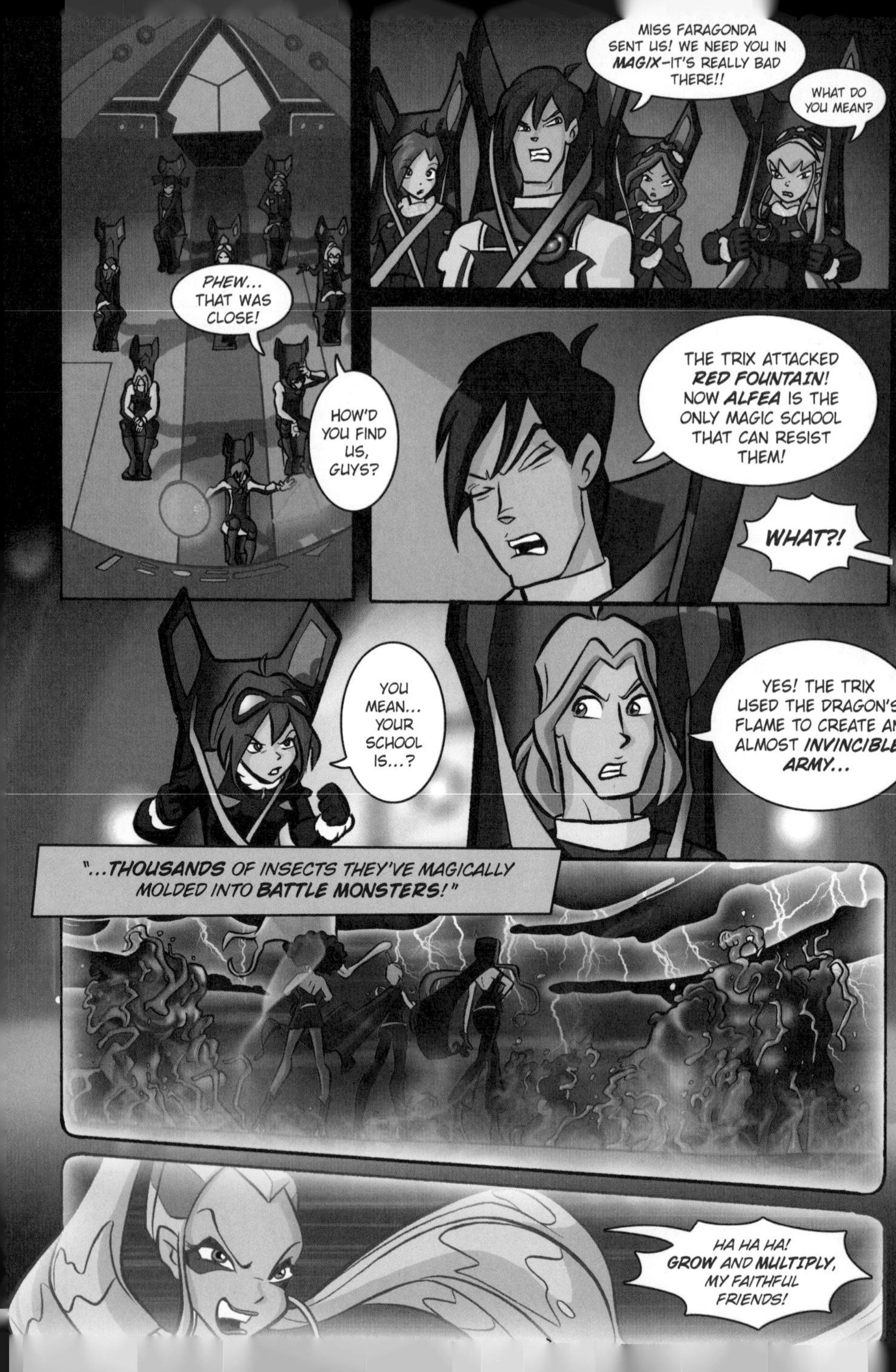
PHEW... THAT WAS CLOSE!
HOW'D YOU FIND US, GUYS?
MISS FARAGONDA SENT US! WE NEED YOU IN MAGIX—IT'S REALLY BAD THERE!!
WHAT DO YOU MEAN?
THE TRIX ATTACKED RED FOUNTAIN! NOW ALFEA IS THE ONLY MAGIC SCHOOL THAT CAN RESIST THEM!
WHAT?!
YOU MEAN... YOUR SCHOOL IS...?
YES! THE TRIX USED THE DRAGON'S FLAME TO CREATE AN ALMOST INVINCIBLE ARMY...
"...THOUSANDS OF INSECTS THEY'VE MAGICALLY MOLDED INTO BATTLE MONSTERS!"
HA HA HA! GROW AND MULTIPLY, MY FAITHFUL FRIENDS!

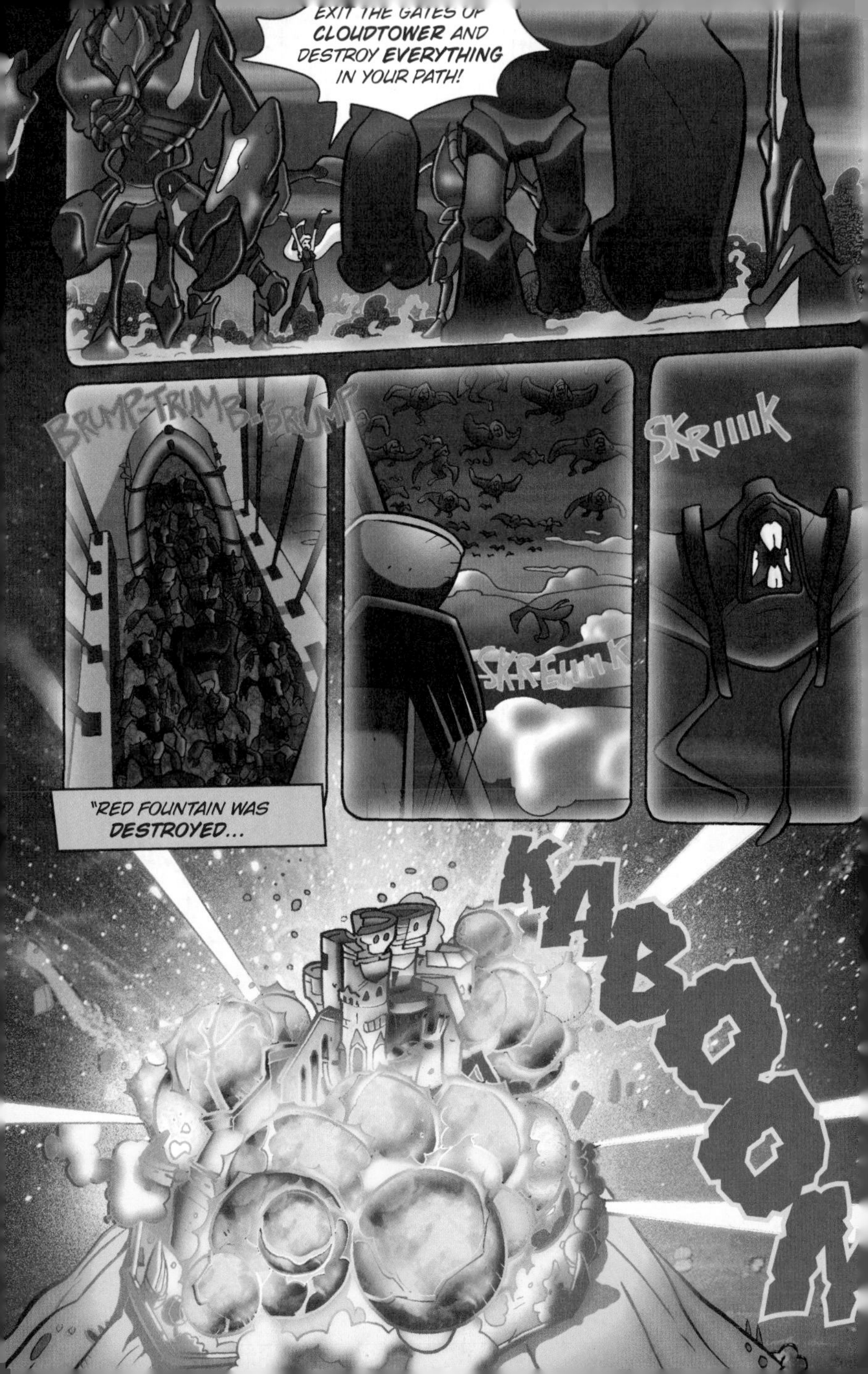
EXIT THE GATES OF CLOUDTOWER AND DESTROY EVERYTHING IN YOUR PATH!
BRUMP-TRUMBL-BRUMP
SKRIIIIK
SKREIIIIIK
"RED FOUNTAIN WAS DESTROYED...
KABOOM

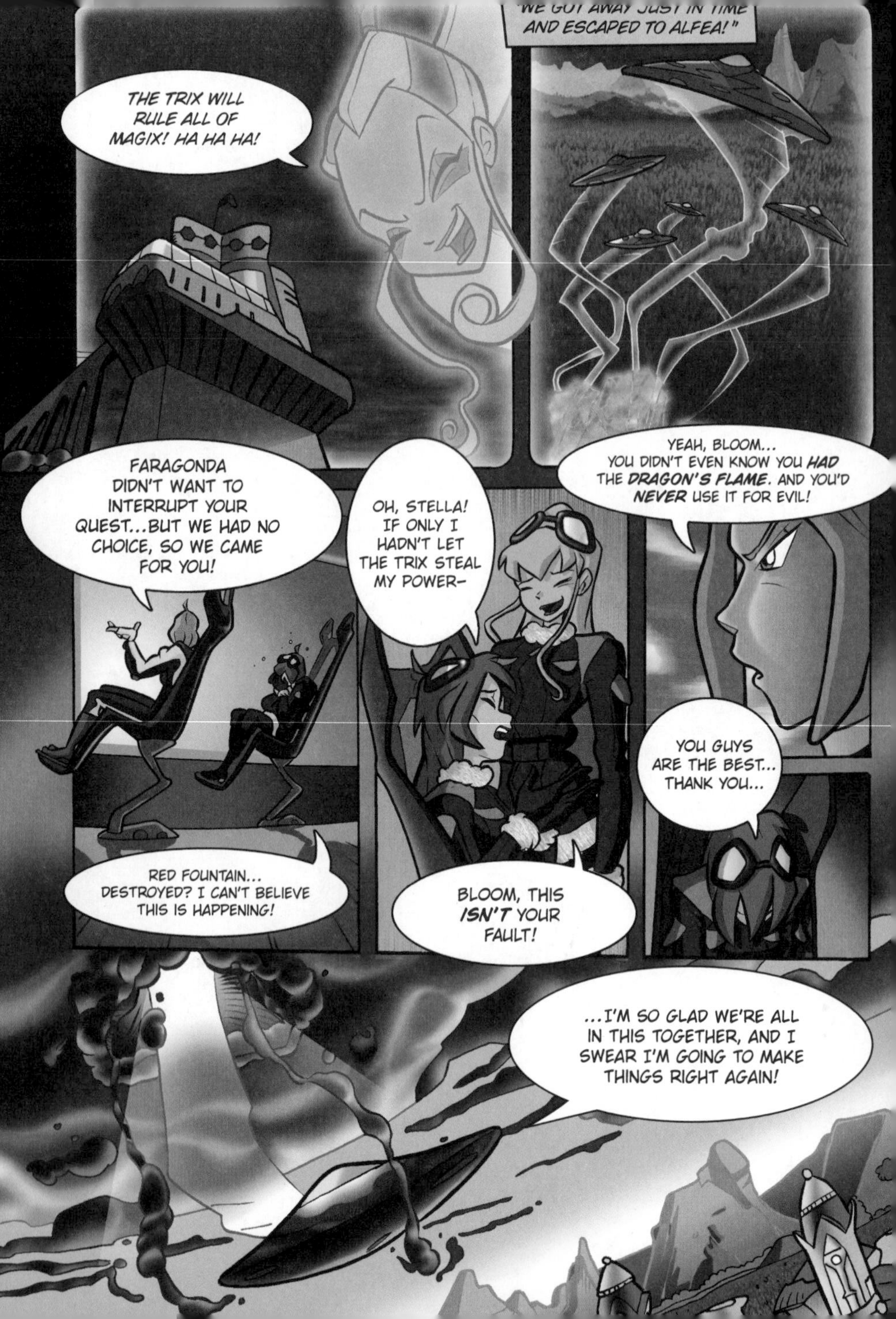
"WE GOT AWAY JUST IN TIME AND ESCAPED TO ALFEA!"
THE TRIX WILL RULE ALL OF MAGIX! HA HA HA!
FARAGONDA DIDN'T WANT TO INTERRUPT YOUR QUEST...BUT WE HAD NO CHOICE, SO WE CAME FOR YOU!
RED FOUNTAIN... DESTROYED? I CAN'T BELIEVE THIS IS HAPPENING!
OH, STELLA! IF ONLY I HADN'T LET THE TRIX STEAL MY POWER–
BLOOM, THIS ISN'T YOUR FAULT!
YEAH, BLOOM... YOU DIDN'T EVEN KNOW YOU HAD THE DRAGON'S FLAME. AND YOU'D NEVER USE IT FOR EVIL!
YOU GUYS ARE THE BEST... THANK YOU...
...I'M SO GLAD WE'RE ALL IN THIS TOGETHER, AND I SWEAR I'M GOING TO MAKE THINGS RIGHT AGAIN!

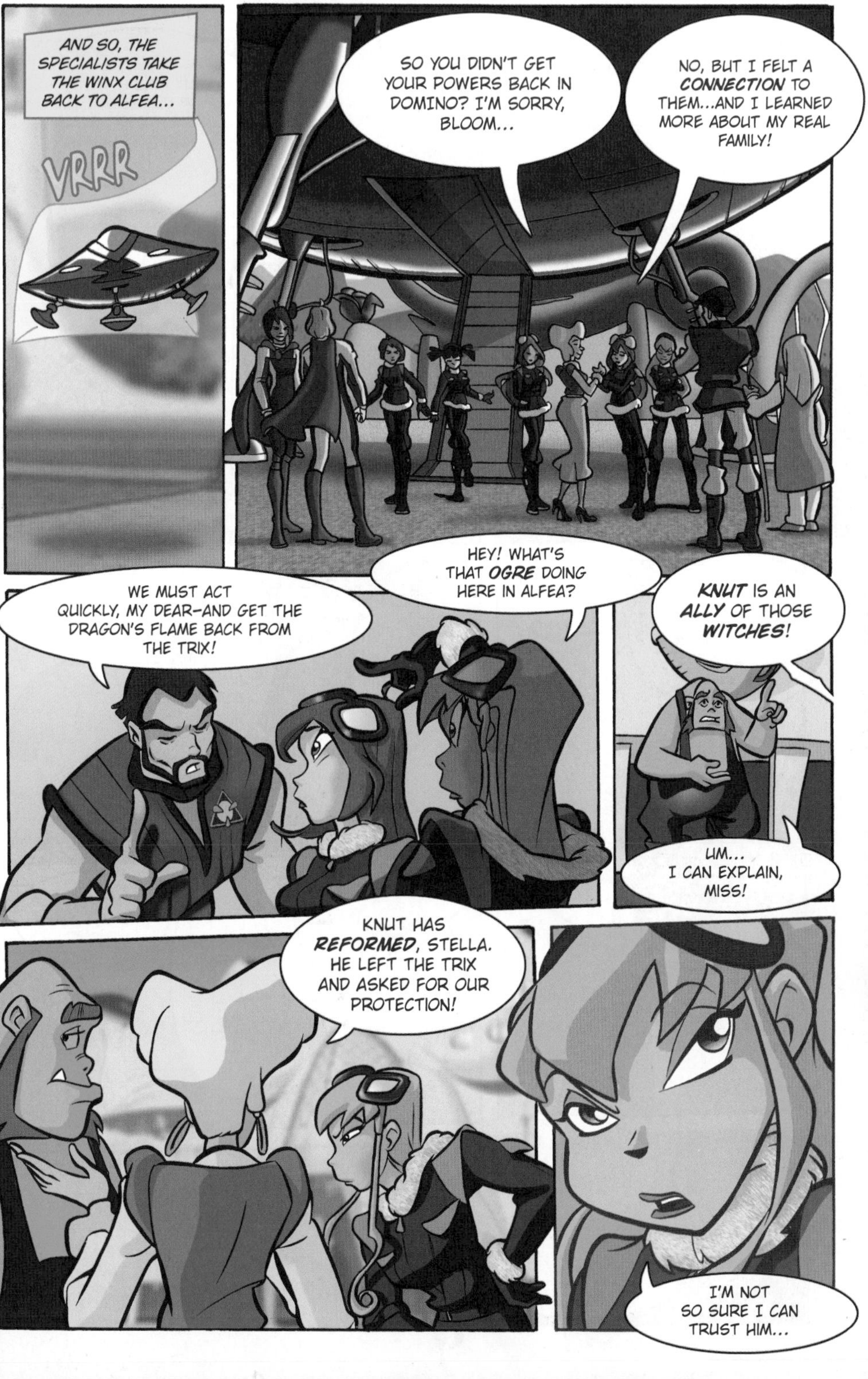

AND SO, THE SPECIALISTS TAKE THE WINX CLUB BACK TO ALFEA...
VRRR
SO YOU DIDN'T GET YOUR POWERS BACK IN DOMINO? I'M SORRY, BLOOM...
NO, BUT I FELT A CONNECTION TO THEM...AND I LEARNED MORE ABOUT MY REAL FAMILY!
WE MUST ACT QUICKLY, MY DEAR–AND GET THE DRAGON'S FLAME BACK FROM THE TRIX!
HEY! WHAT'S THAT OGRE DOING HERE IN ALFEA?
KNUT IS AN ALLY OF THOSE WITCHES!
UM... I CAN EXPLAIN, MISS!
KNUT HAS REFORMED, STELLA. HE LEFT THE TRIX AND ASKED FOR OUR PROTECTION!
I'M NOT SO SURE I CAN TRUST HIM...

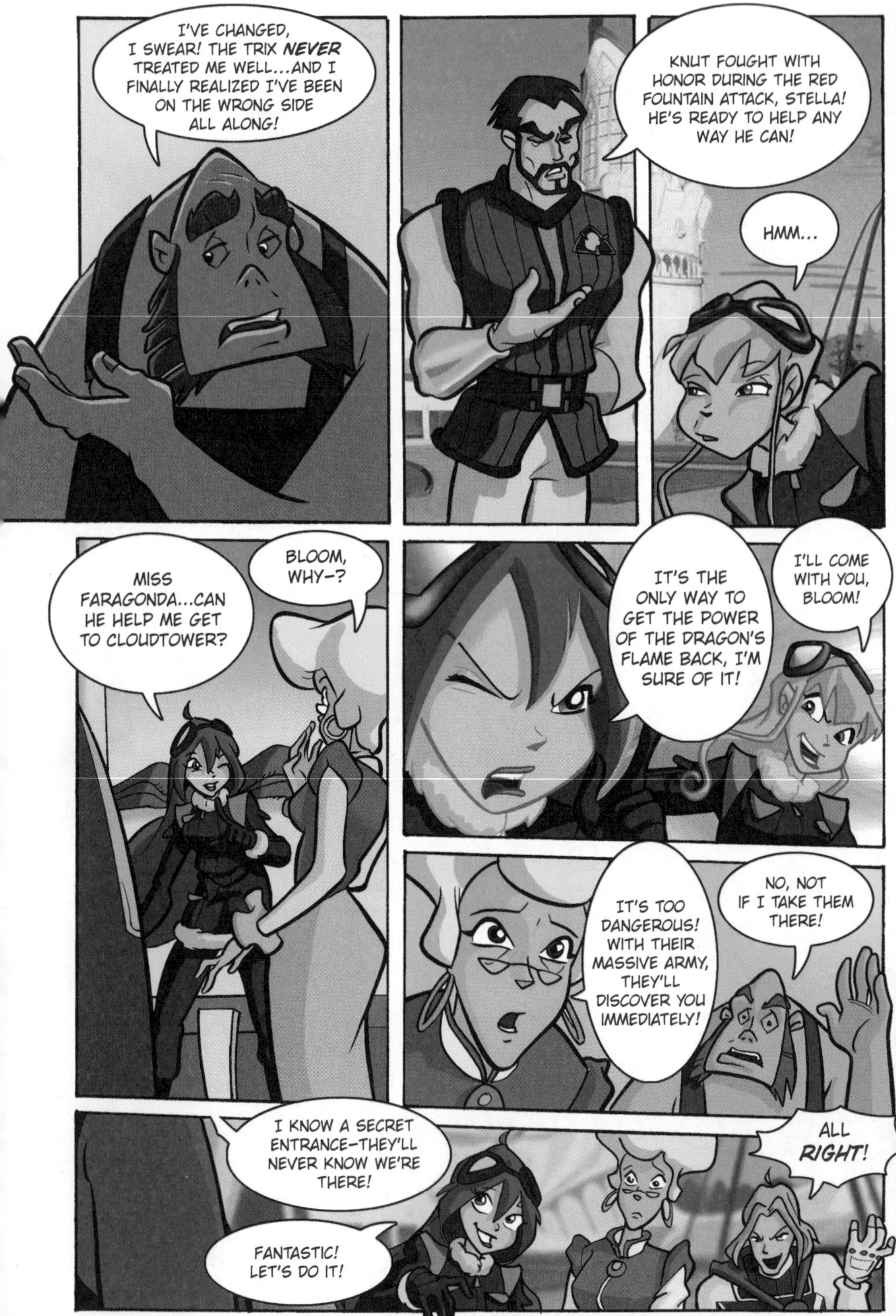

I'VE CHANGED, I SWEAR! THE TRIX NEVER TREATED ME WELL...AND I FINALLY REALIZED I'VE BEEN ON THE WRONG SIDE ALL ALONG!
KNUT FOUGHT WITH HONOR DURING THE RED FOUNTAIN ATTACK, STELLA! HE'S READY TO HELP ANY WAY HE CAN!
HMM...
MISS FARAGONDA...CAN HE HELP ME GET TO CLOUDTOWER?
BLOOM, WHY-?
IT'S THE ONLY WAY TO GET THE POWER OF THE DRAGON'S FLAME BACK, I'M SURE OF IT!
I'LL COME WITH YOU, BLOOM!
IT'S TOO DANGEROUS! WITH THEIR MASSIVE ARMY, THEY'LL DISCOVER YOU IMMEDIATELY!
NO, NOT IF I TAKE THEM THERE!
I KNOW A SECRET ENTRANCE-THEY'LL NEVER KNOW WE'RE THERE!
FANTASTIC! LET'S DO IT!
ALL RIGHT!

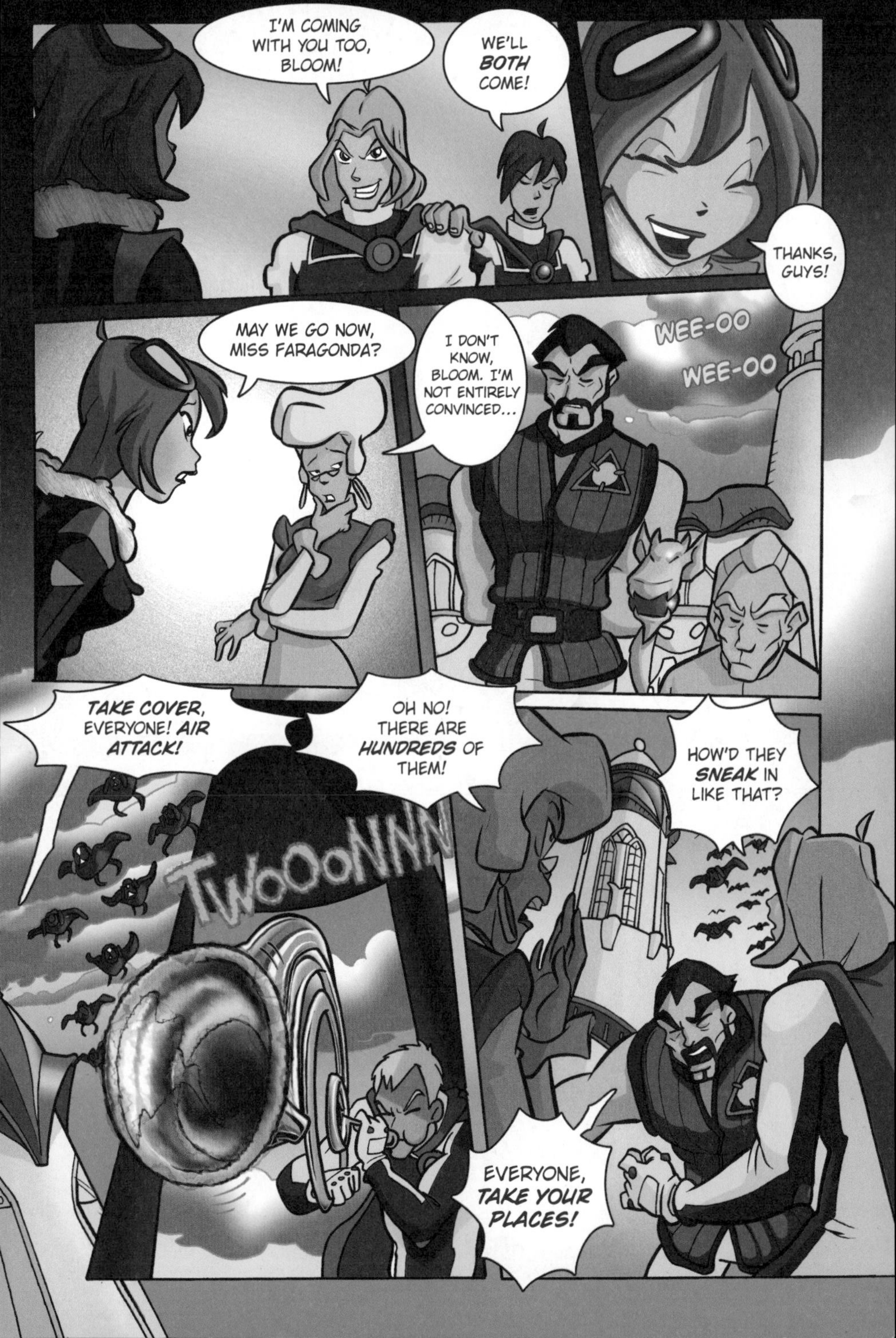
I'M COMING WITH YOU TOO, BLOOM!
WE'LL BOTH COME!
THANKS, GUYS!
MAY WE GO NOW, MISS FARAGONDA?
I DON'T KNOW, BLOOM. I'M NOT ENTIRELY CONVINCED...
WEE-OO
WEE-OO
TAKE COVER, EVERYONE! AIR ATTACK!
OH NO! THERE ARE HUNDREDS OF THEM!
TWOOOONNN
HOW'D THEY SNEAK IN LIKE THAT?
EVERYONE, TAKE YOUR PLACES!

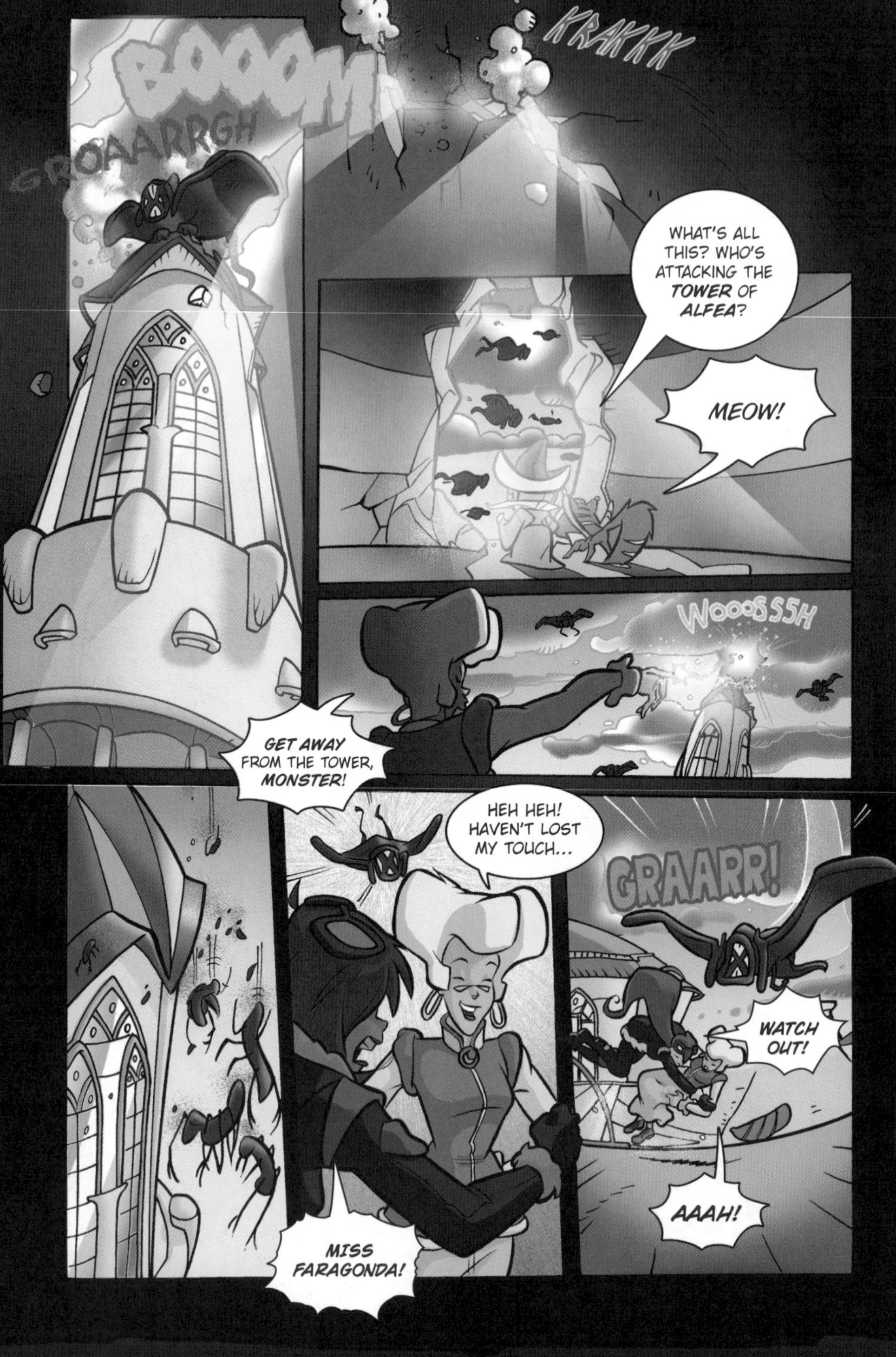
BOOOM
KRAKKK
GROAARRGH
WHAT'S ALL THIS? WHO'S ATTACKING THE TOWER OF ALFEA?
MEOW!
WOOOSSSH
GET AWAY FROM THE TOWER, MONSTER!
HEH HEH! HAVEN'T LOST MY TOUCH...
MISS FARAGONDA!
GRAARR!
WATCH OUT!
AAAH!

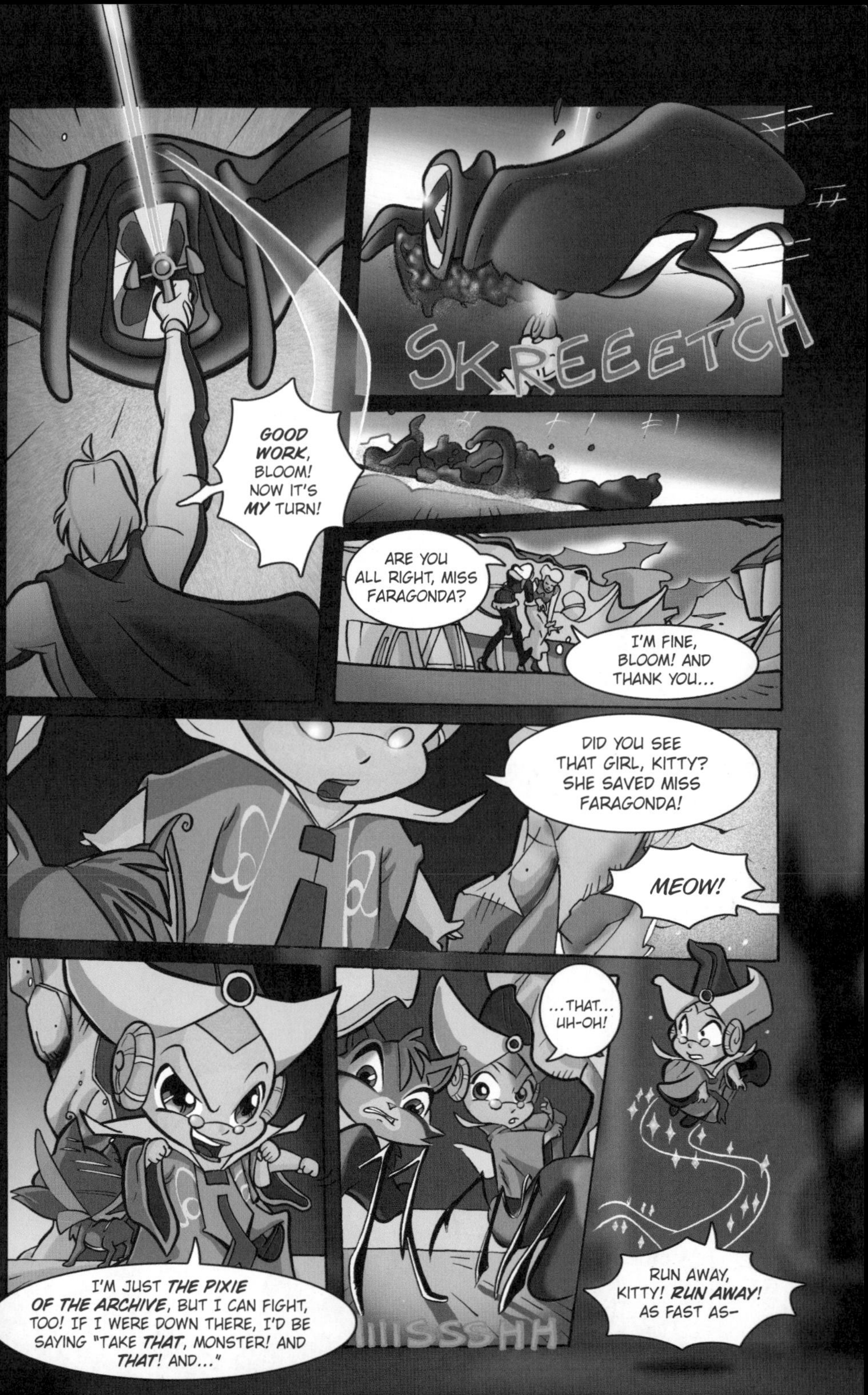
SKREEETCH
GOOD WORK, BLOOM! NOW IT'S MY TURN!
ARE YOU ALL RIGHT, MISS FARAGONDA?
I'M FINE, BLOOM! AND THANK YOU...
DID YOU SEE THAT GIRL, KITTY? SHE SAVED MISS FARAGONDA!
MEOW!
I'M JUST THE PIXIE OF THE ARCHIVE, BUT I CAN FIGHT, TOO! IF I WERE DOWN THERE, I'D BE SAYING "TAKE THAT, MONSTER! AND THAT! AND..."
...THAT... UH-OH!
IIIISSSSHH
RUN AWAY, KITTY! RUN AWAY! AS FAST AS-

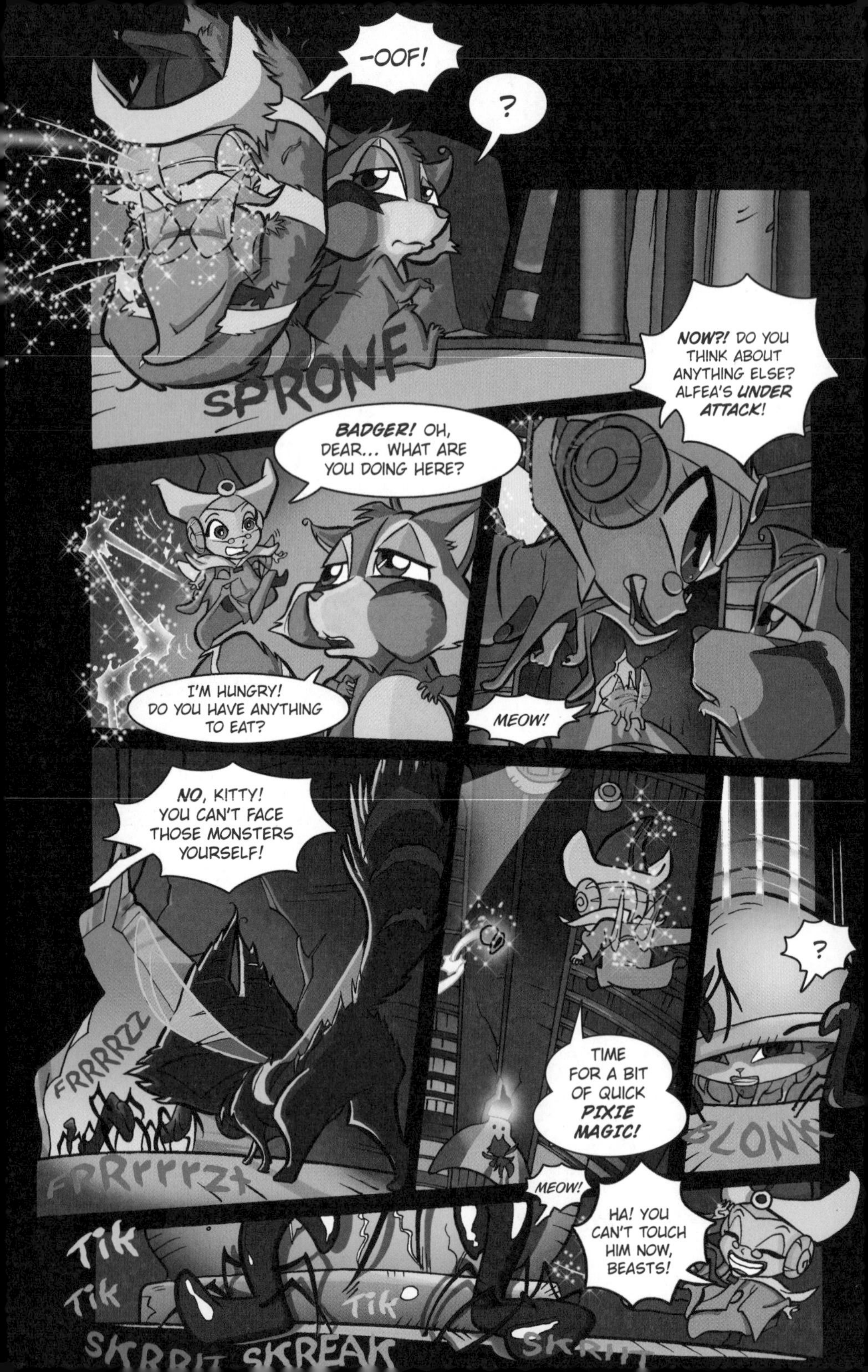

-OOF!
?
SPRONF
NOW?! DO YOU THINK ABOUT ANYTHING ELSE? ALFEA'S UNDER ATTACK!
BADGER! OH, DEAR... WHAT ARE YOU DOING HERE?
I'M HUNGRY! DO YOU HAVE ANYTHING TO EAT?
MEOW!
NO, KITTY! YOU CAN'T FACE THOSE MONSTERS YOURSELF!
FRRRRZZ
FRRrrrzt
?
TIME FOR A BIT OF QUICK PIXIE MAGIC!
BLONK
MEOW!
HA! YOU CAN'T TOUCH HIM NOW, BEASTS!
TIK
TIK
TIK
SKREAK

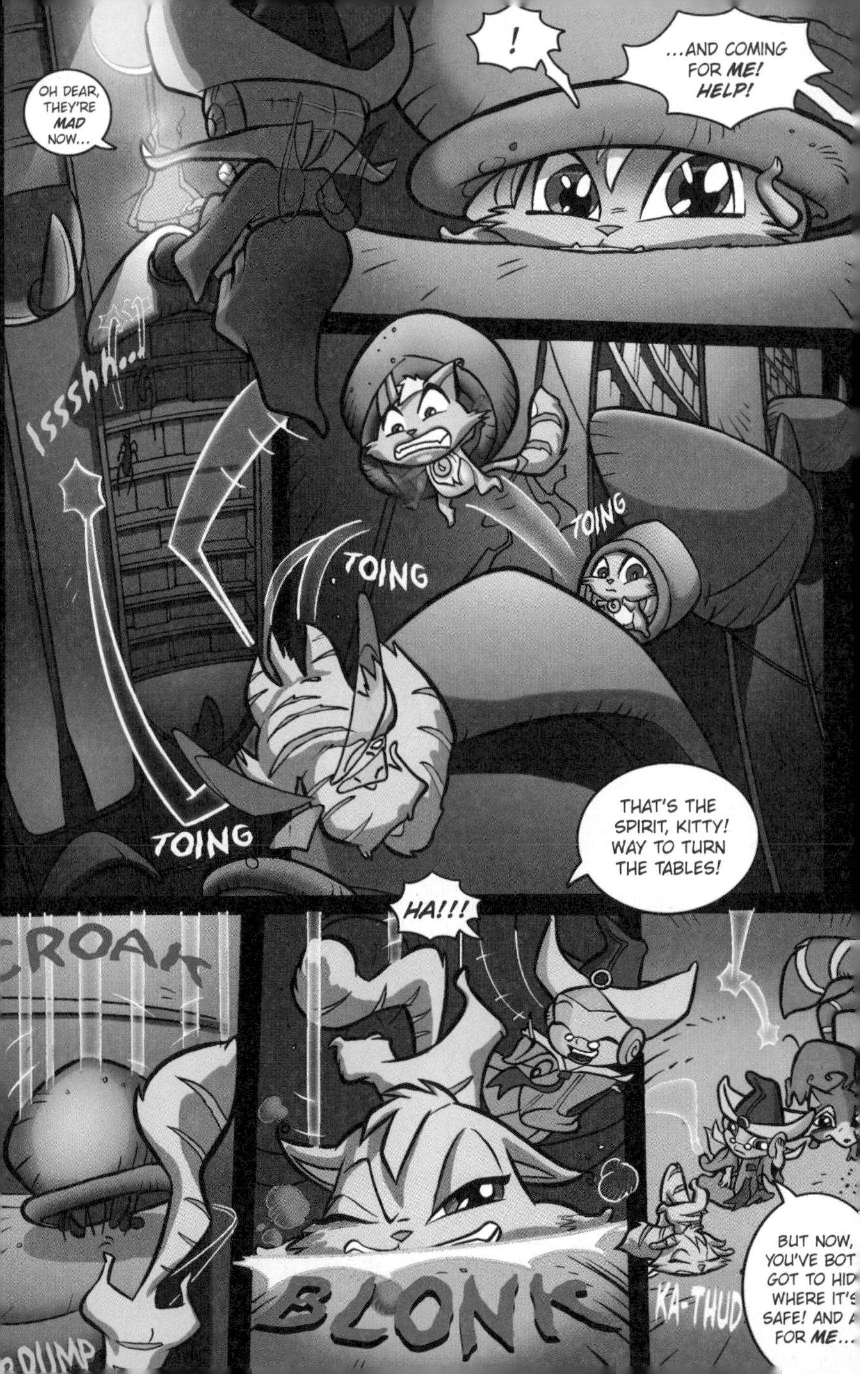
OH DEAR, THEY'RE MAD NOW...
!
...AND COMING FOR ME! HELP!
ISSSHH...
TOING
TOING
TOING
THAT'S THE SPIRIT, KITTY! WAY TO TURN THE TABLES!
CROAK
BRUMP
HA!!!
BLONK
KA-THUD
BUT NOW, YOU'VE BOT GOT TO HID WHERE IT'S SAFE! AND A FOR ME...

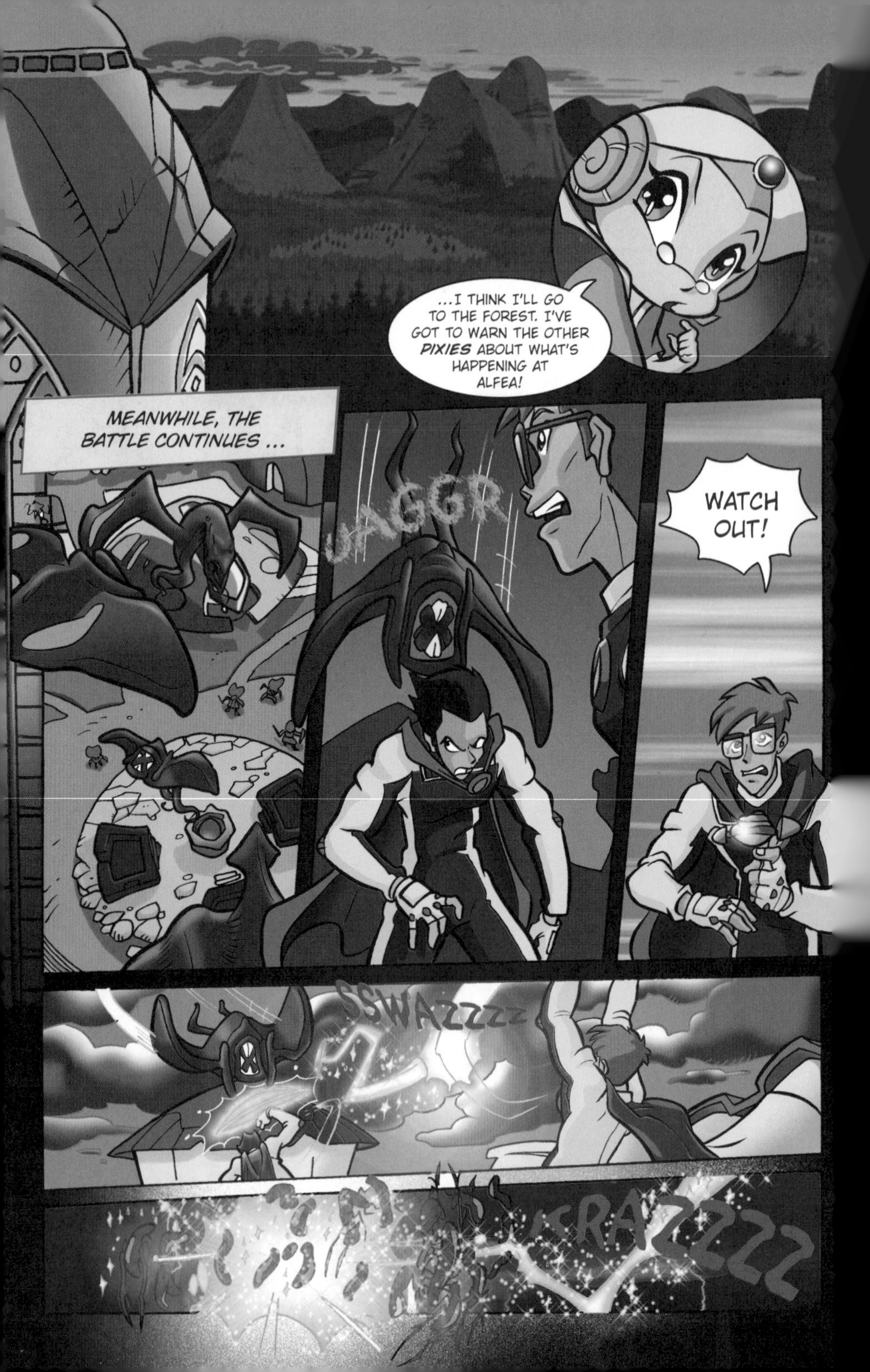

...I THINK I'LL GO TO THE FOREST. I'VE GOT TO WARN THE OTHER PIXIES ABOUT WHAT'S HAPPENING AT ALFEA!
MEANWHILE, THE BATTLE CONTINUES ...
UAGGR
WATCH OUT!
SSWAZZZZ
KRAZZZZZ

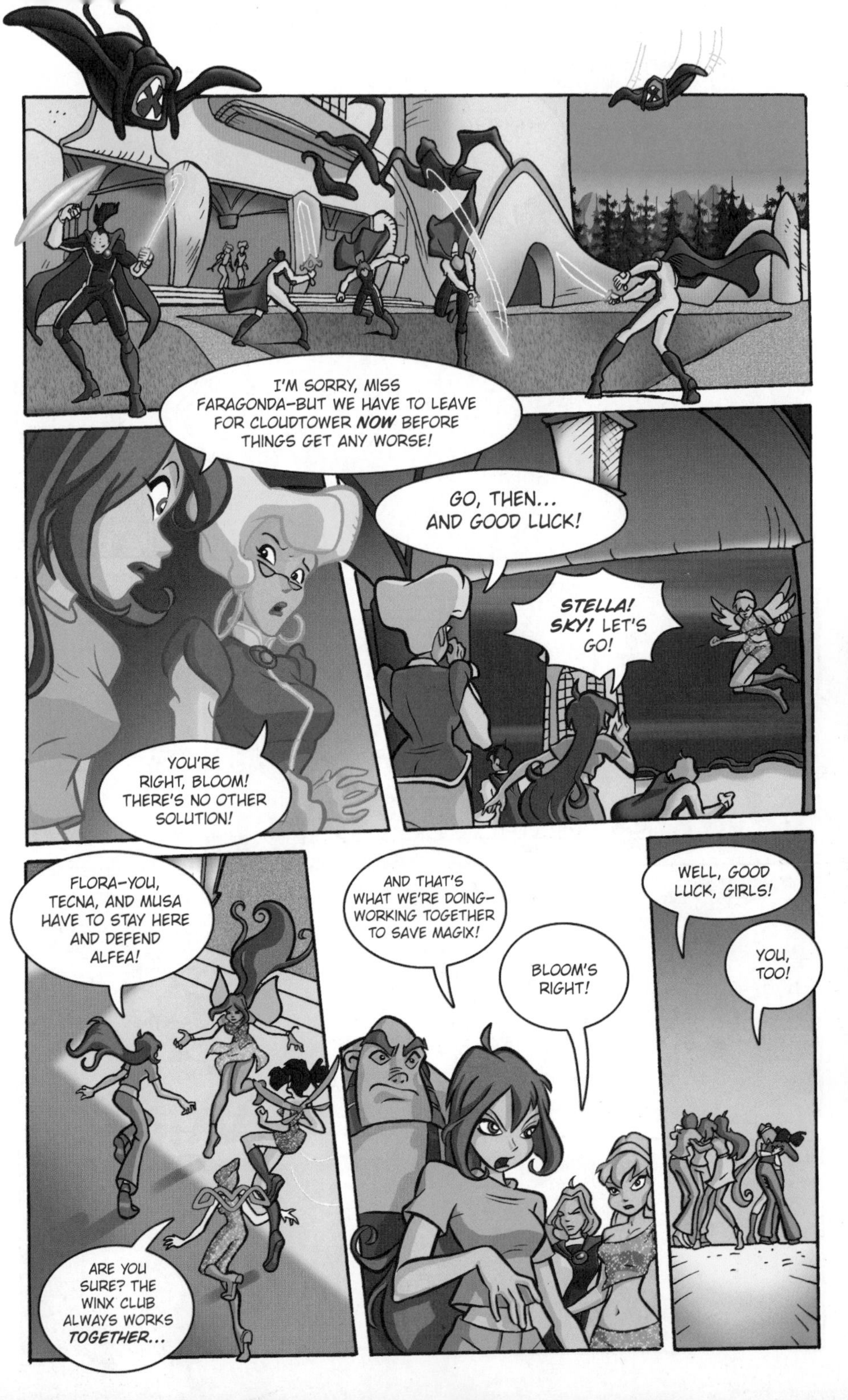
I'M SORRY, MISS FARAGONDA—BUT WE HAVE TO LEAVE FOR CLOUDTOWER NOW BEFORE THINGS GET ANY WORSE!
YOU'RE RIGHT, BLOOM! THERE'S NO OTHER SOLUTION!
GO, THEN... AND GOOD LUCK!
STELLA! SKY! LET'S GO!
FLORA—YOU, TECNA, AND MUSA HAVE TO STAY HERE AND DEFEND ALFEA!
ARE YOU SURE? THE WINX CLUB ALWAYS WORKS TOGETHER...
AND THAT'S WHAT WE'RE DOING-WORKING TOGETHER TO SAVE MAGIX!
BLOOM'S RIGHT!
WELL, GOOD LUCK, GIRLS!
YOU, TOO!

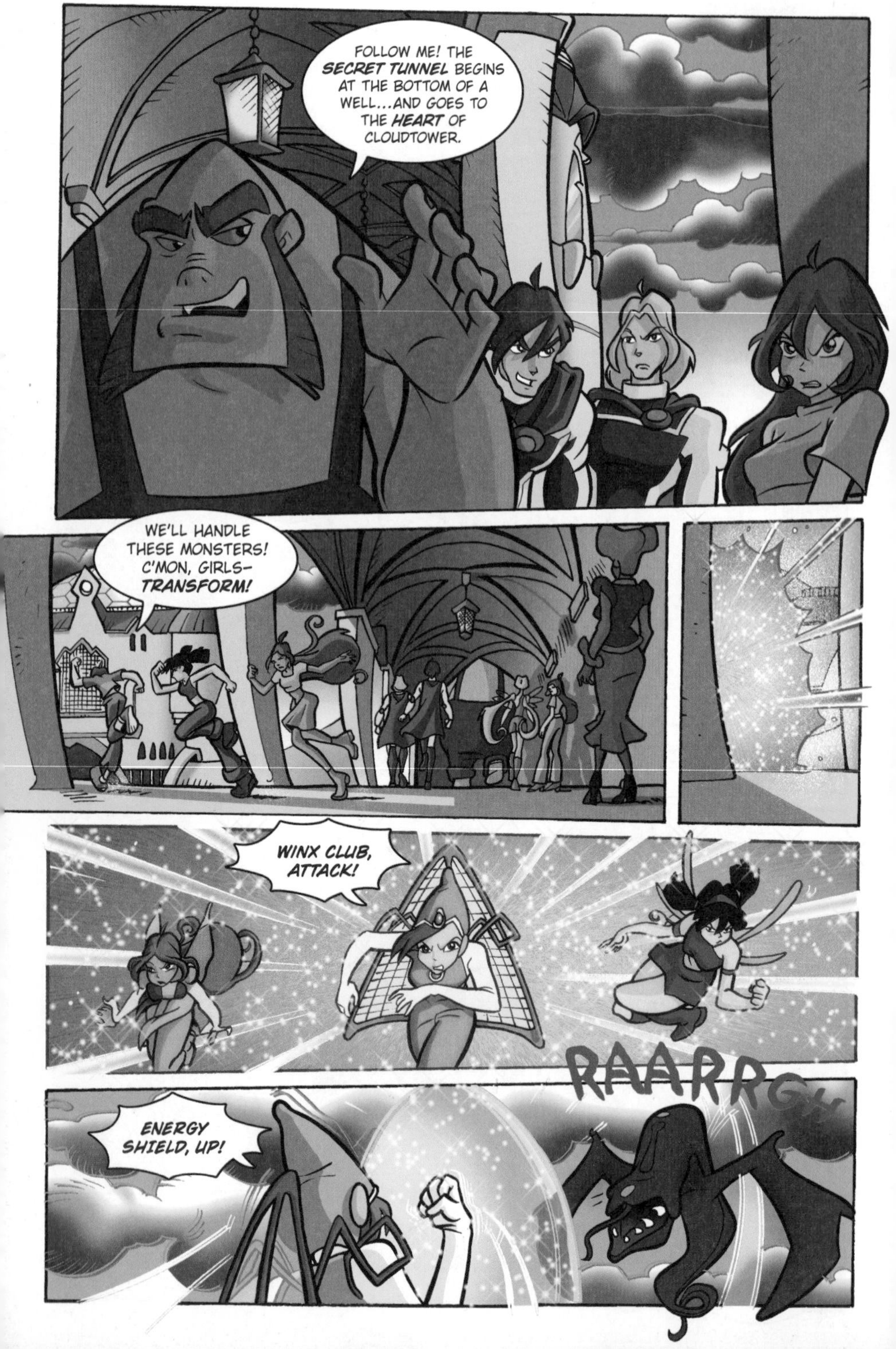
FOLLOW ME! THE SECRET TUNNEL BEGINS AT THE BOTTOM OF A WELL...AND GOES TO THE HEART OF CLOUDTOWER.
WE'LL HANDLE THESE MONSTERS! C'MON, GIRLS-TRANSFORM!
WINX CLUB, ATTACK!
RAARRGH
ENERGY SHIELD, UP!

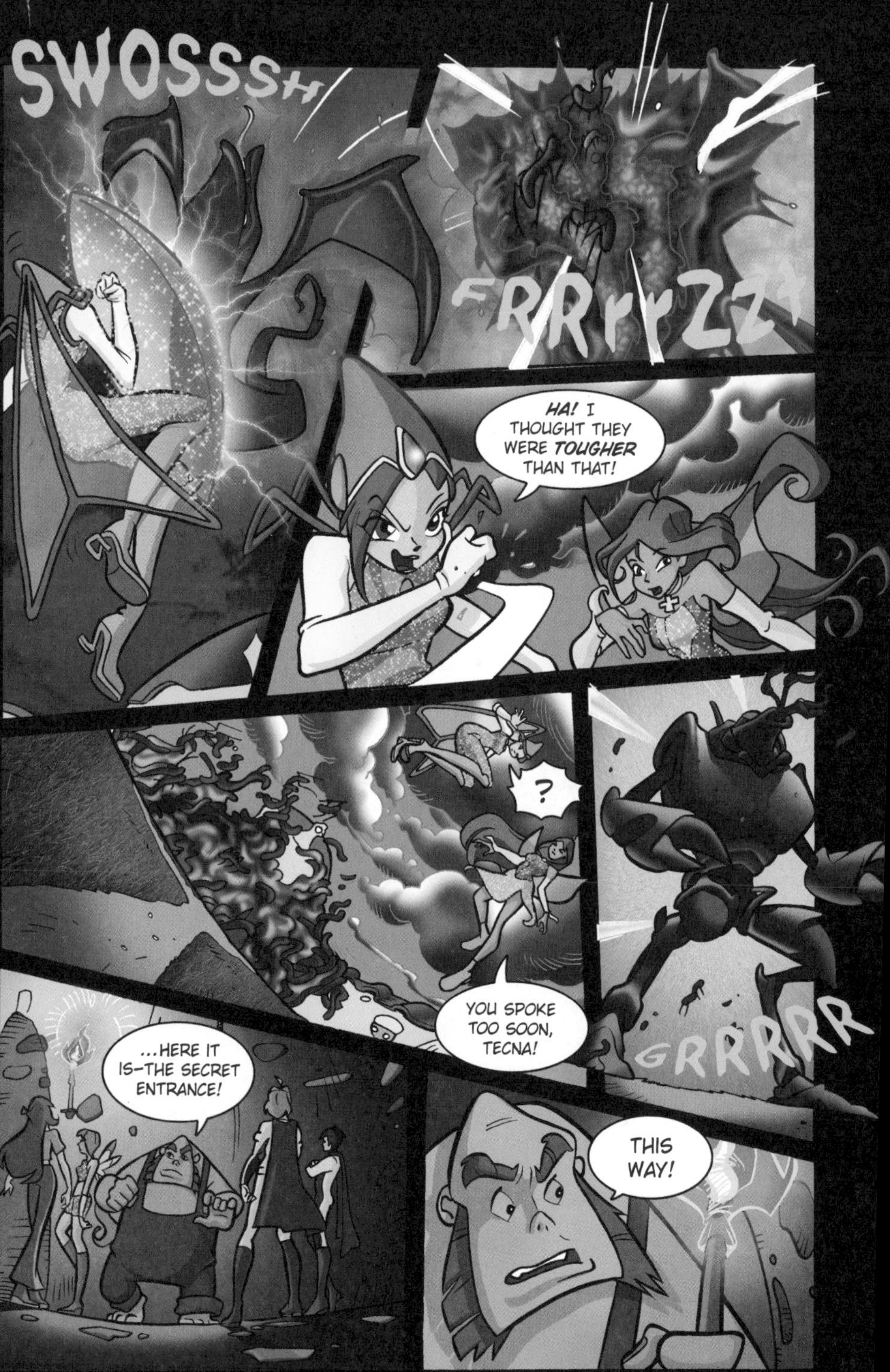
SWOSSSH
FRRrrZZ
HA! I THOUGHT THEY WERE TOUGHER THAN THAT!
?
GRRRRR
YOU SPOKE TOO SOON, TECNA!
...HERE IT IS—THE SECRET ENTRANCE!
THIS WAY!

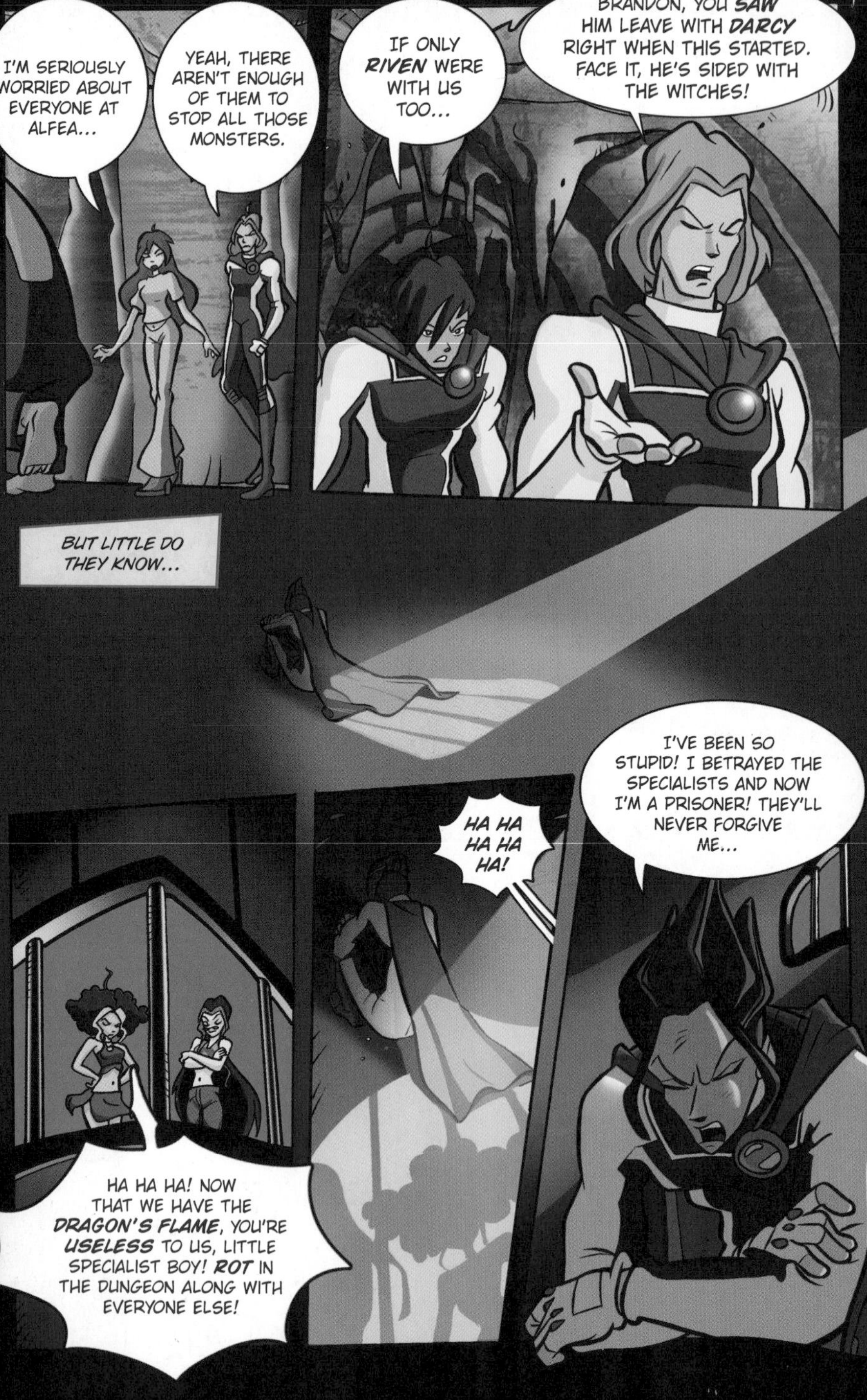
I'M SERIOUSLY WORRIED ABOUT EVERYONE AT ALFEA...
YEAH, THERE AREN'T ENOUGH OF THEM TO STOP ALL THOSE MONSTERS.
IF ONLY RIVEN WERE WITH US TOO...
BRANDON, YOU SAW HIM LEAVE WITH DARCY RIGHT WHEN THIS STARTED. FACE IT, HE'S SIDED WITH THE WITCHES!
BUT LITTLE DO THEY KNOW...
HA HA HA! NOW THAT WE HAVE THE DRAGON'S FLAME, YOU'RE USELESS TO US, LITTLE SPECIALIST BOY! ROT IN THE DUNGEON ALONG WITH EVERYONE ELSE!
HA HA HA HA HA!
I'VE BEEN SO STUPID! I BETRAYED THE SPECIALISTS AND NOW I'M A PRISONER! THEY'LL NEVER FORGIVE ME...

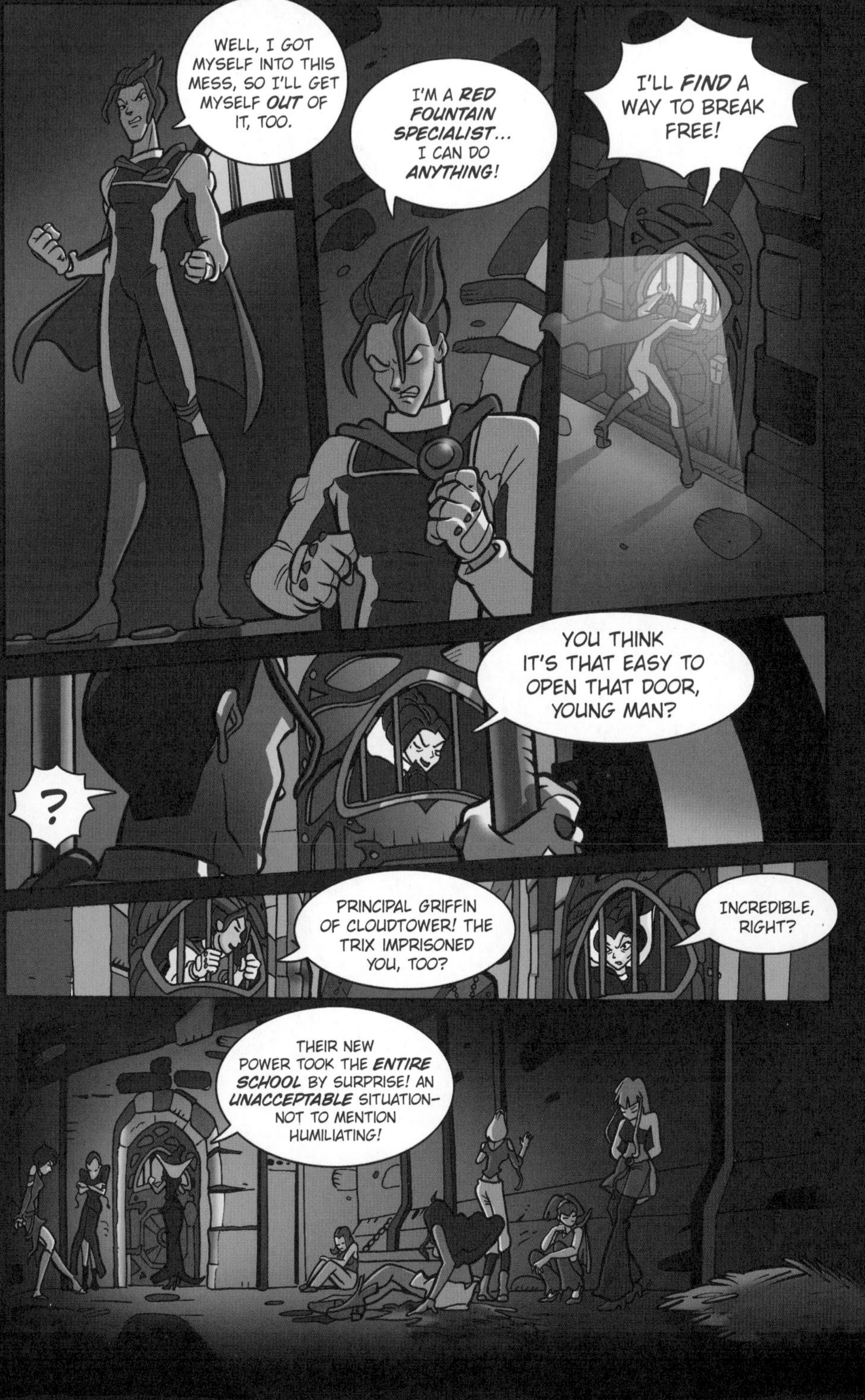
WELL, I GOT MYSELF INTO THIS MESS, SO I'LL GET MYSELF OUT OF IT, TOO.
I'M A RED FOUNTAIN SPECIALIST... I CAN DO ANYTHING!
I'LL FIND A WAY TO BREAK FREE!
YOU THINK IT'S THAT EASY TO OPEN THAT DOOR, YOUNG MAN?
?
PRINCIPAL GRIFFIN OF CLOUDTOWER! THE TRIX IMPRISONED YOU, TOO?
INCREDIBLE, RIGHT?
THEIR NEW POWER TOOK THE ENTIRE SCHOOL BY SURPRISE! AN UNACCEPTABLE SITUATION— NOT TO MENTION HUMILIATING!

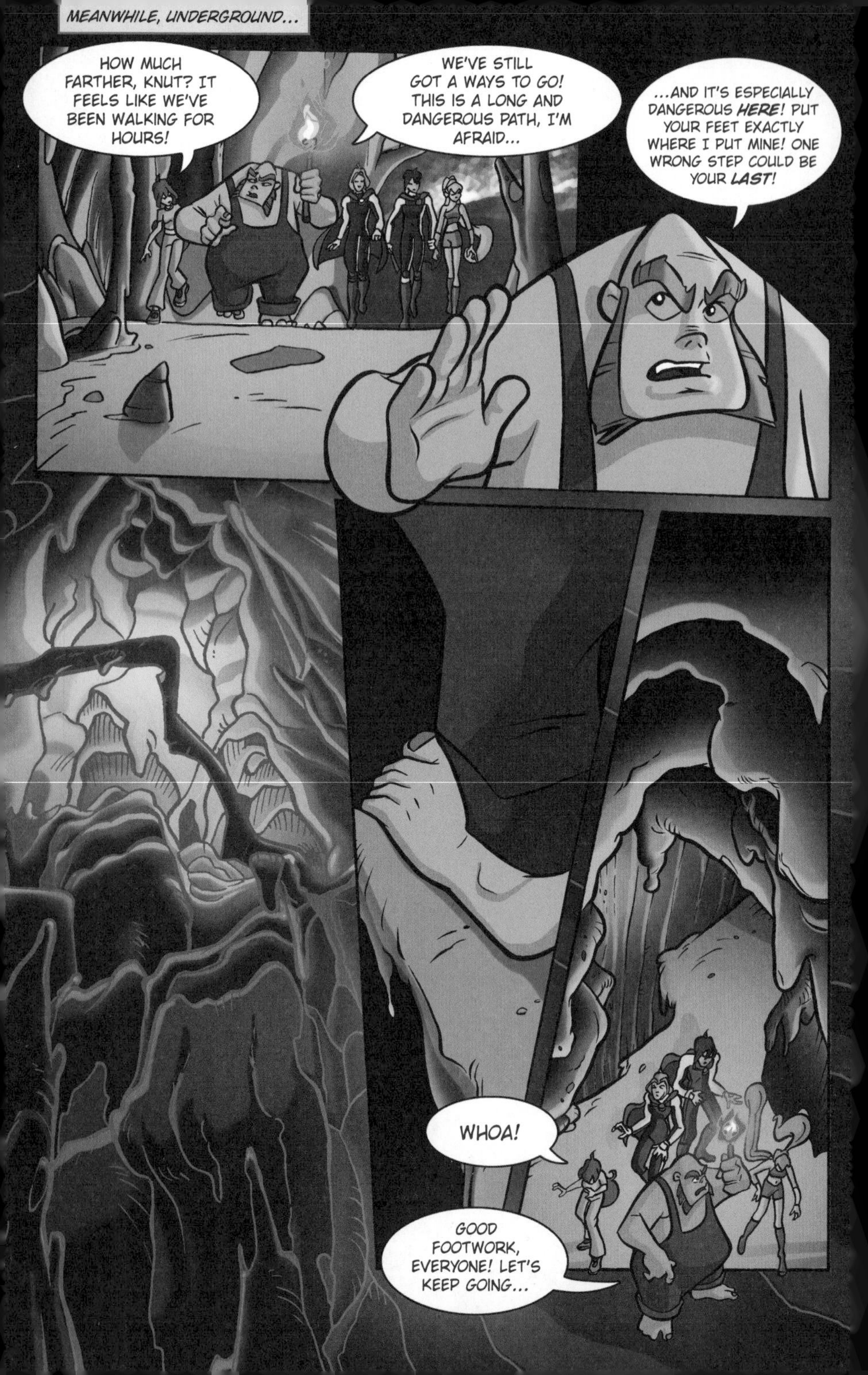
MEANWHILE, UNDERGROUND...
HOW MUCH FARTHER, KNUT? IT FEELS LIKE WE'VE BEEN WALKING FOR HOURS!
WE'VE STILL GOT A WAYS TO GO! THIS IS A LONG AND DANGEROUS PATH, I'M AFRAID...
...AND IT'S ESPECIALLY DANGEROUS HERE! PUT YOUR FEET EXACTLY WHERE I PUT MINE! ONE WRONG STEP COULD BE YOUR LAST!
WHOA!
GOOD FOOTWORK, EVERYONE! LET'S KEEP GOING...

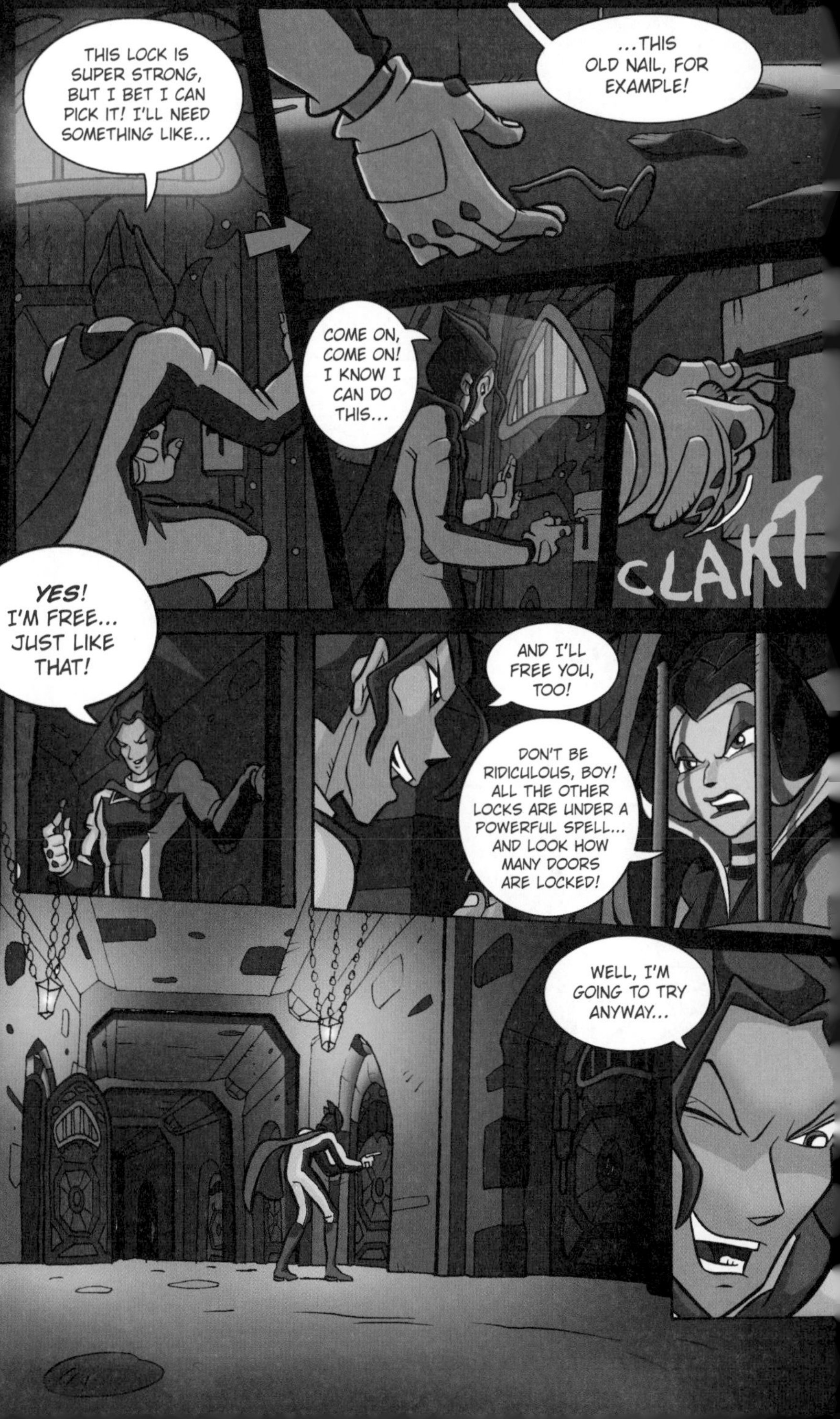
THIS LOCK IS SUPER STRONG, BUT I BET I CAN PICK IT! I'LL NEED SOMETHING LIKE…
…THIS OLD NAIL, FOR EXAMPLE!
COME ON, COME ON! I KNOW I CAN DO THIS…
CLAKT
YES! I'M FREE… JUST LIKE THAT!
AND I'LL FREE YOU, TOO!
DON'T BE RIDICULOUS, BOY! ALL THE OTHER LOCKS ARE UNDER A POWERFUL SPELL… AND LOOK HOW MANY DOORS ARE LOCKED!
WELL, I'M GOING TO TRY ANYWAY…

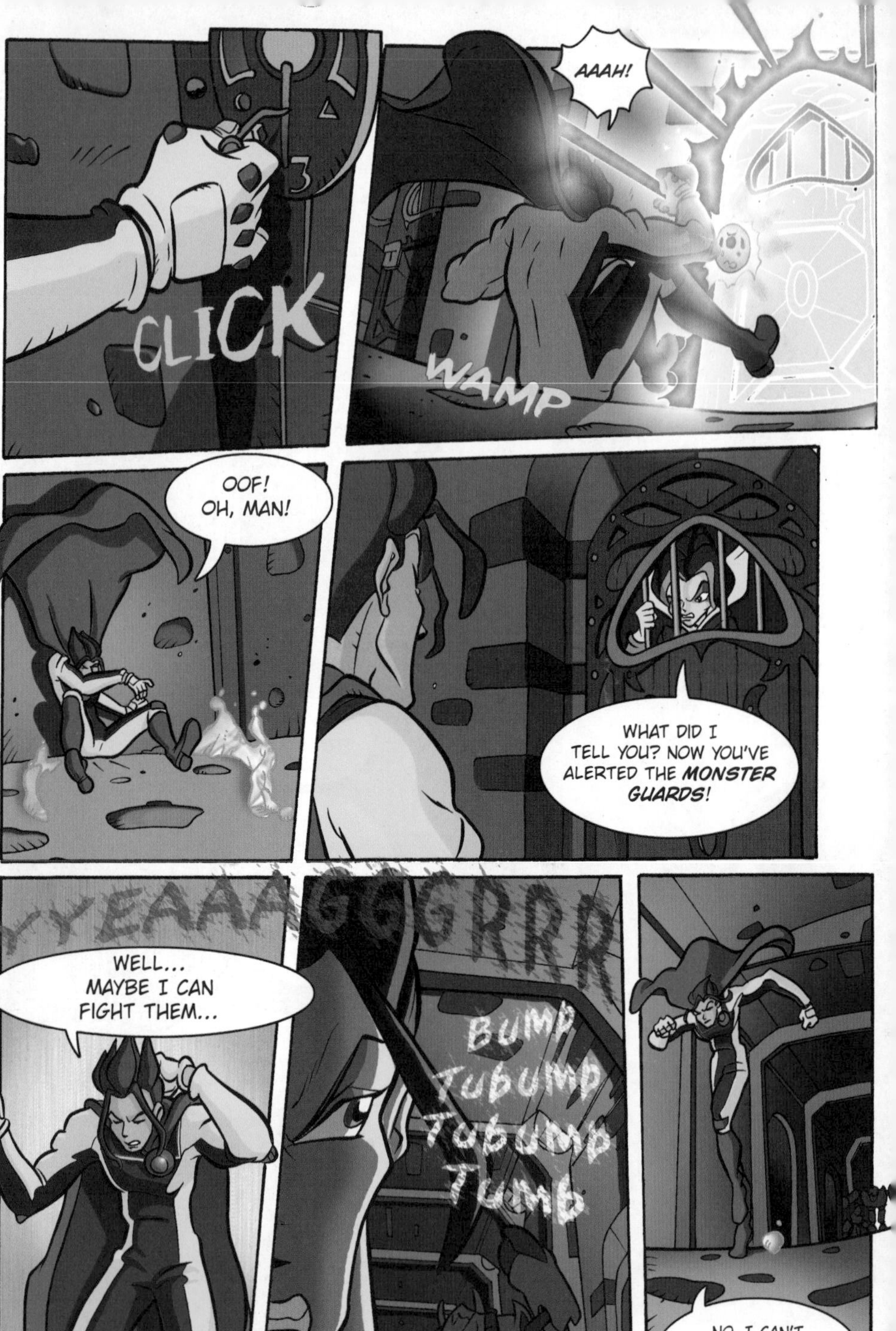
CLICK
AAAH!
WAMP
OOF! OH, MAN!
WHAT DID I TELL YOU? NOW YOU'VE ALERTED THE MONSTER GUARDS!
YYEAAAGGGGRRR
WELL... MAYBE I CAN FIGHT THEM...
BUMP TUBUMP TUBUMP TUMB
NO, I CAN'T DO IT ALONE—I HAVE TO RUN FOR IT!

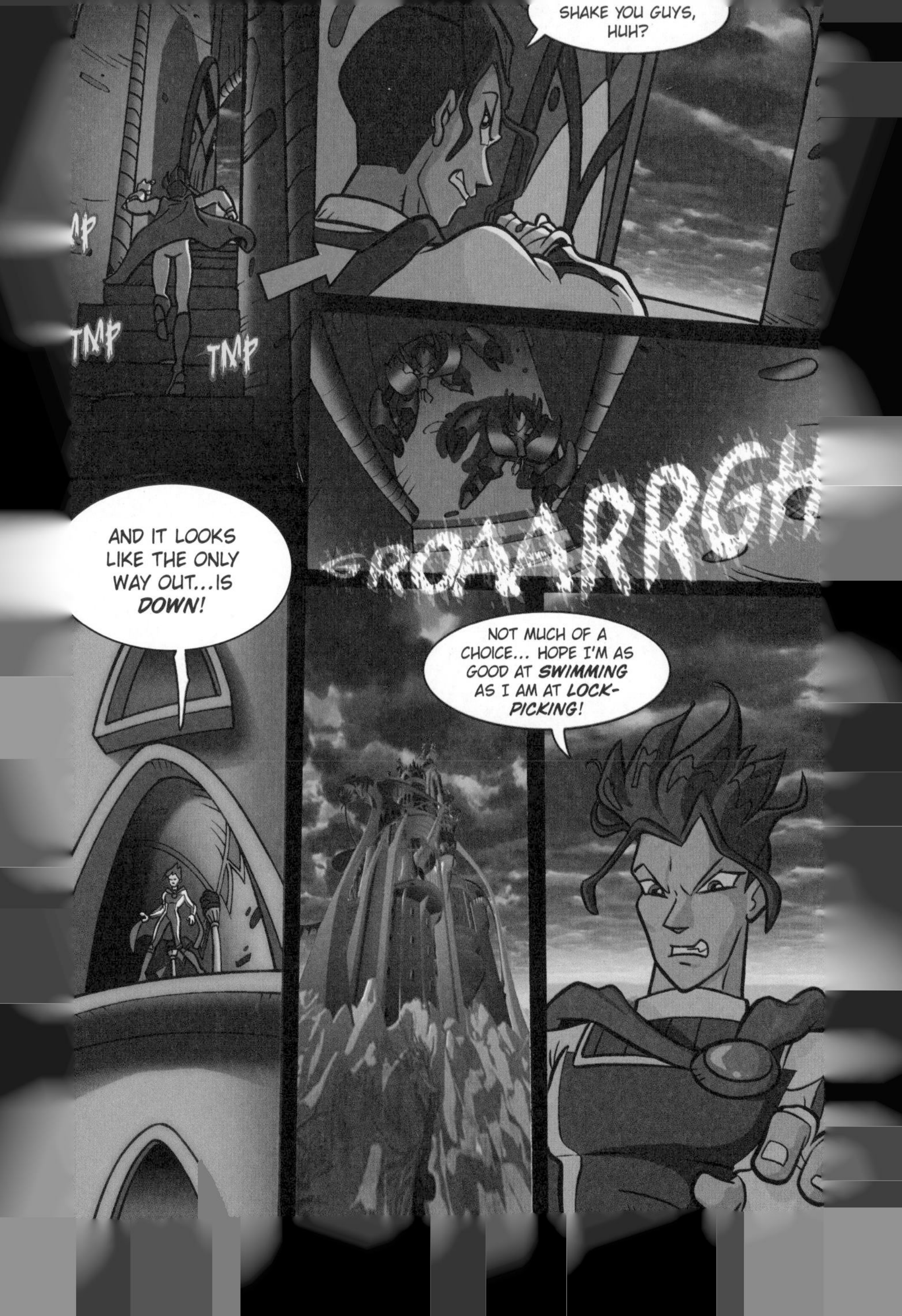
SHAKE YOU GUYS, HUH?
TMP
TMP
GROAARRGH
AND IT LOOKS LIKE THE ONLY WAY OUT...IS DOWN!
NOT MUCH OF A CHOICE... HOPE I'M AS GOOD AT SWIMMING AS I AM AT LOCK-PICKING!

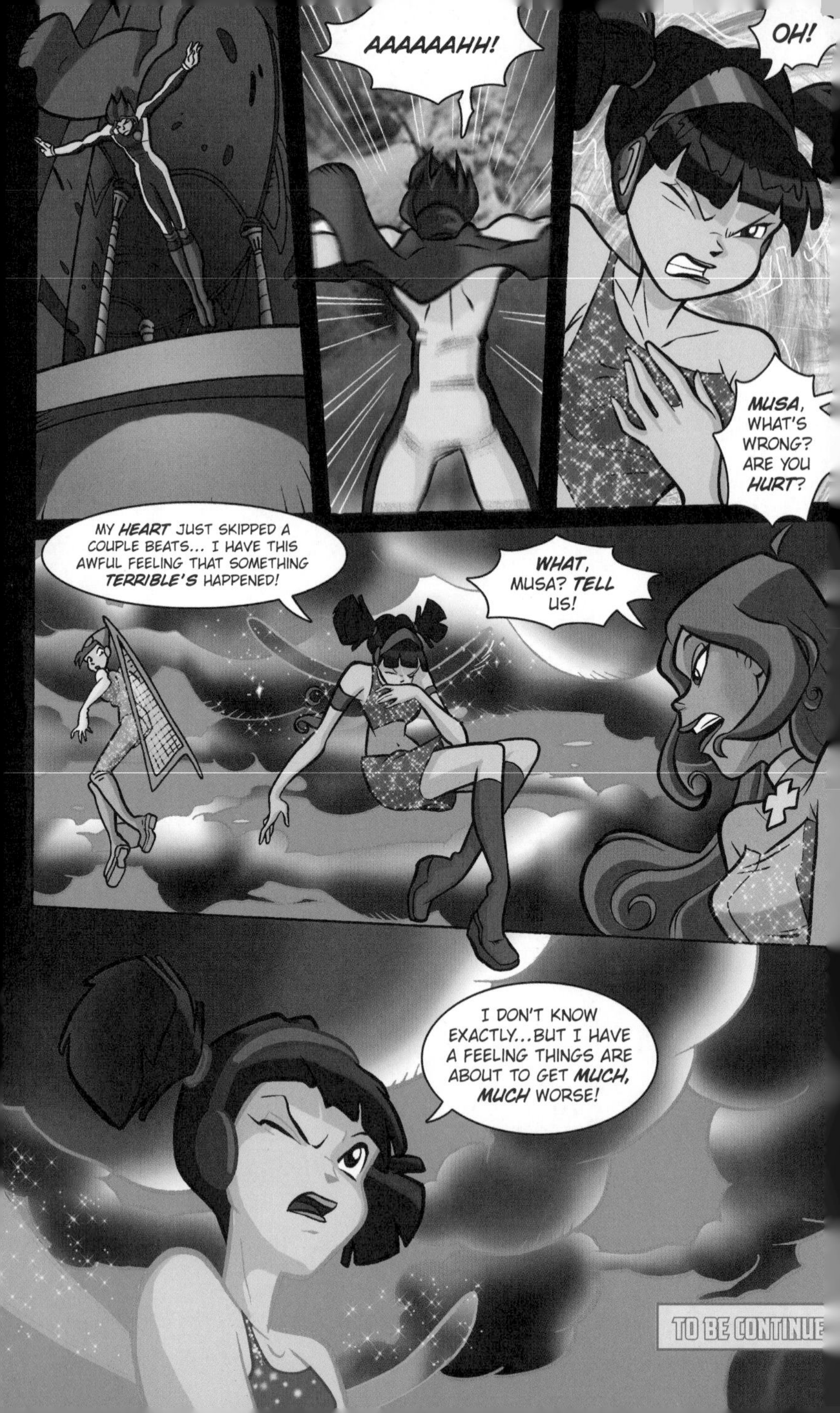
AAAAAAHH!
OH!
MUSA, WHAT'S WRONG? ARE YOU HURT?
MY HEART JUST SKIPPED A COUPLE BEATS... I HAVE THIS AWFUL FEELING THAT SOMETHING TERRIBLE'S HAPPENED!
WHAT, MUSA? TELL US!
I DON'T KNOW EXACTLY...BUT I HAVE A FEELING THINGS ARE ABOUT TO GET MUCH, MUCH WORSE!
TO BE CONTINUE

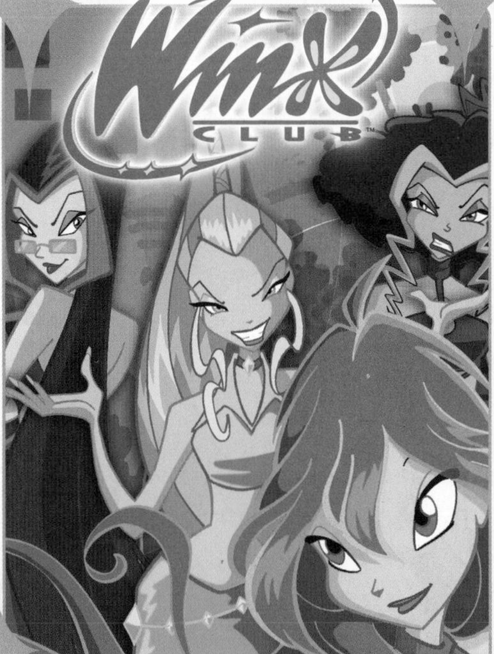
Winx CLUB

Magic Battle

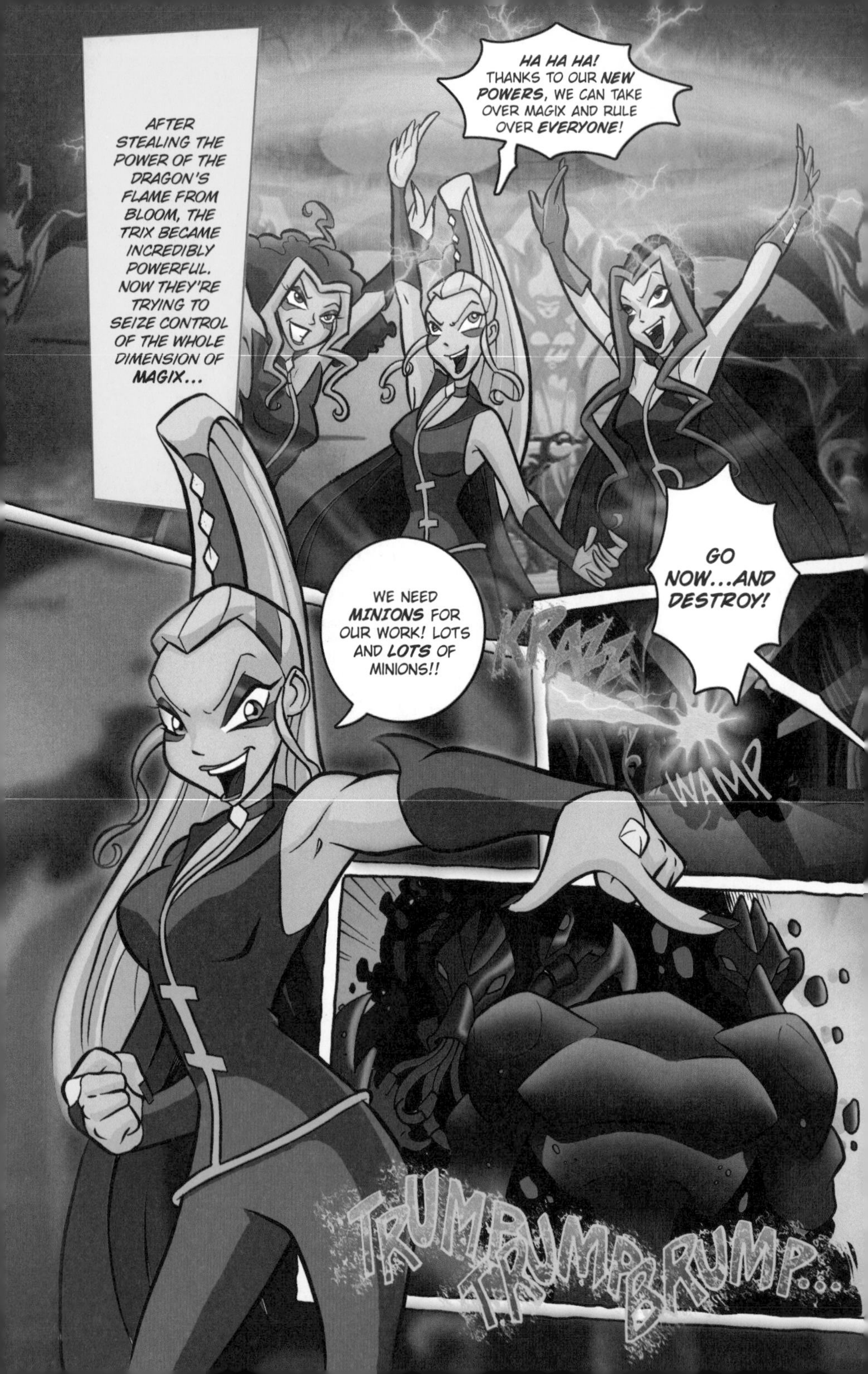
AFTER STEALING THE POWER OF THE DRAGON'S FLAME FROM BLOOM, THE TRIX BECAME INCREDIBLY POWERFUL. NOW THEY'RE TRYING TO SEIZE CONTROL OF THE WHOLE DIMENSION OF MAGIX...
HA HA HA! THANKS TO OUR NEW POWERS, WE CAN TAKE OVER MAGIX AND RULE OVER EVERYONE!
WE NEED MINIONS FOR OUR WORK! LOTS AND LOTS OF MINIONS!!
GO NOW...AND DESTROY!
KRAZZ
WAMP
TRUMP TRUMP BRUMP...

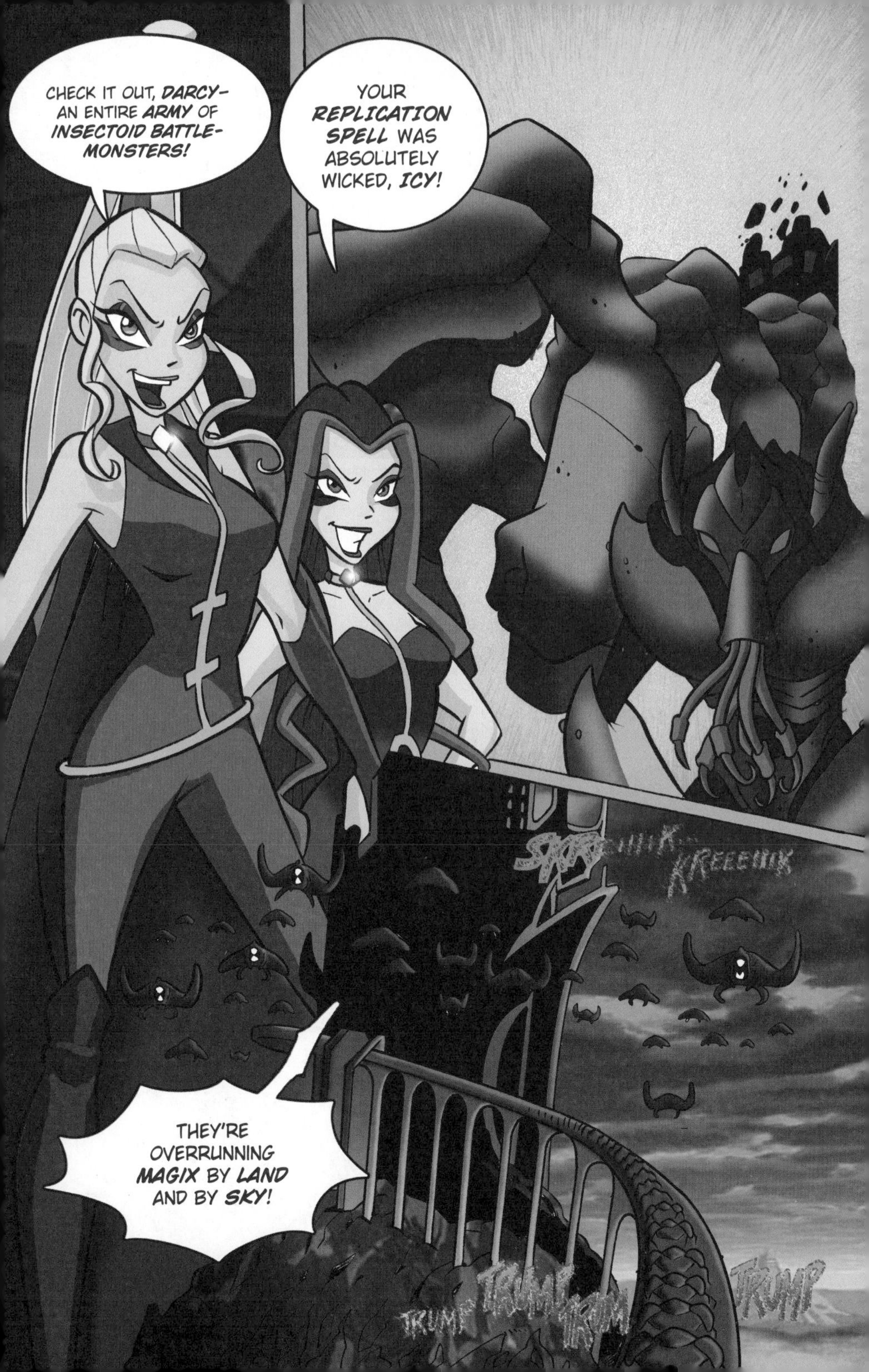
CHECK IT OUT, DARCY— AN ENTIRE ARMY OF INSECTOID BATTLE-MONSTERS!
YOUR REPLICATION SPELL WAS ABSOLUTELY WICKED, ICY!
SKREEEHHK... KREEEHHK
THEY'RE OVERRUNNING MAGIX BY LAND AND BY SKY!
TRUMP TRUMP TRUMP
TRUMP

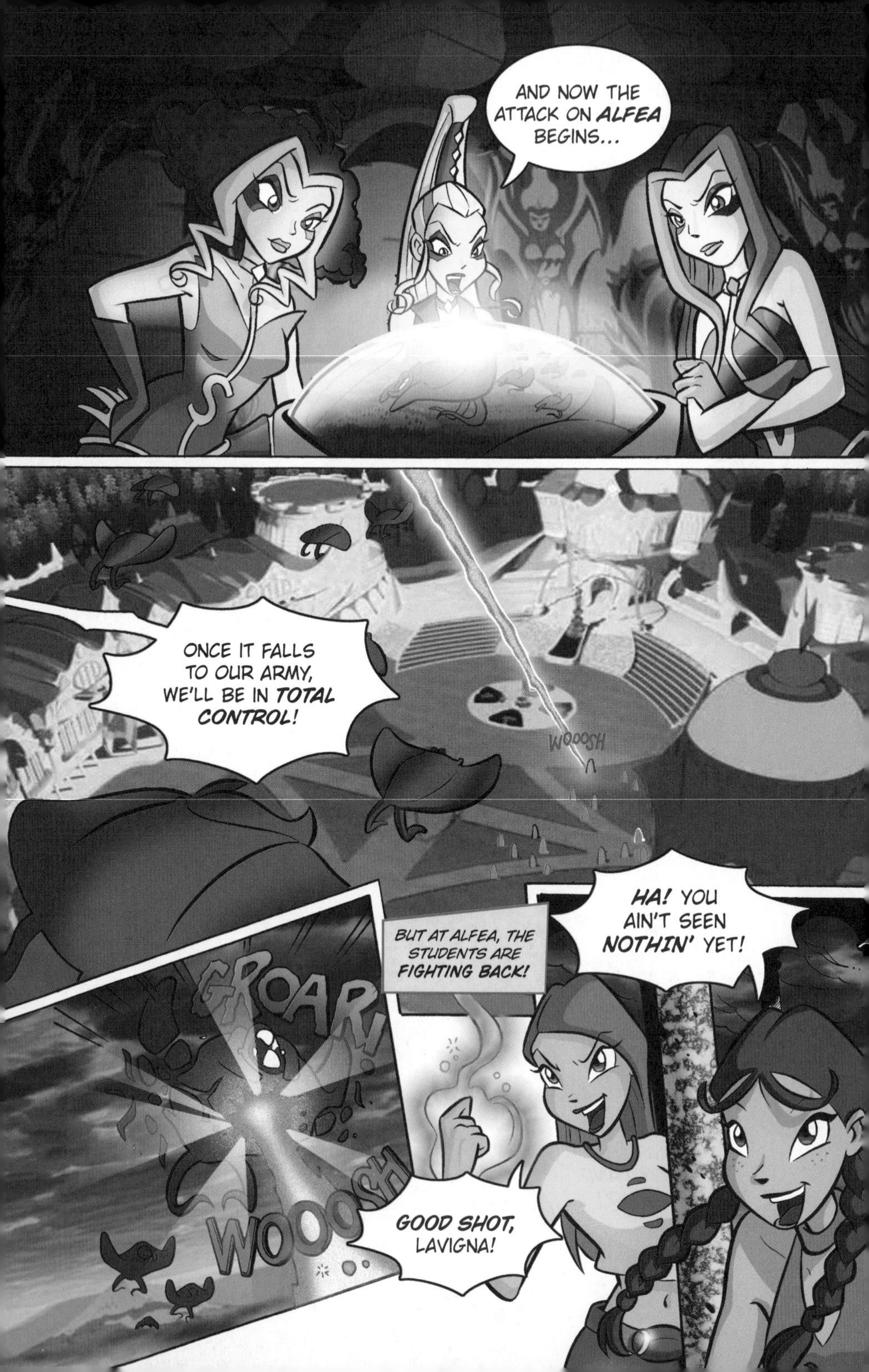
AND NOW THE ATTACK ON ALFEA BEGINS...
ONCE IT FALLS TO OUR ARMY, WE'LL BE IN TOTAL CONTROL!
WOOOSH
BUT AT ALFEA, THE STUDENTS ARE FIGHTING BACK!
HA! YOU AIN'T SEEN NOTHIN' YET!
GROAR!
WOOOSH
GOOD SHOT, LAVIGNA!

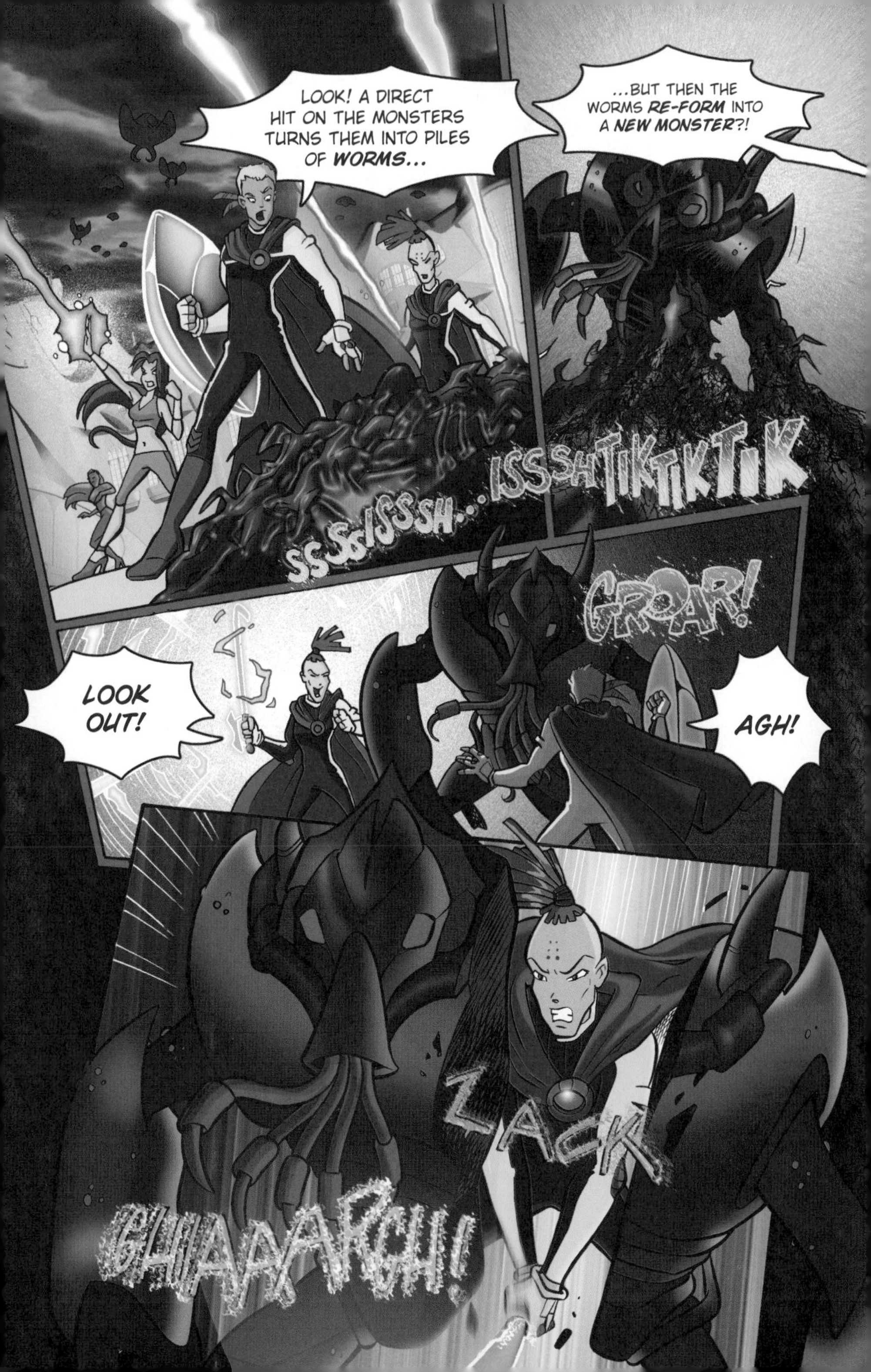
LOOK! A DIRECT HIT ON THE MONSTERS TURNS THEM INTO PILES OF WORMS...
...BUT THEN THE WORMS RE-FORM INTO A NEW MONSTER?!
SSSSISSSH...ISSSH
TIKTIKTIK
GROAR!
LOOK OUT!
AGH!
ZACK
GHAAARGH!

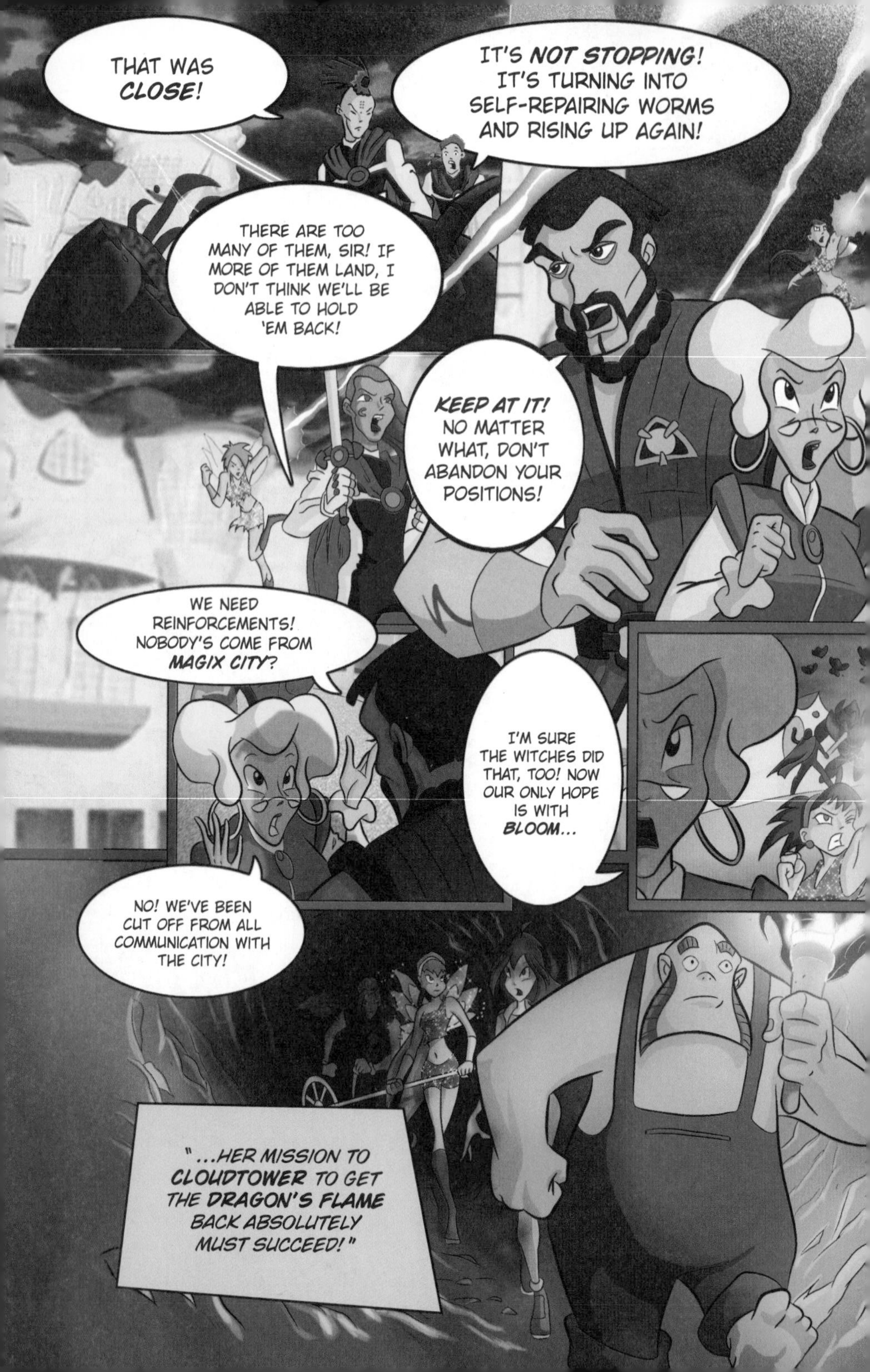
THAT WAS CLOSE!
IT'S NOT STOPPING! IT'S TURNING INTO SELF-REPAIRING WORMS AND RISING UP AGAIN!
THERE ARE TOO MANY OF THEM, SIR! IF MORE OF THEM LAND, I DON'T THINK WE'LL BE ABLE TO HOLD 'EM BACK!
KEEP AT IT! NO MATTER WHAT, DON'T ABANDON YOUR POSITIONS!
WE NEED REINFORCEMENTS! NOBODY'S COME FROM MAGIX CITY?
NO! WE'VE BEEN CUT OFF FROM ALL COMMUNICATION WITH THE CITY!
I'M SURE THE WITCHES DID THAT, TOO! NOW OUR ONLY HOPE IS WITH BLOOM...
"...HER MISSION TO CLOUDTOWER TO GET THE DRAGON'S FLAME BACK ABSOLUTELY MUST SUCCEED!"

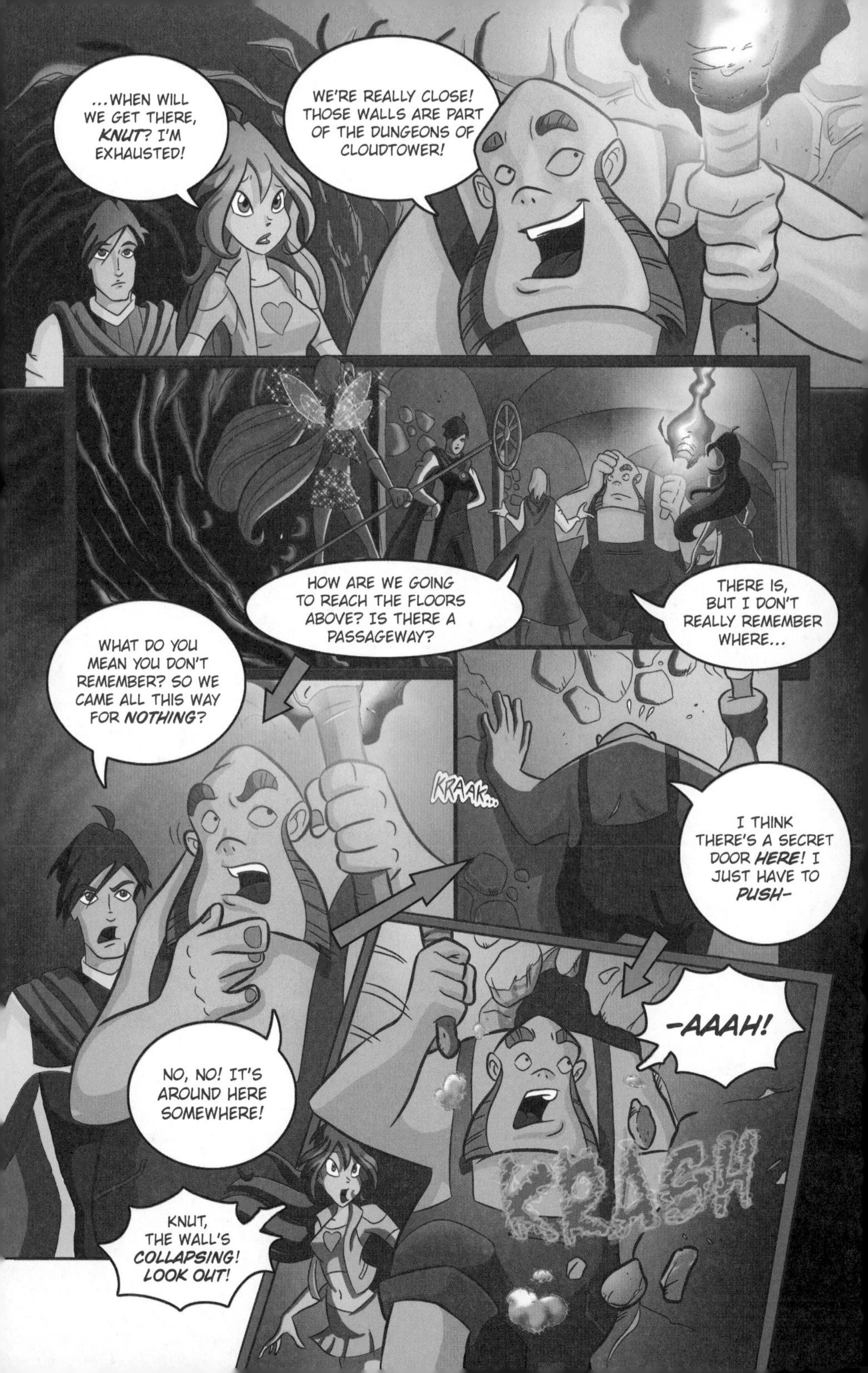
...WHEN WILL WE GET THERE, *KNUT*? I'M EXHAUSTED!
WE'RE REALLY CLOSE! THOSE WALLS ARE PART OF THE DUNGEONS OF CLOUDTOWER!
HOW ARE WE GOING TO REACH THE FLOORS ABOVE? IS THERE A PASSAGEWAY?
THERE IS, BUT I DON'T REALLY REMEMBER WHERE...
WHAT DO YOU MEAN YOU DON'T REMEMBER? SO WE CAME ALL THIS WAY FOR *NOTHING*?
NO, NO! IT'S AROUND HERE SOMEWHERE!
KRAAK...
I THINK THERE'S A SECRET DOOR *HERE*! I JUST HAVE TO *PUSH*-
-AAAH!
KNUT, THE WALL'S *COLLAPSING*! *LOOK OUT*!

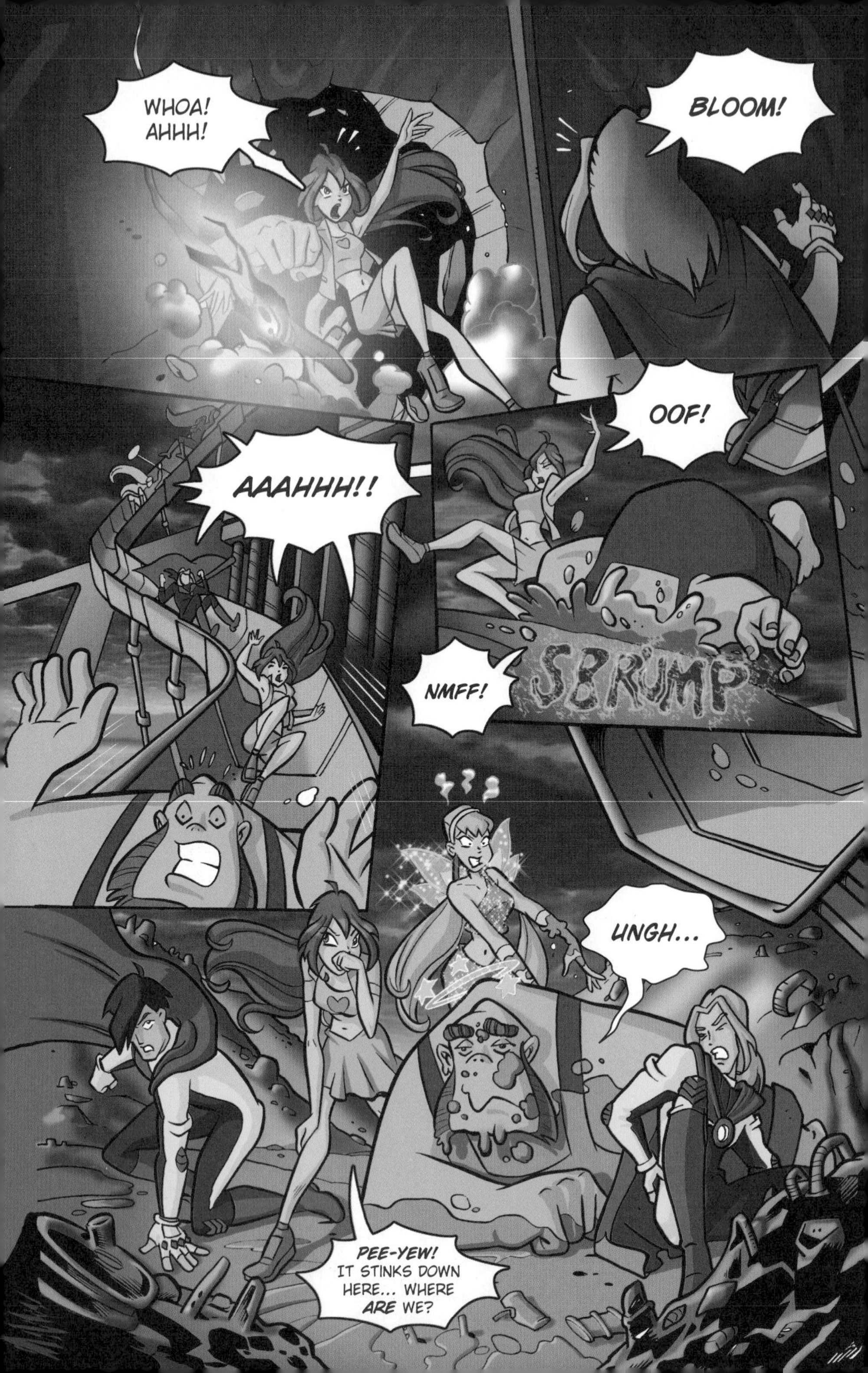
WHOA! AHHH!
BLOOM!
AAAHHH!!
OOF!
SCRUMP
NMFF!
UNGH...
PEE-YEW! IT STINKS DOWN HERE... WHERE ARE WE?

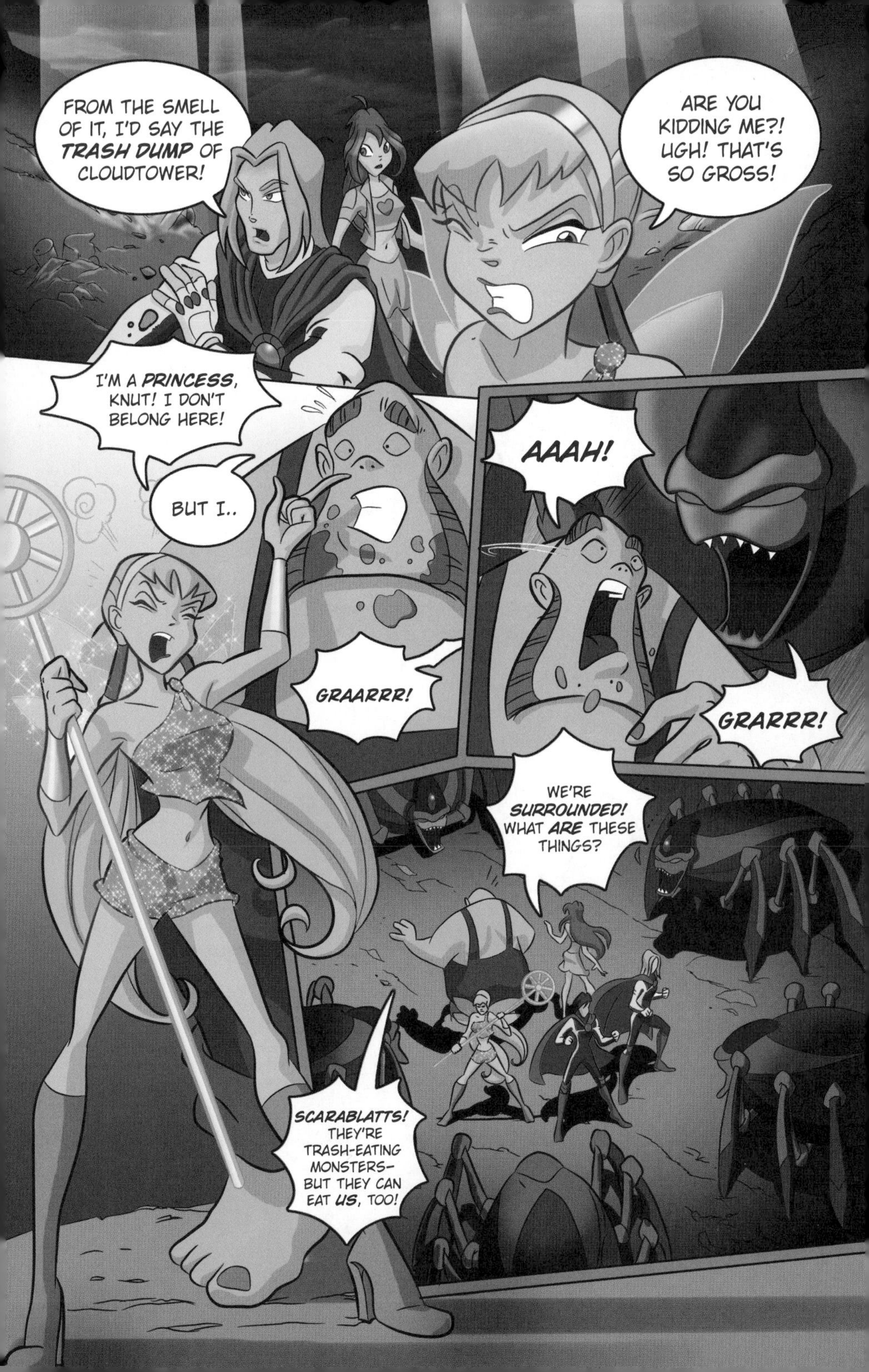
FROM THE SMELL OF IT, I'D SAY THE TRASH DUMP OF CLOUDTOWER!
ARE YOU KIDDING ME?! UGH! THAT'S SO GROSS!
I'M A PRINCESS, KNUT! I DON'T BELONG HERE!
BUT I..
AAAH!
GRAARRR!
GRARRR!
WE'RE SURROUNDED! WHAT ARE THESE THINGS?
SCARABLATTS! THEY'RE TRASH-EATING MONSTERS-BUT THEY CAN EAT US, TOO!

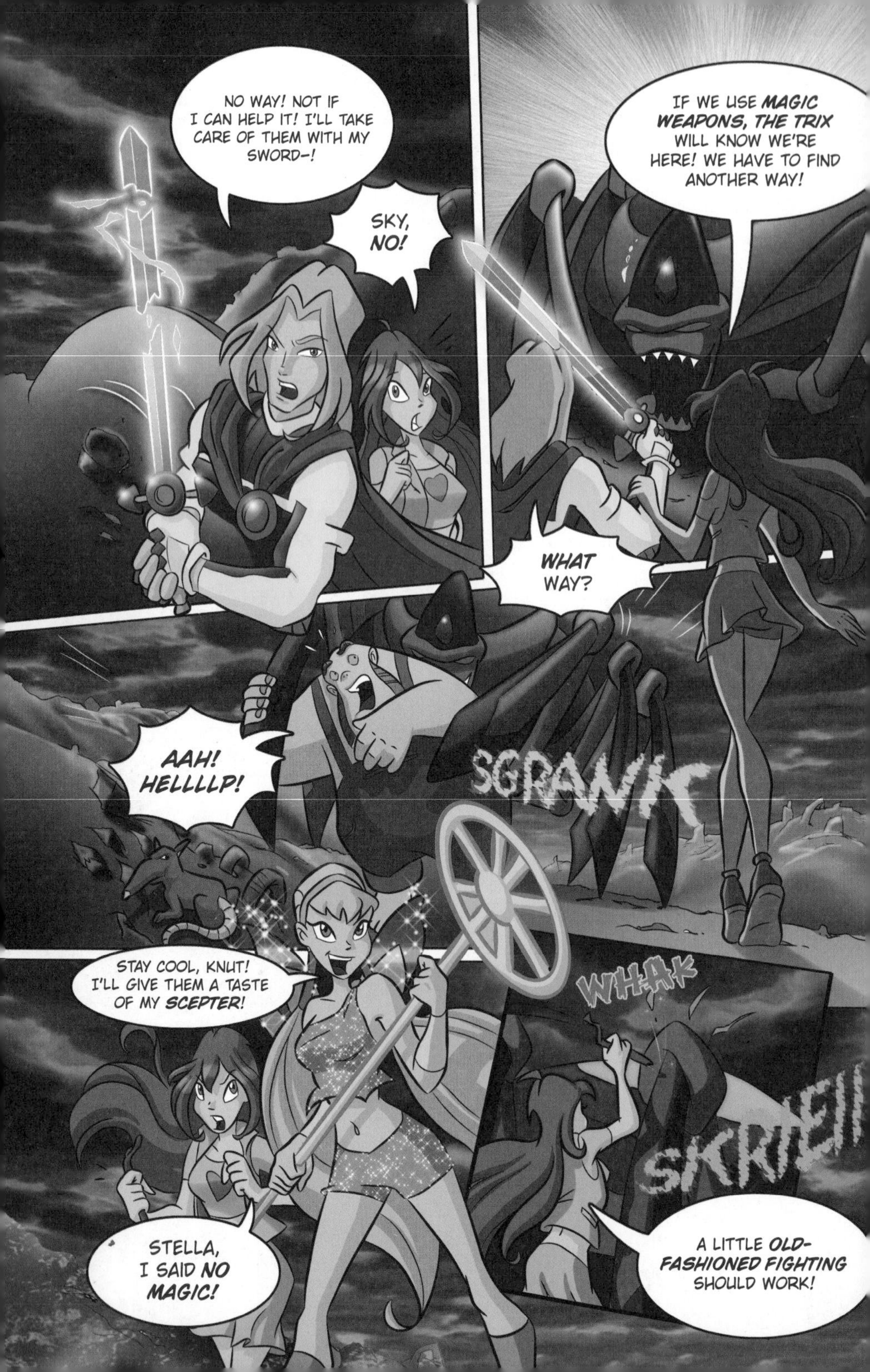
NO WAY! NOT IF I CAN HELP IT! I'LL TAKE CARE OF THEM WITH MY SWORD-!
SKY, NO!
IF WE USE MAGIC WEAPONS, THE TRIX WILL KNOW WE'RE HERE! WE HAVE TO FIND ANOTHER WAY!
WHAT WAY?
AAH! HELLLLP!
SGRAWK
STAY COOL, KNUT! I'LL GIVE THEM A TASTE OF MY SCEPTER!
WHAK
SKRIEII
STELLA, I SAID NO MAGIC!
A LITTLE OLD-FASHIONED FIGHTING SHOULD WORK!

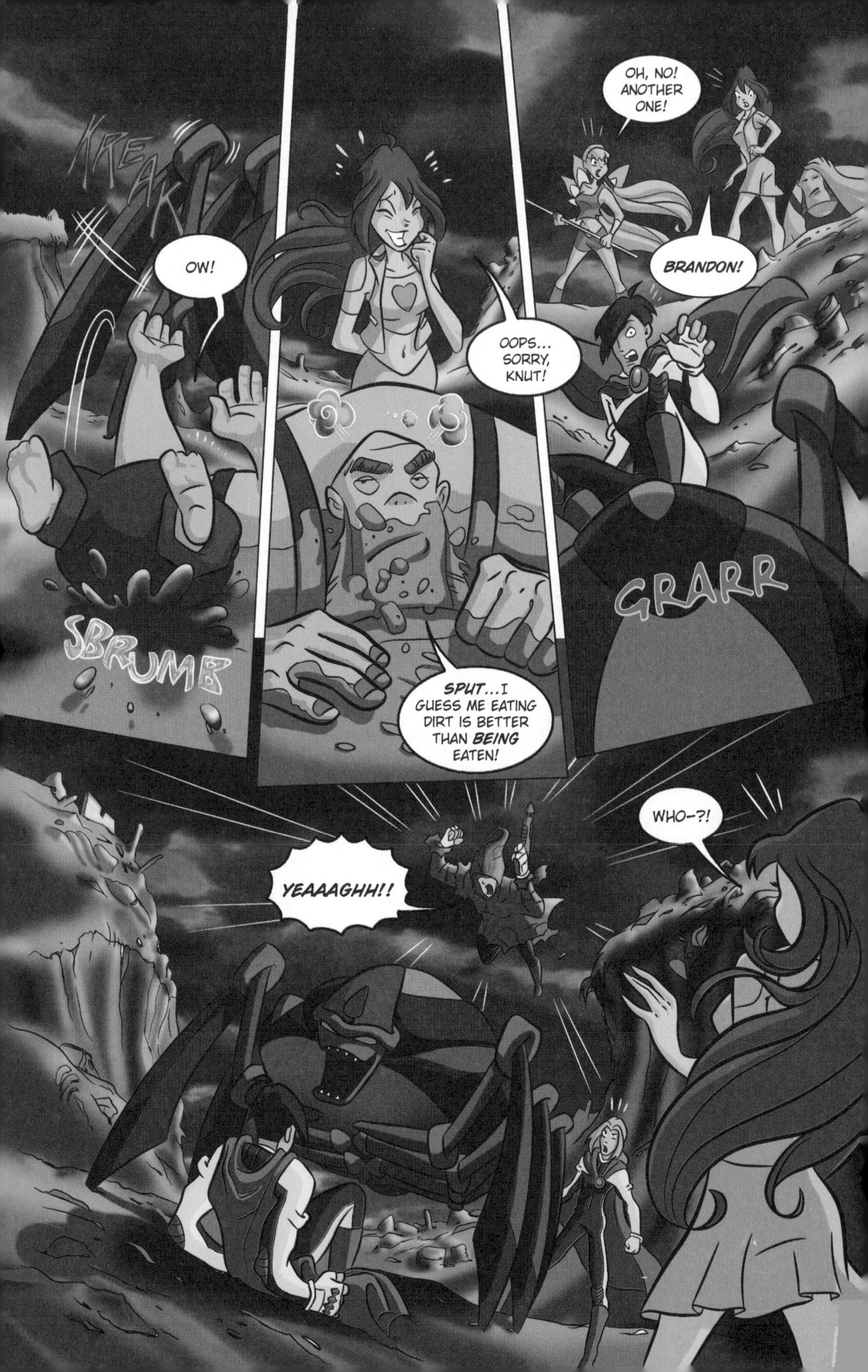
KREAK
OW!
SBRUMB
OOPS... SORRY, KNUT!
SPUT...I GUESS ME EATING DIRT IS BETTER THAN BEING EATEN!
OH, NO! ANOTHER ONE!
BRANDON!
GRARR
YEAAAGHH!!
WHO-?!

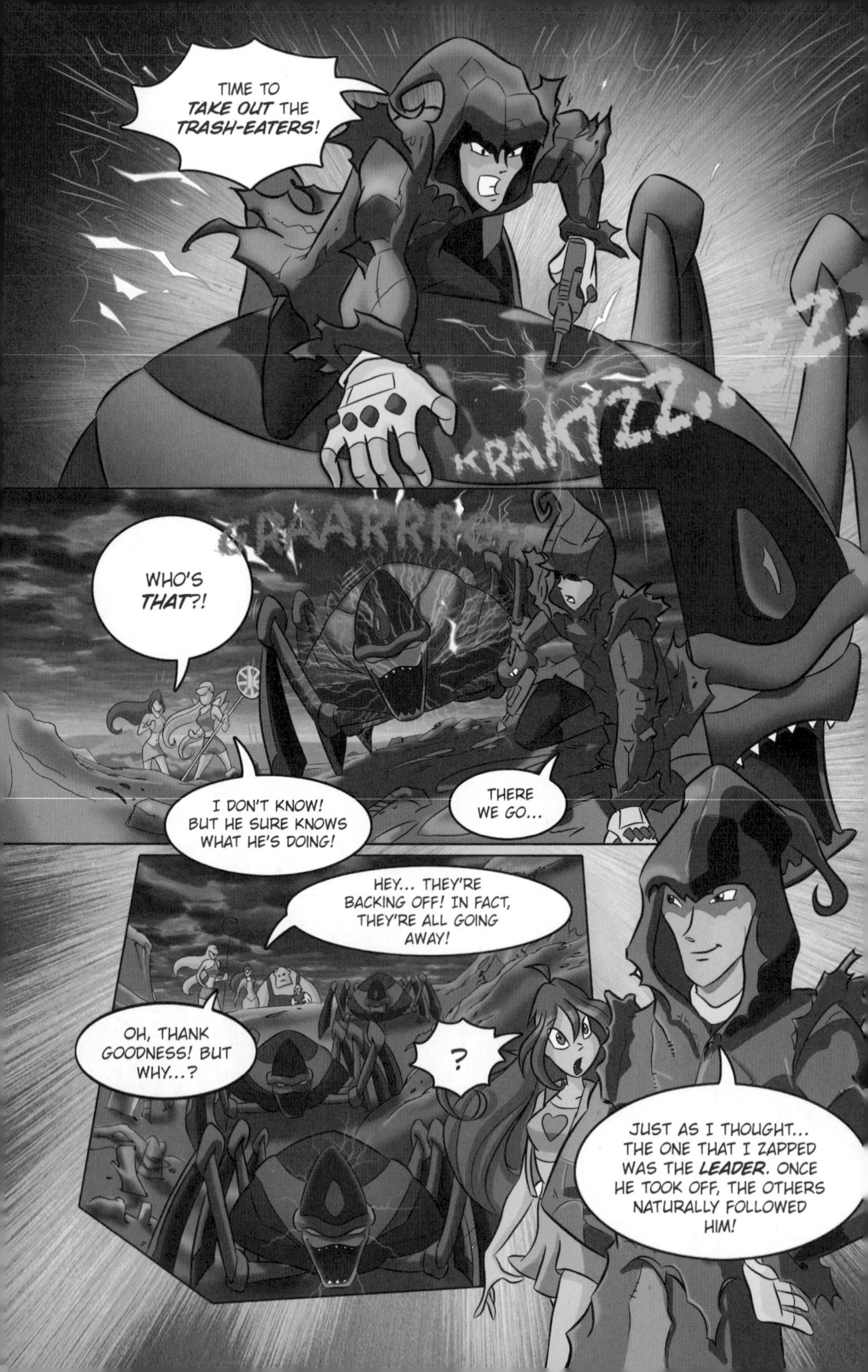
TIME TO TAKE OUT THE TRASH-EATERS!
KRAKZZ...ZZZ
GRAARRRGH
WHO'S THAT?!
I DON'T KNOW! BUT HE SURE KNOWS WHAT HE'S DOING!
THERE WE GO...
HEY... THEY'RE BACKING OFF! IN FACT, THEY'RE ALL GOING AWAY!
OH, THANK GOODNESS! BUT WHY...?
?
JUST AS I THOUGHT... THE ONE THAT I ZAPPED WAS THE LEADER. ONCE HE TOOK OFF, THE OTHERS NATURALLY FOLLOWED HIM!

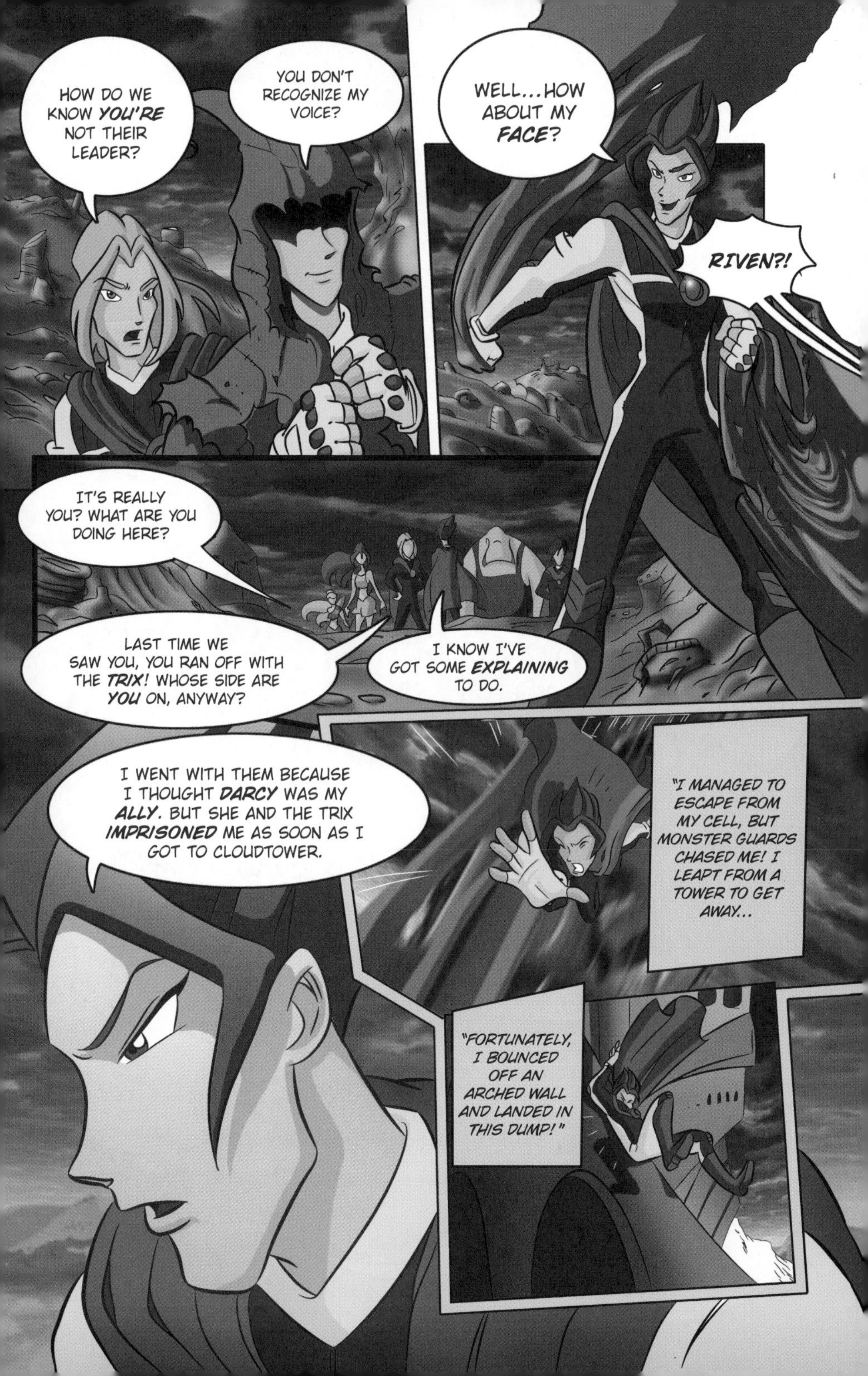
HOW DO WE KNOW YOU'RE NOT THEIR LEADER?
YOU DON'T RECOGNIZE MY VOICE?
WELL...HOW ABOUT MY FACE?
RIVEN?!
IT'S REALLY YOU? WHAT ARE YOU DOING HERE?
LAST TIME WE SAW YOU, YOU RAN OFF WITH THE TRIX! WHOSE SIDE ARE YOU ON, ANYWAY?
I KNOW I'VE GOT SOME EXPLAINING TO DO.
I WENT WITH THEM BECAUSE I THOUGHT DARCY WAS MY ALLY. BUT SHE AND THE TRIX IMPRISONED ME AS SOON AS I GOT TO CLOUDTOWER.
"I MANAGED TO ESCAPE FROM MY CELL, BUT MONSTER GUARDS CHASED ME! I LEAPT FROM A TOWER TO GET AWAY...
"FORTUNATELY, I BOUNCED OFF AN ARCHED WALL AND LANDED IN THIS DUMP!"

I HAD TO DISGUISE MYSELF TO HIDE FROM THE SCARABLATTS... AND I STUDIED THEIR STRENGTHS AND WEAKNESSES.
SO THAT WEAPON YOU JUST USED...?
OH, I JUST MADE IT OUT OF SCRAP METAL FROM THE DUMP...
YOU MADE THAT YOURSELF? THAT'S AMAZING!
I GUESS YOU WERE PAYING ATTENTION TO ALL THOSE LESSONS ABOUT **CAMOUFLAGE** AND **INFILTRATION**!
AND YOU USED **TECHNOLOGY** AS WELL! **INSTRUCTOR CODATORTA** WOULD BE PROUD!
THE SPECIALISTS **NEED** YOU! I HOPE YOU'LL COME BACK!
I DON'T KNOW... I MADE A LOT OF MISTAKES WITH YOU GUYS...
THAT'S ALL IN THE PAST. HOW ABOUT WE START OVER, RIVEN?
I...I'D LIKE THAT. THANKS, **SKY**. IT WOULD BE GREAT TO BE A SPECIALIST AGAIN.
NOW—LET'S GET OUT OF HERE! WE'VE STILL GOT A MAJOR MISSION TO COMPLETE!

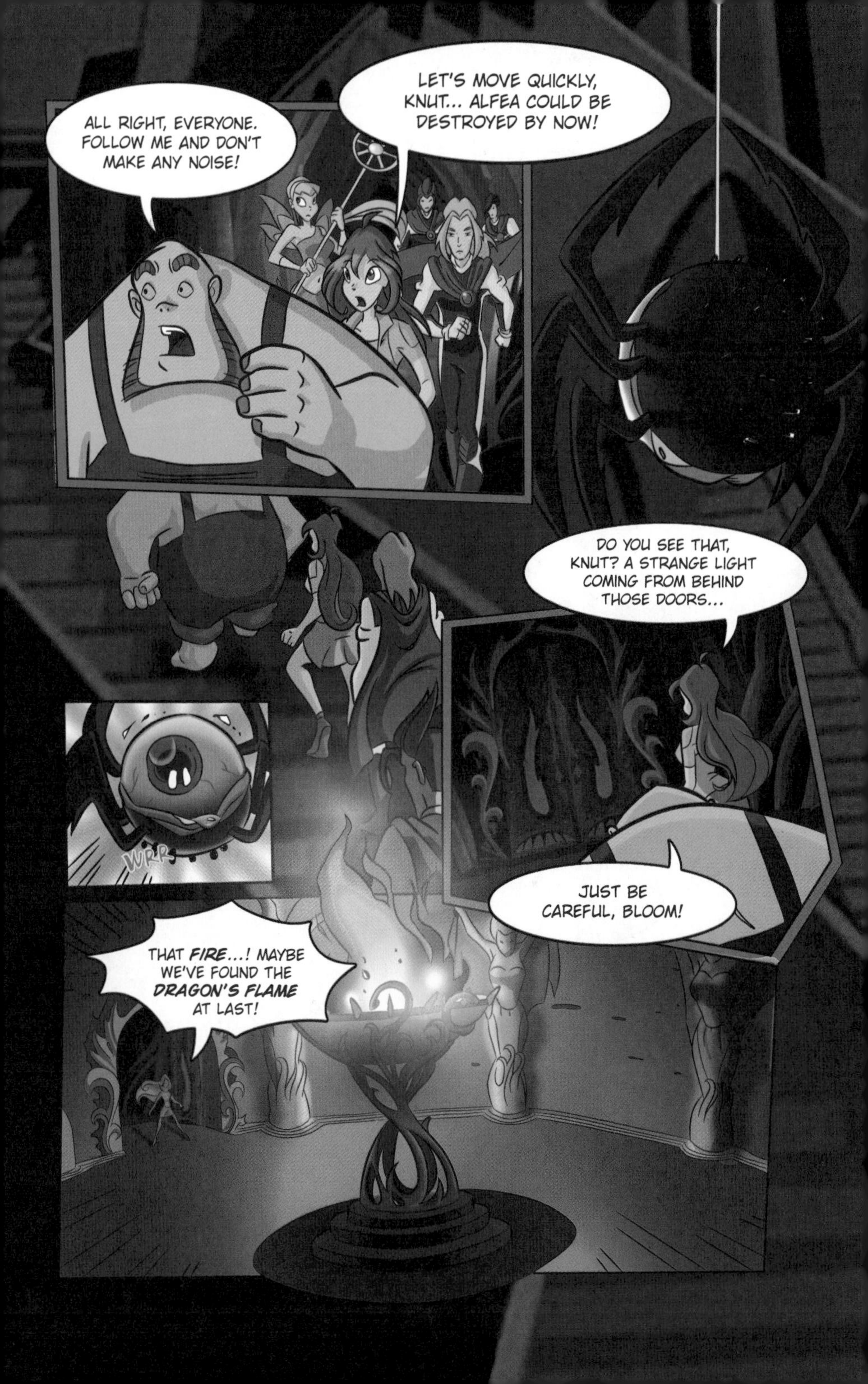
ALL RIGHT, EVERYONE. FOLLOW ME AND DON'T MAKE ANY NOISE!
LET'S MOVE QUICKLY, KNUT... ALFEA COULD BE DESTROYED BY NOW!
DO YOU SEE THAT, KNUT? A STRANGE LIGHT COMING FROM BEHIND THOSE DOORS...
WRR
JUST BE CAREFUL, BLOOM!
THAT FIRE...! MAYBE WE'VE FOUND THE DRAGON'S FLAME AT LAST!

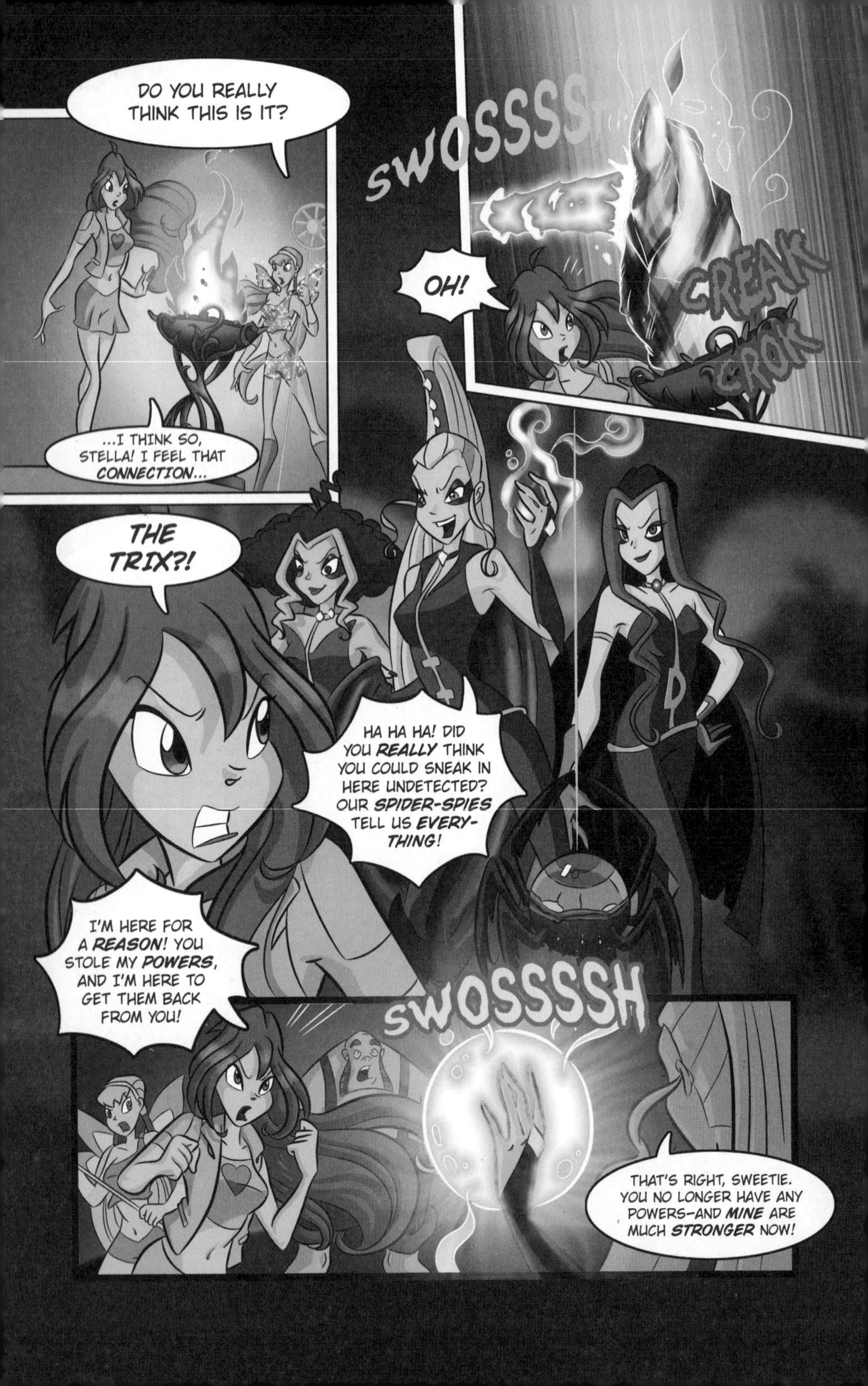
DO YOU REALLY THINK THIS IS IT?
...I THINK SO, STELLA! I FEEL THAT CONNECTION...
SWOSSSSS
OH!
CREAK
CROK
THE TRIX?!
HA HA HA! DID YOU REALLY THINK YOU COULD SNEAK IN HERE UNDETECTED? OUR SPIDER-SPIES TELL US EVERY-THING!
I'M HERE FOR A REASON! YOU STOLE MY POWERS, AND I'M HERE TO GET THEM BACK FROM YOU!
SWOSSSSH
THAT'S RIGHT, SWEETIE. YOU NO LONGER HAVE ANY POWERS—AND MINE ARE MUCH STRONGER NOW!

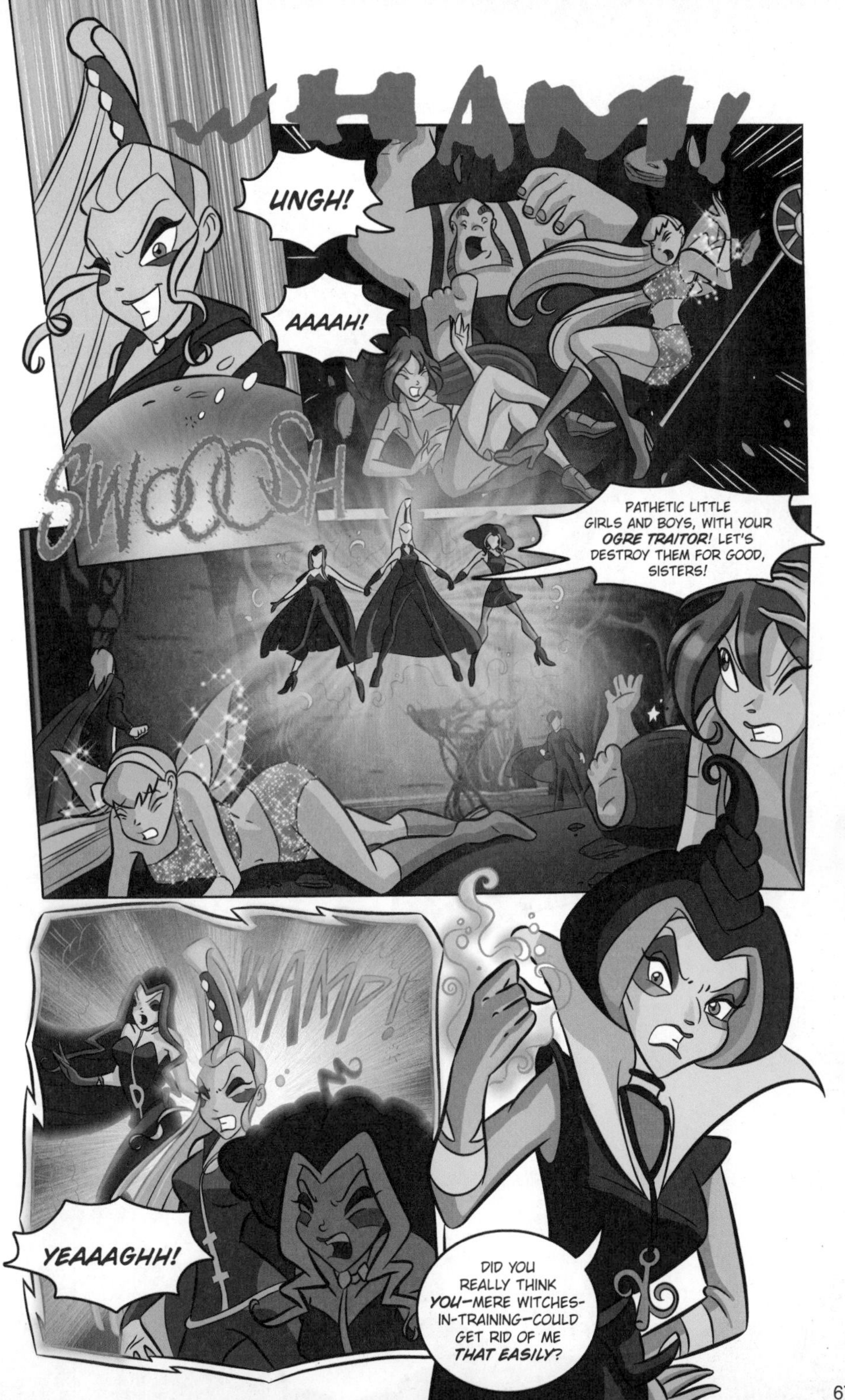
WHAM!
UNGH!
AAAAH!
SWOOSH
PATHETIC LITTLE GIRLS AND BOYS, WITH YOUR *OGRE TRAITOR*! LET'S DESTROY THEM FOR GOOD, SISTERS!
WAMP!
YEAAAGHH!
DID YOU REALLY THINK *YOU*—MERE WITCHES-IN-TRAINING—COULD GET RID OF ME *THAT EASILY*?

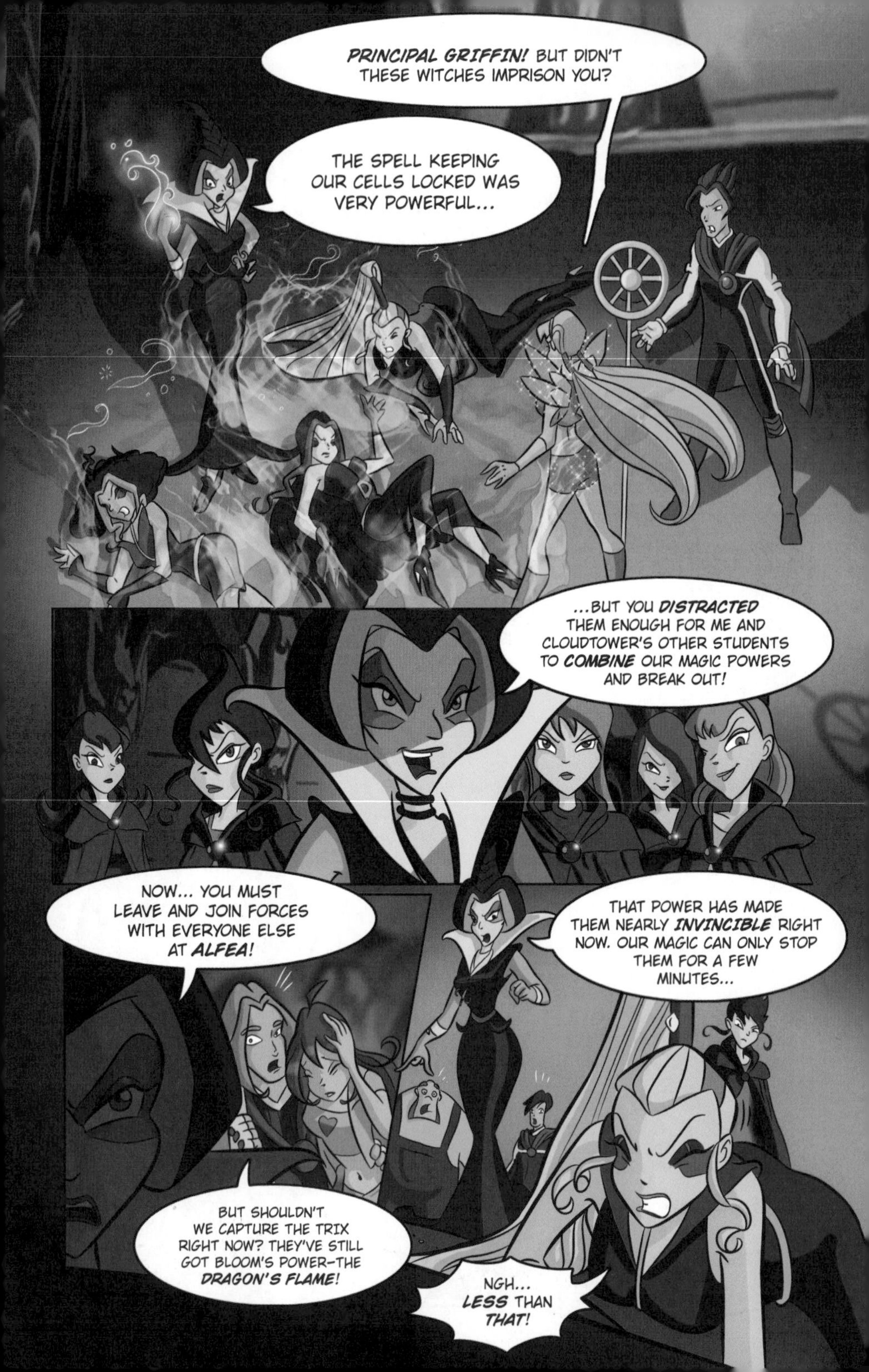
PRINCIPAL GRIFFIN! BUT DIDN'T THESE WITCHES IMPRISON YOU?
THE SPELL KEEPING OUR CELLS LOCKED WAS VERY POWERFUL...
...BUT YOU DISTRACTED THEM ENOUGH FOR ME AND CLOUDTOWER'S OTHER STUDENTS TO COMBINE OUR MAGIC POWERS AND BREAK OUT!
NOW... YOU MUST LEAVE AND JOIN FORCES WITH EVERYONE ELSE AT ALFEA!
THAT POWER HAS MADE THEM NEARLY INVINCIBLE RIGHT NOW. OUR MAGIC CAN ONLY STOP THEM FOR A FEW MINUTES...
BUT SHOULDN'T WE CAPTURE THE TRIX RIGHT NOW? THEY'VE STILL GOT BLOOM'S POWER–THE DRAGON'S FLAME!
NGH... LESS THAN THAT!

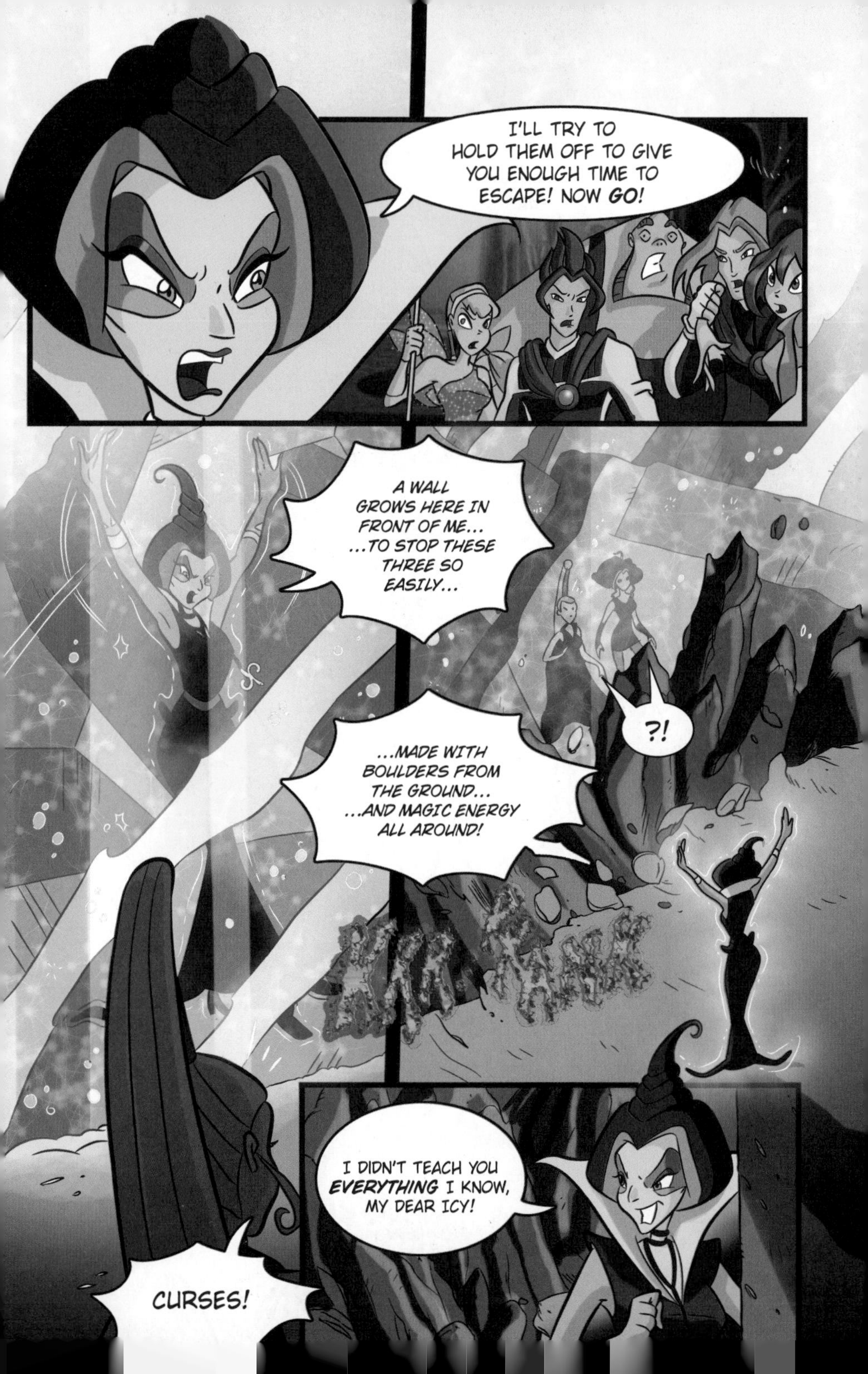
I'LL TRY TO HOLD THEM OFF TO GIVE YOU ENOUGH TIME TO ESCAPE! NOW GO!
A WALL GROWS HERE IN FRONT OF ME... ...TO STOP THESE THREE SO EASILY...
?!
...MADE WITH BOULDERS FROM THE GROUND... ...AND MAGIC ENERGY ALL AROUND!
I DIDN'T TEACH YOU EVERYTHING I KNOW, MY DEAR ICY!
CURSES!

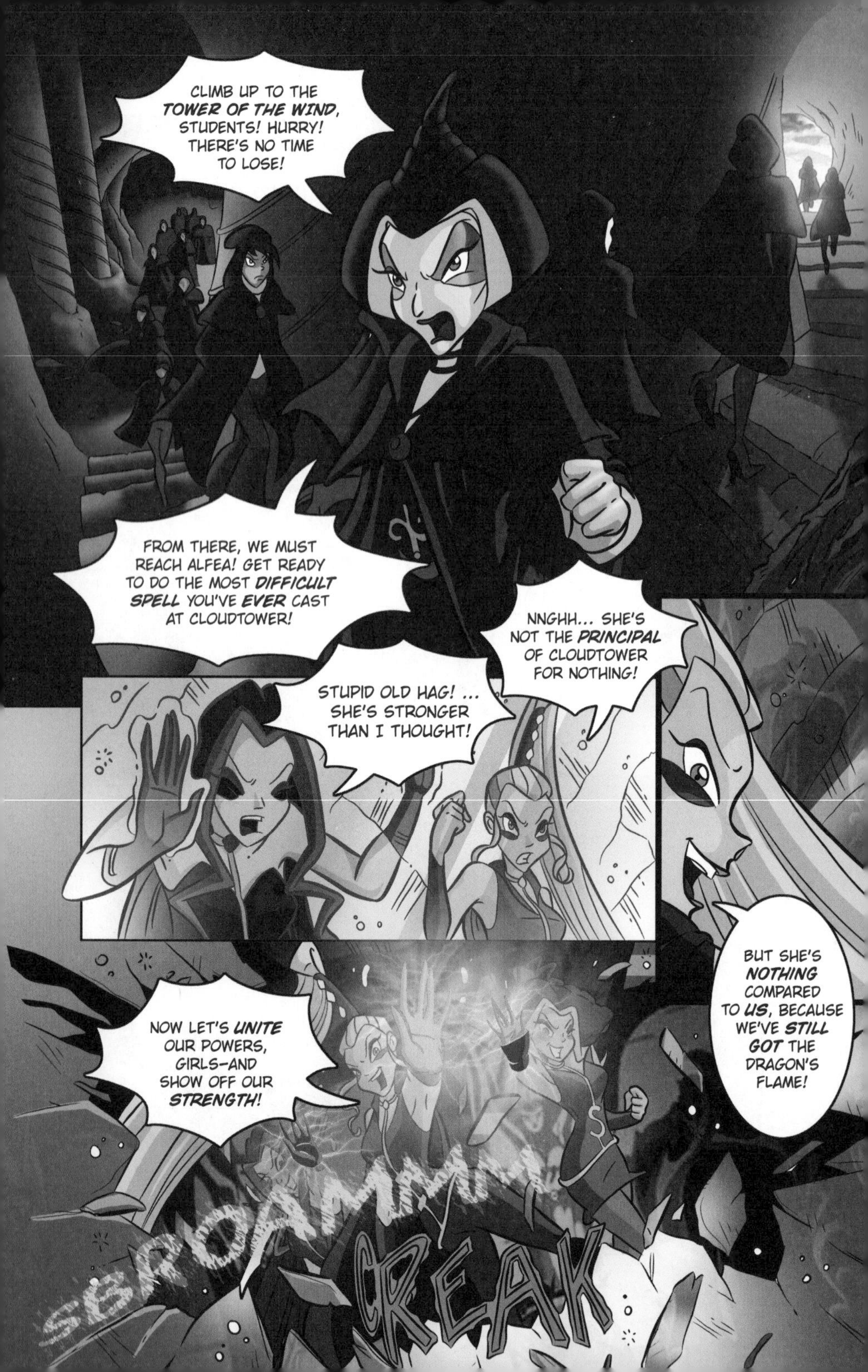
CLIMB UP TO THE TOWER OF THE WIND, STUDENTS! HURRY! THERE'S NO TIME TO LOSE!
FROM THERE, WE MUST REACH ALFEA! GET READY TO DO THE MOST DIFFICULT SPELL YOU'VE EVER CAST AT CLOUDTOWER!
NNGHH... SHE'S NOT THE PRINCIPAL OF CLOUDTOWER FOR NOTHING!
STUPID OLD HAG! ... SHE'S STRONGER THAN I THOUGHT!
BUT SHE'S NOTHING COMPARED TO US, BECAUSE WE'VE STILL GOT THE DRAGON'S FLAME!
NOW LET'S UNITE OUR POWERS, GIRLS—AND SHOW OFF OUR STRENGTH!
CREAK

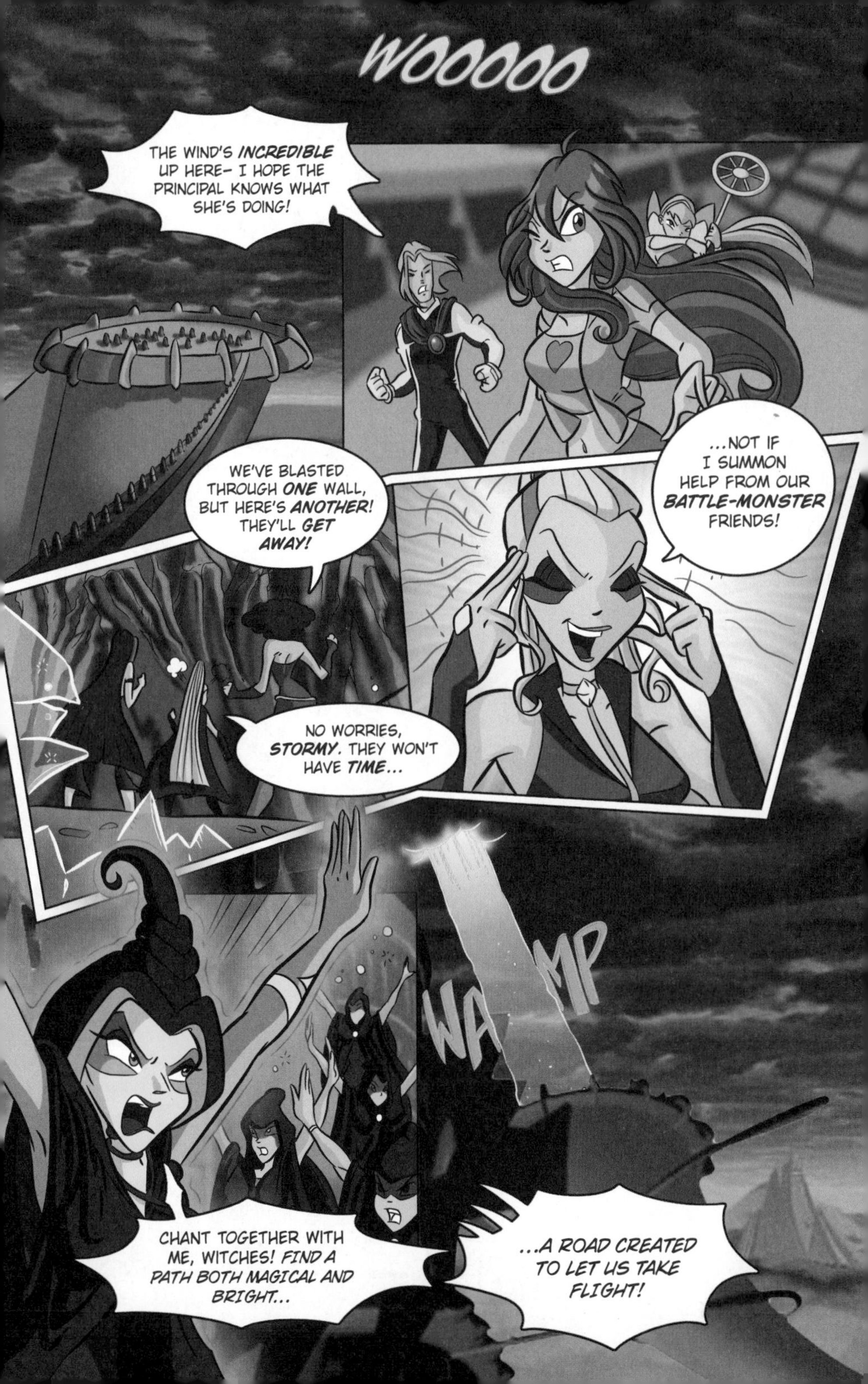
WOOOOO
THE WIND'S INCREDIBLE UP HERE– I HOPE THE PRINCIPAL KNOWS WHAT SHE'S DOING!
WE'VE BLASTED THROUGH ONE WALL, BUT HERE'S ANOTHER! THEY'LL GET AWAY!
NO WORRIES, STORMY. THEY WON'T HAVE TIME...
...NOT IF I SUMMON HELP FROM OUR BATTLE-MONSTER FRIENDS!
CHANT TOGETHER WITH ME, WITCHES! FIND A PATH BOTH MAGICAL AND BRIGHT...
WAMP
...A ROAD CREATED TO LET US TAKE FLIGHT!

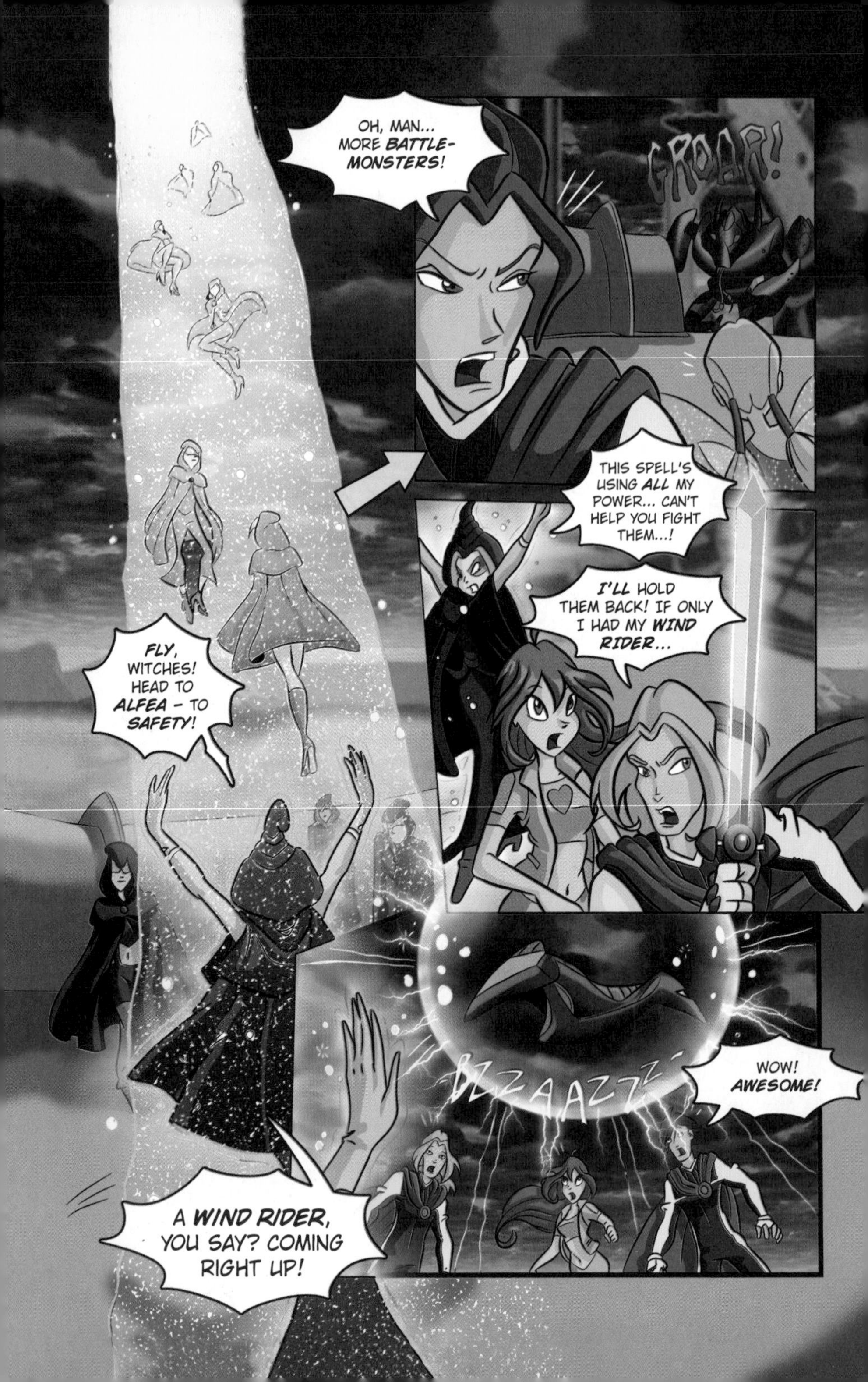
OH, MAN... MORE BATTLE-MONSTERS!
GROAR!
THIS SPELL'S USING ALL MY POWER... CAN'T HELP YOU FIGHT THEM...!
I'LL HOLD THEM BACK! IF ONLY I HAD MY WIND RIDER...
FLY, WITCHES! HEAD TO ALFEA – TO SAFETY!
BZZAAZZZ
WOW! AWESOME!
A WIND RIDER, YOU SAY? COMING RIGHT UP!

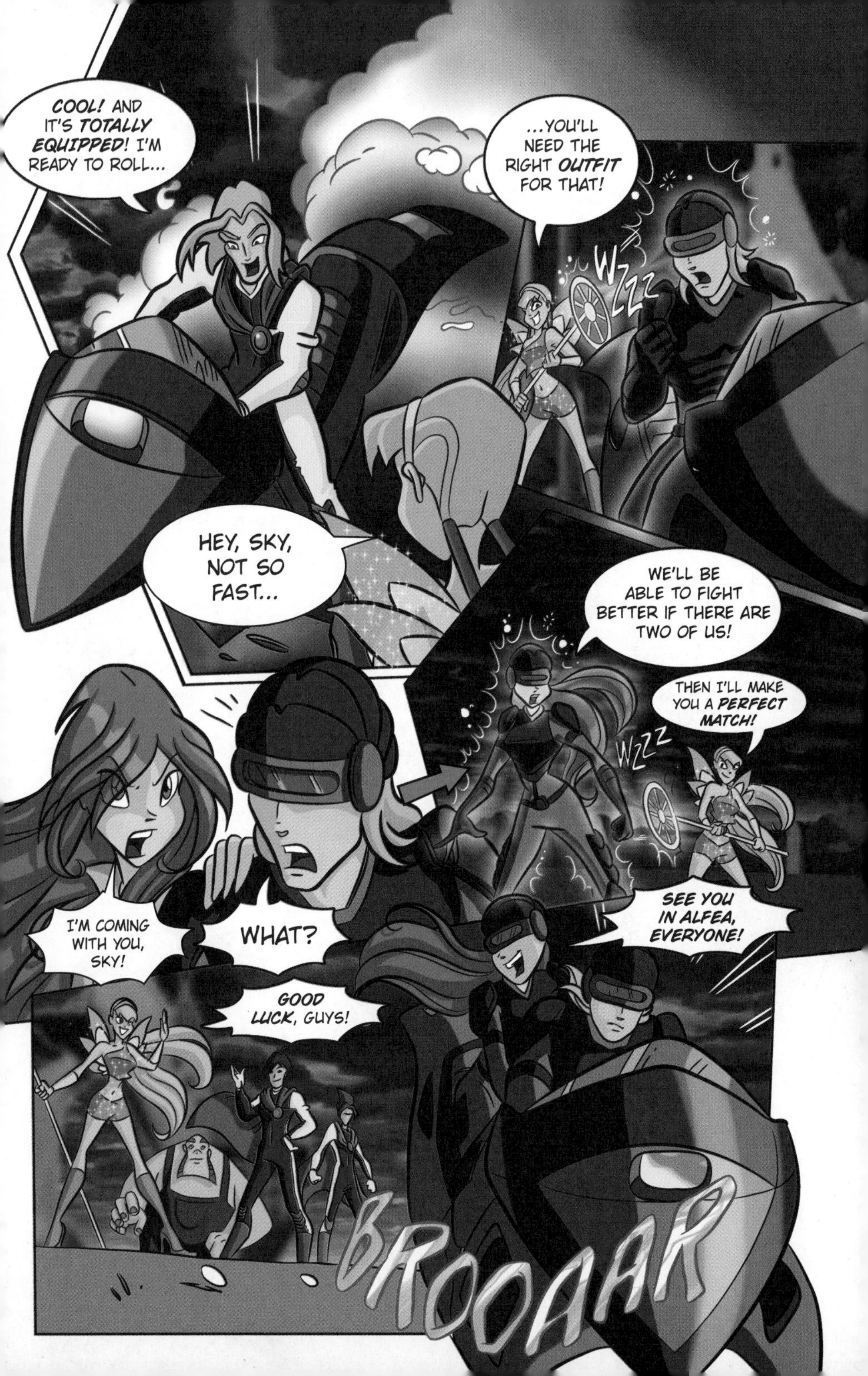
COOL! AND IT'S TOTALLY EQUIPPED! I'M READY TO ROLL...
...YOU'LL NEED THE RIGHT OUTFIT FOR THAT!
WZZZ
HEY, SKY, NOT SO FAST...
WE'LL BE ABLE TO FIGHT BETTER IF THERE ARE TWO OF US!
THEN I'LL MAKE YOU A PERFECT MATCH!
WZZZ
I'M COMING WITH YOU, SKY!
WHAT?
SEE YOU IN ALFEA, EVERYONE!
GOOD LUCK, GUYS!
BROOAAR

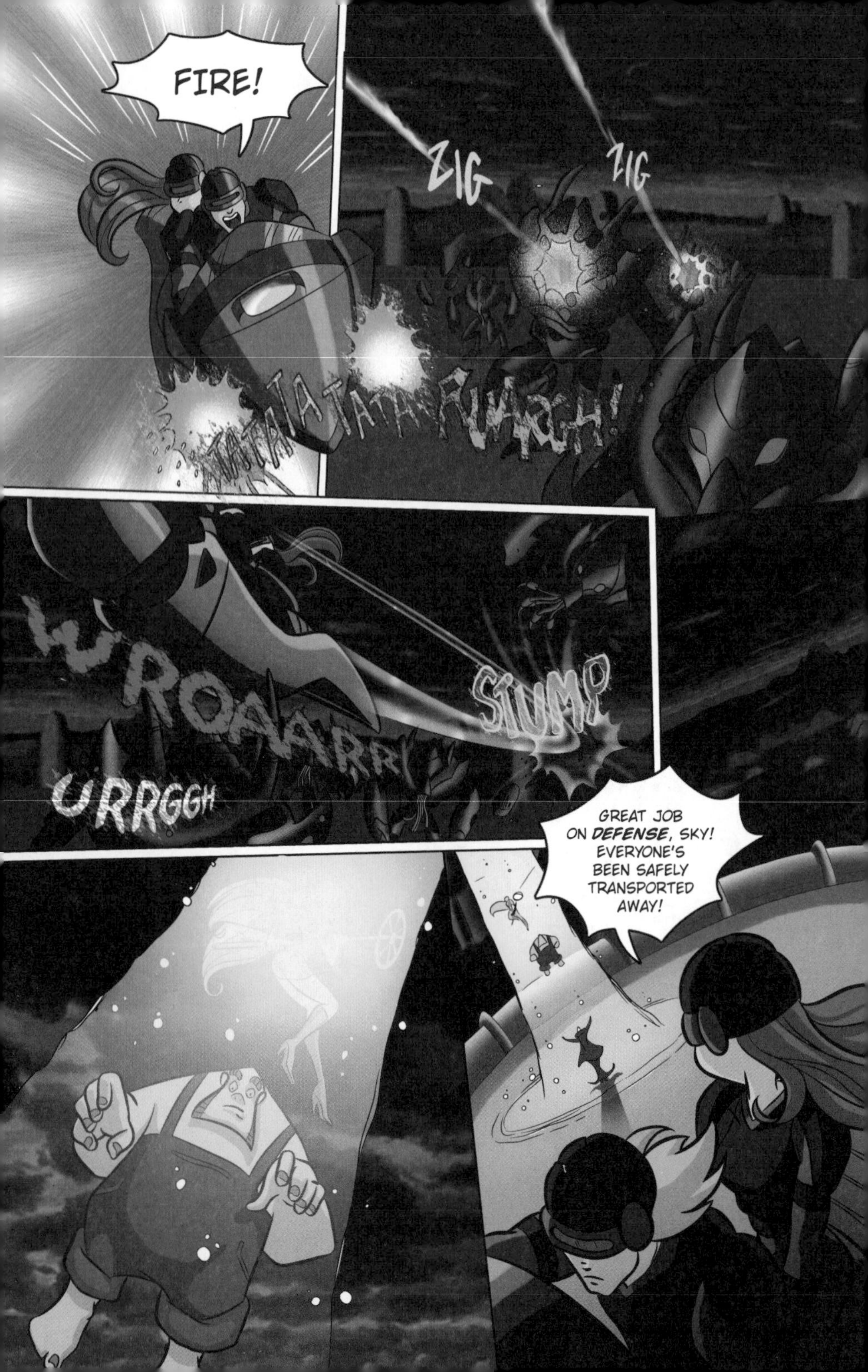
FIRE!
ZIG
ZIG
TATATATATA
FWASH!
WROAARR
STUMP
URRGGH
GREAT JOB ON DEFENSE, SKY! EVERYONE'S BEEN SAFELY TRANSPORTED AWAY!

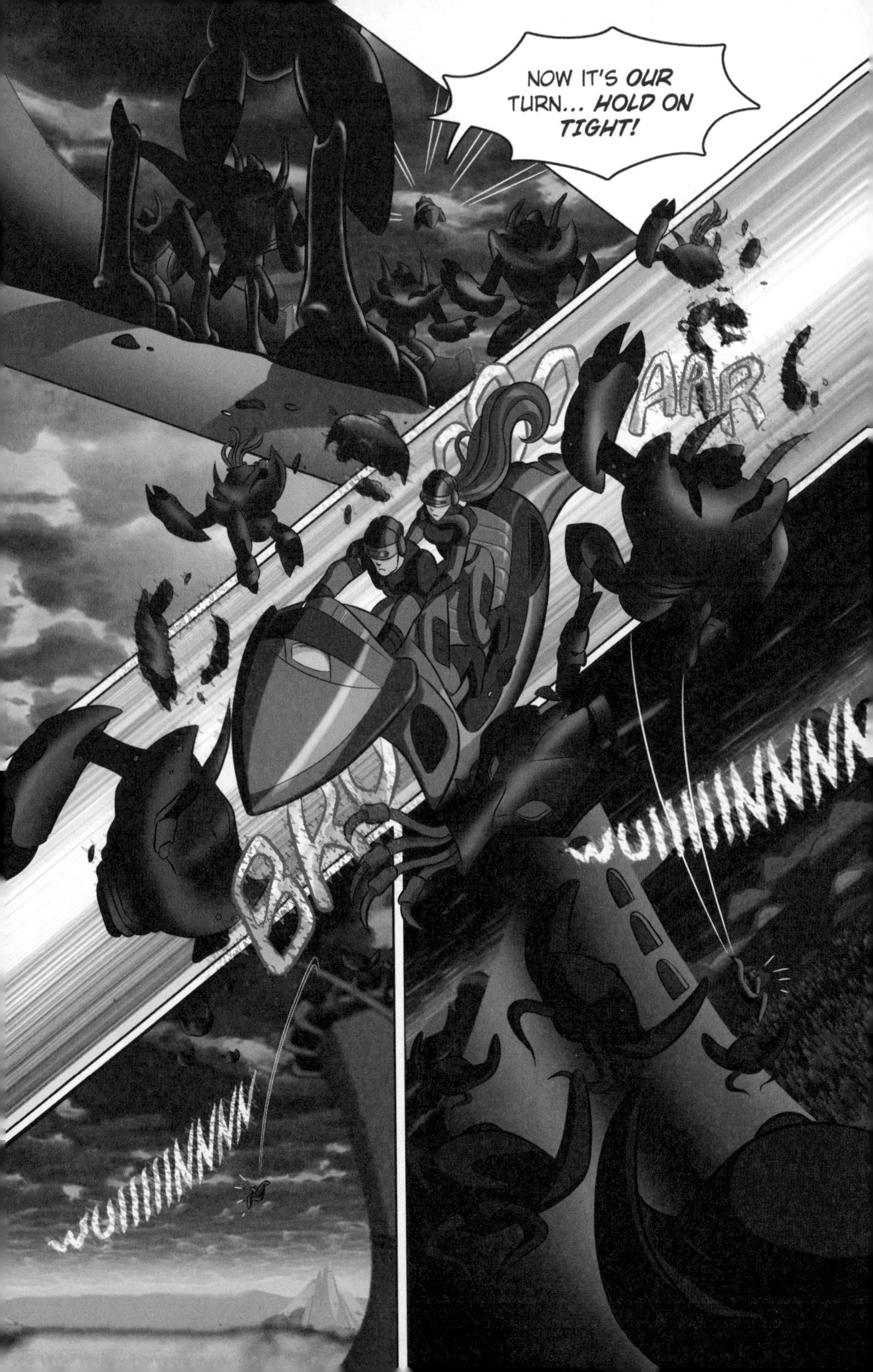
NOW IT'S OUR TURN... HOLD ON TIGHT!

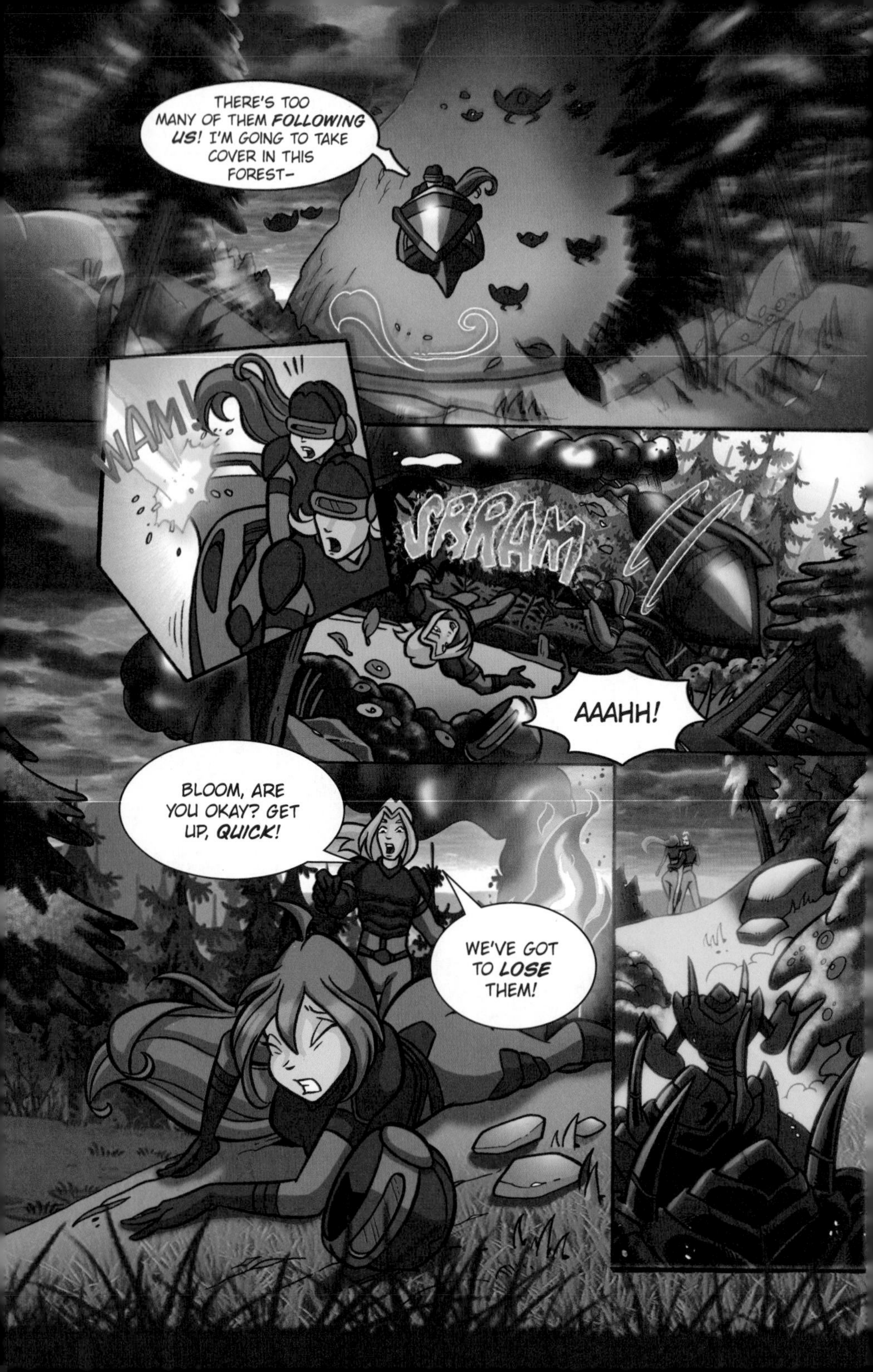
THERE'S TOO MANY OF THEM FOLLOWING US! I'M GOING TO TAKE COVER IN THIS FOREST–
WAM!
SBRAM
AAAHH!
BLOOM, ARE YOU OKAY? GET UP, QUICK!
WE'VE GOT TO LOSE THEM!

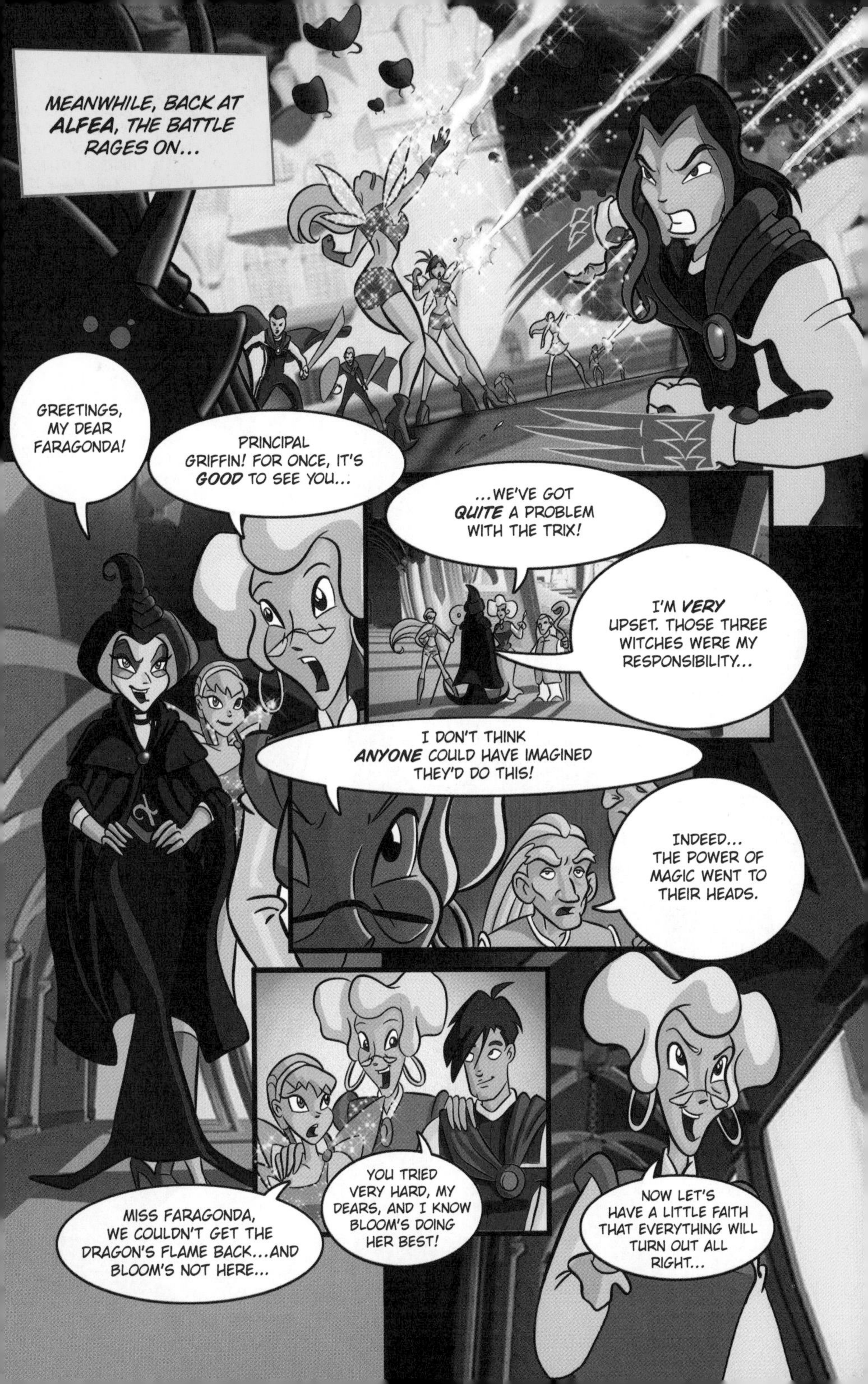
MEANWHILE, BACK AT ALFEA, THE BATTLE RAGES ON...
GREETINGS, MY DEAR FARAGONDA!
PRINCIPAL GRIFFIN! FOR ONCE, IT'S GOOD TO SEE YOU...
...WE'VE GOT QUITE A PROBLEM WITH THE TRIX!
I'M VERY UPSET. THOSE THREE WITCHES WERE MY RESPONSIBILITY...
I DON'T THINK ANYONE COULD HAVE IMAGINED THEY'D DO THIS!
INDEED... THE POWER OF MAGIC WENT TO THEIR HEADS.
MISS FARAGONDA, WE COULDN'T GET THE DRAGON'S FLAME BACK...AND BLOOM'S NOT HERE...
YOU TRIED VERY HARD, MY DEARS, AND I KNOW BLOOM'S DOING HER BEST!
NOW LET'S HAVE A LITTLE FAITH THAT EVERYTHING WILL TURN OUT ALL RIGHT...

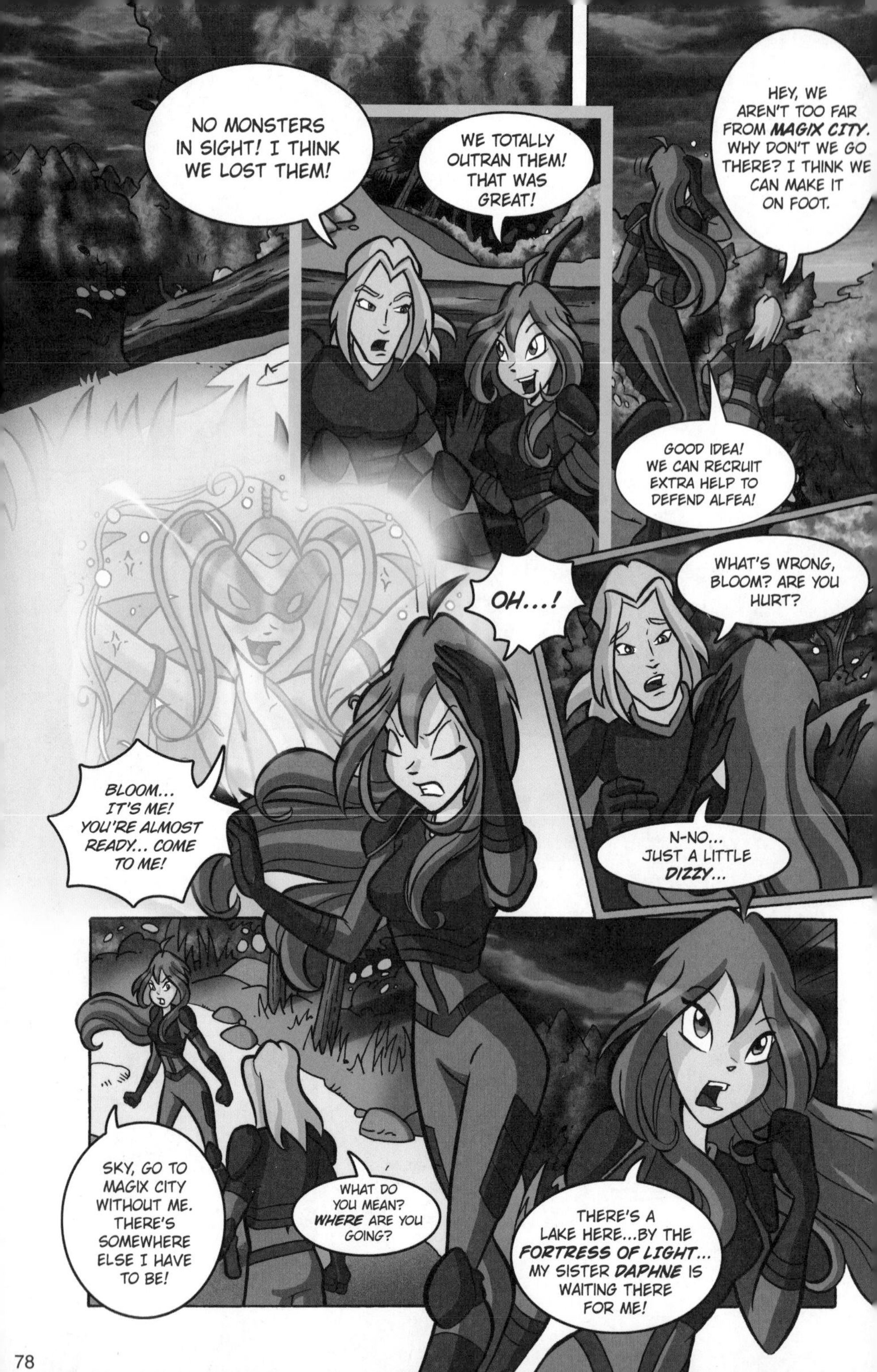
NO MONSTERS IN SIGHT! I THINK WE LOST THEM!
WE TOTALLY OUTRAN THEM! THAT WAS GREAT!
HEY, WE AREN'T TOO FAR FROM MAGIX CITY. WHY DON'T WE GO THERE? I THINK WE CAN MAKE IT ON FOOT.
GOOD IDEA! WE CAN RECRUIT EXTRA HELP TO DEFEND ALFEA!
OH...!
WHAT'S WRONG, BLOOM? ARE YOU HURT?
BLOOM... IT'S ME! YOU'RE ALMOST READY... COME TO ME!
N-NO... JUST A LITTLE DIZZY...
SKY, GO TO MAGIX CITY WITHOUT ME. THERE'S SOMEWHERE ELSE I HAVE TO BE!
WHAT DO YOU MEAN? WHERE ARE YOU GOING?
THERE'S A LAKE HERE...BY THE FORTRESS OF LIGHT... MY SISTER DAPHNE IS WAITING THERE FOR ME!

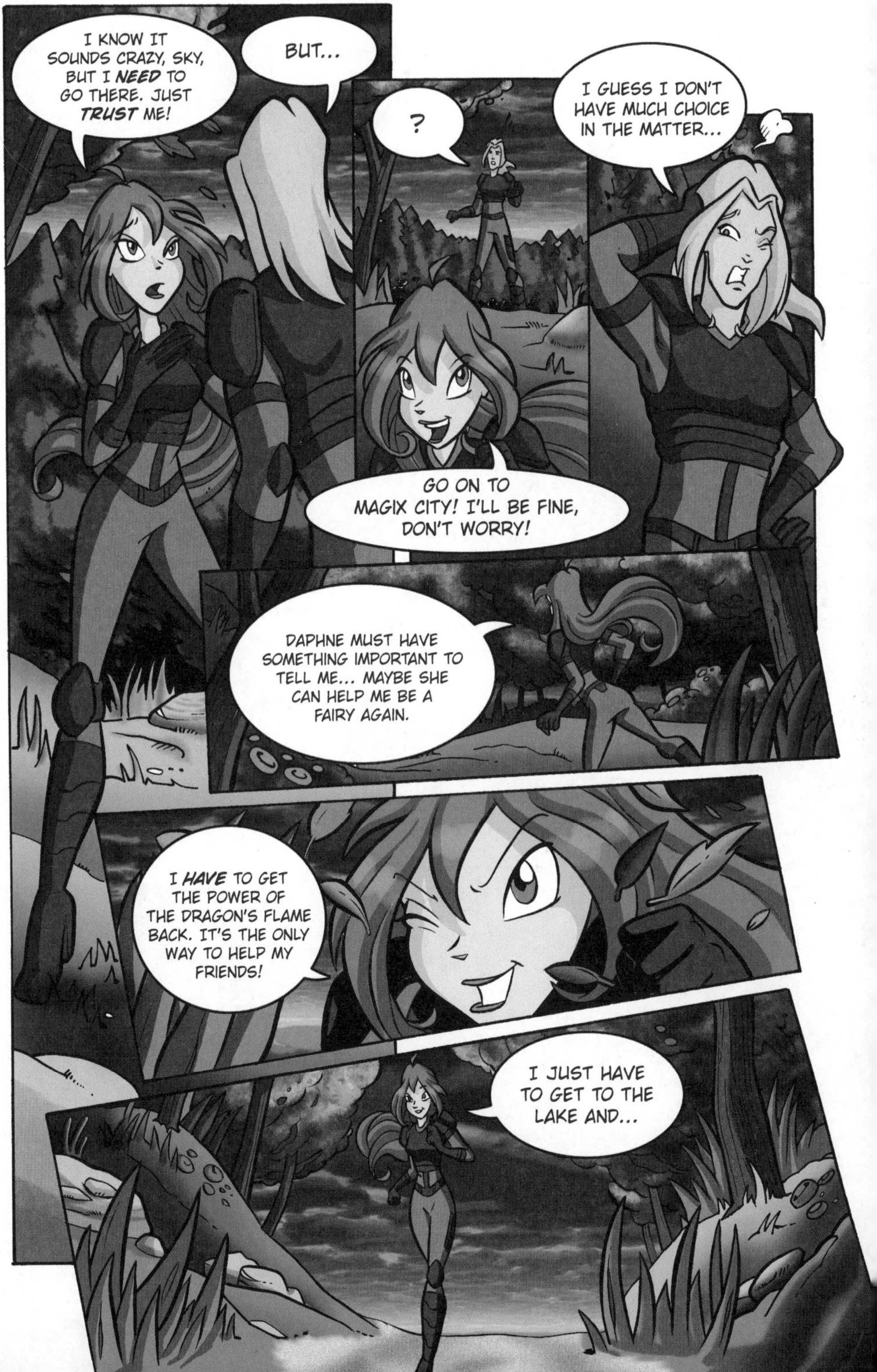
I KNOW IT SOUNDS CRAZY, SKY, BUT I NEED TO GO THERE. JUST TRUST ME!
BUT...
?
I GUESS I DON'T HAVE MUCH CHOICE IN THE MATTER...
GO ON TO MAGIX CITY! I'LL BE FINE, DON'T WORRY!
DAPHNE MUST HAVE SOMETHING IMPORTANT TO TELL ME... MAYBE SHE CAN HELP ME BE A FAIRY AGAIN.
I HAVE TO GET THE POWER OF THE DRAGON'S FLAME BACK. IT'S THE ONLY WAY TO HELP MY FRIENDS!
I JUST HAVE TO GET TO THE LAKE AND...

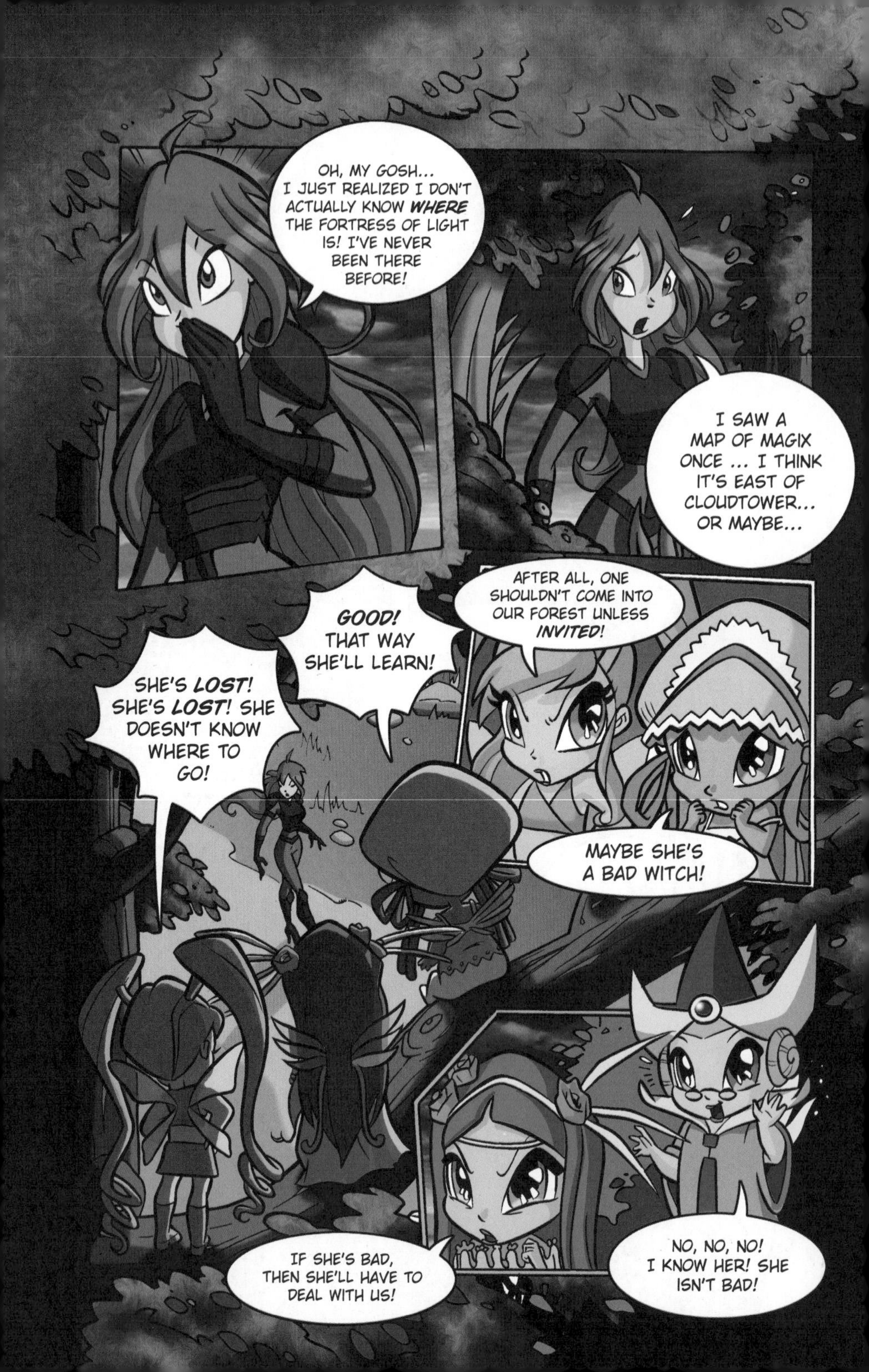
OH, MY GOSH... I JUST REALIZED I DON'T ACTUALLY KNOW WHERE THE FORTRESS OF LIGHT IS! I'VE NEVER BEEN THERE BEFORE!
I SAW A MAP OF MAGIX ONCE ... I THINK IT'S EAST OF CLOUDTOWER... OR MAYBE...
AFTER ALL, ONE SHOULDN'T COME INTO OUR FOREST UNLESS INVITED!
GOOD! THAT WAY SHE'LL LEARN!
SHE'S LOST! SHE'S LOST! SHE DOESN'T KNOW WHERE TO GO!
MAYBE SHE'S A BAD WITCH!
IF SHE'S BAD, THEN SHE'LL HAVE TO DEAL WITH US!
NO, NO, NO! I KNOW HER! SHE ISN'T BAD!

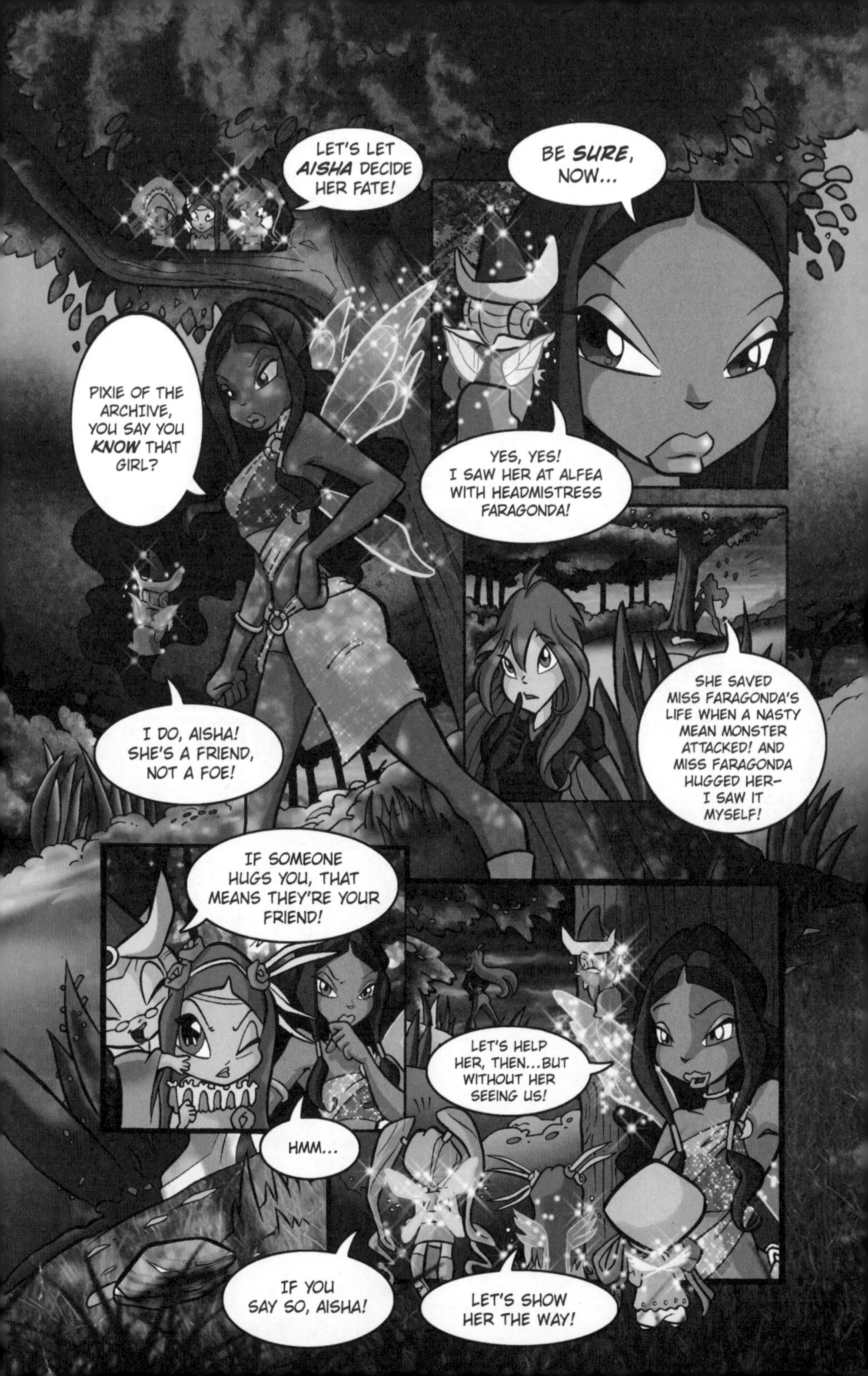
LET'S LET AISHA DECIDE HER FATE!
BE SURE, NOW...
PIXIE OF THE ARCHIVE, YOU SAY YOU KNOW THAT GIRL?
YES, YES! I SAW HER AT ALFEA WITH HEADMISTRESS FARAGONDA!
I DO, AISHA! SHE'S A FRIEND, NOT A FOE!
SHE SAVED MISS FARAGONDA'S LIFE WHEN A NASTY MEAN MONSTER ATTACKED! AND MISS FARAGONDA HUGGED HER– I SAW IT MYSELF!
IF SOMEONE HUGS YOU, THAT MEANS THEY'RE YOUR FRIEND!
HMM...
LET'S HELP HER, THEN...BUT WITHOUT HER SEEING US!
IF YOU SAY SO, AISHA!
LET'S SHOW HER THE WAY!

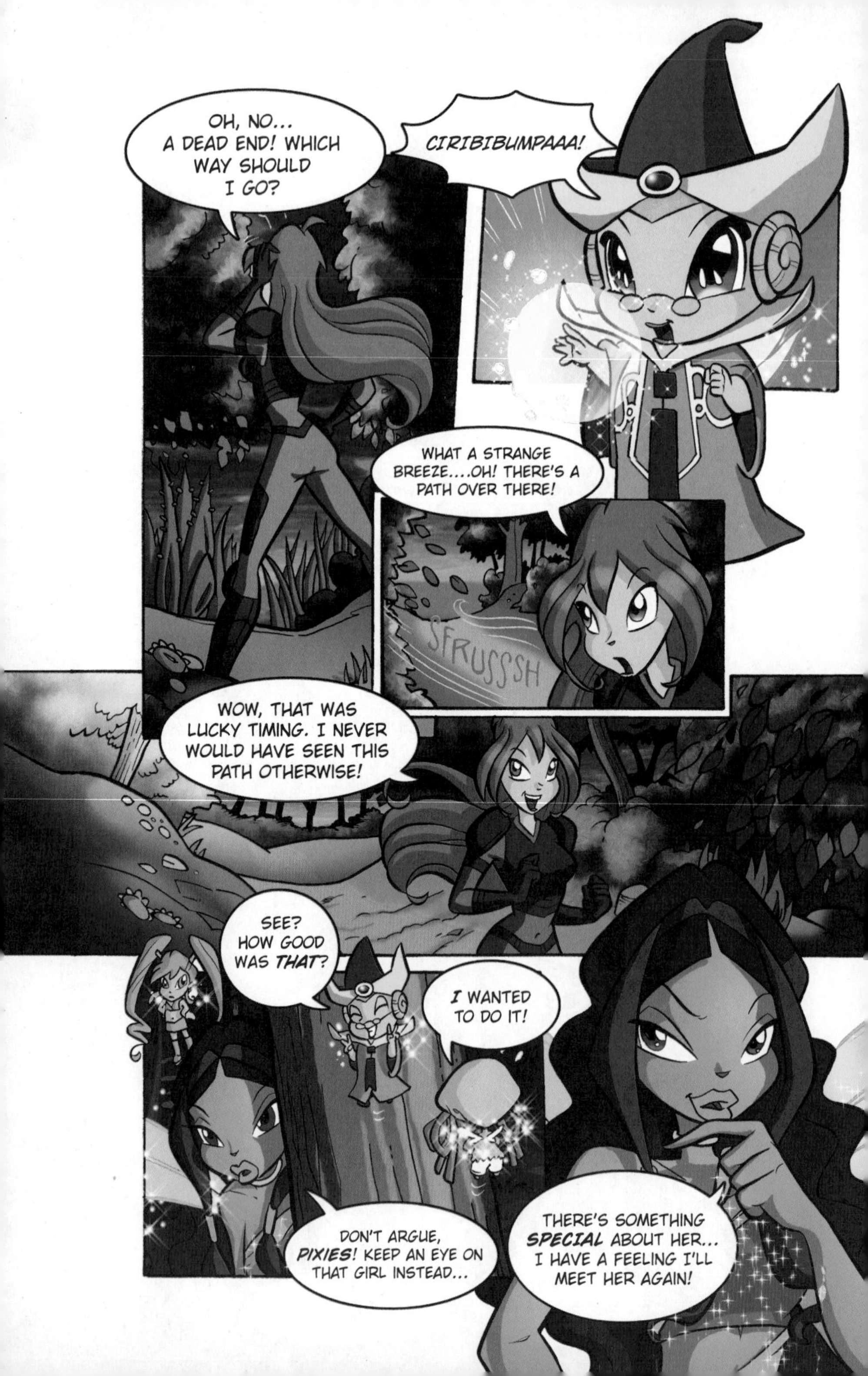
OH, NO... A DEAD END! WHICH WAY SHOULD I GO?
CIRIBIBUMPAAA!
WHAT A STRANGE BREEZE....OH! THERE'S A PATH OVER THERE!
SFRUSSSH
WOW, THAT WAS LUCKY TIMING. I NEVER WOULD HAVE SEEN THIS PATH OTHERWISE!
SEE? HOW GOOD WAS THAT?
I WANTED TO DO IT!
DON'T ARGUE, PIXIES! KEEP AN EYE ON THAT GIRL INSTEAD...
THERE'S SOMETHING SPECIAL ABOUT HER... I HAVE A FEELING I'LL MEET HER AGAIN!

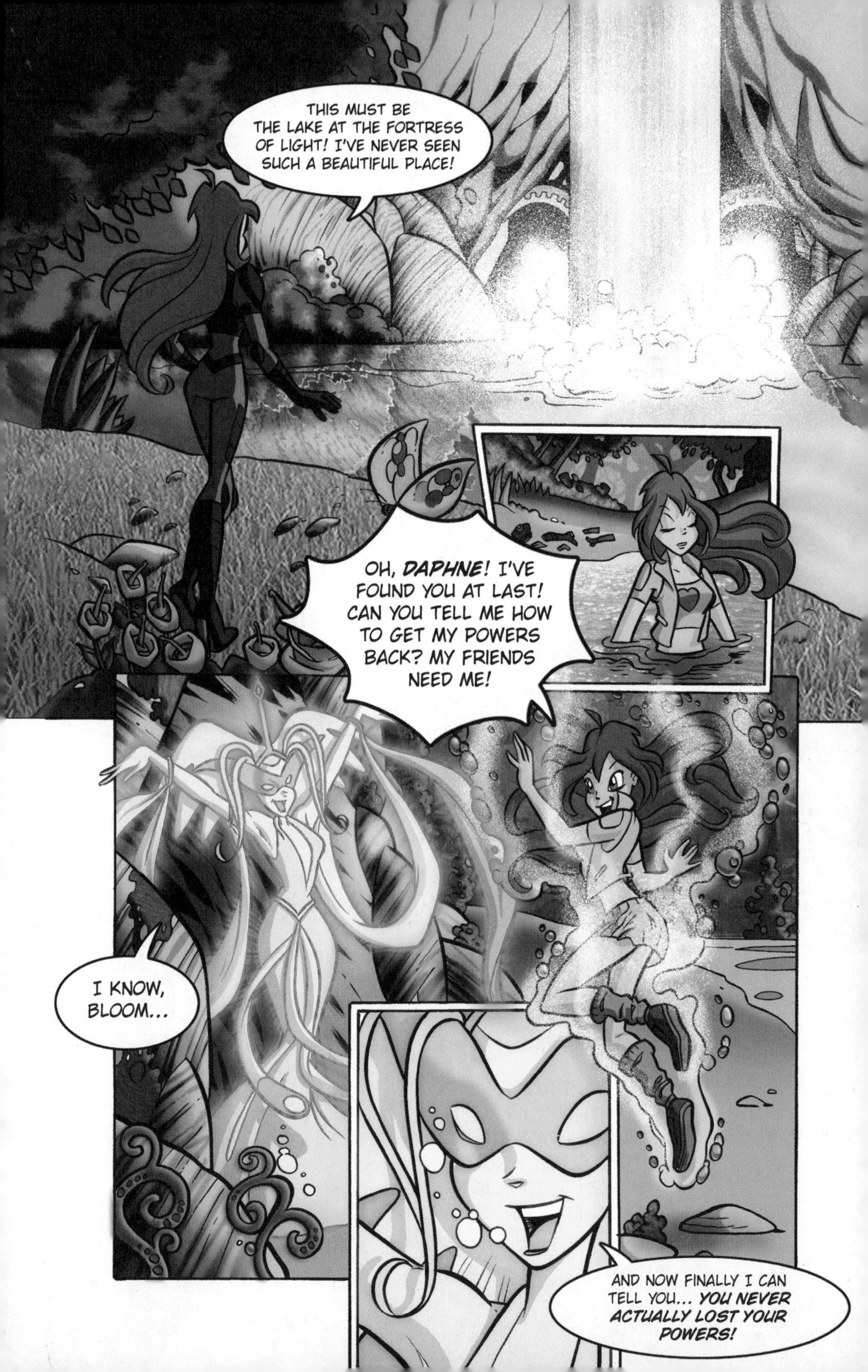
THIS MUST BE THE LAKE AT THE FORTRESS OF LIGHT! I'VE NEVER SEEN SUCH A BEAUTIFUL PLACE!
OH, DAPHNE! I'VE FOUND YOU AT LAST! CAN YOU TELL ME HOW TO GET MY POWERS BACK? MY FRIENDS NEED ME!
I KNOW, BLOOM...
AND NOW FINALLY I CAN TELL YOU... YOU NEVER ACTUALLY LOST YOUR POWERS!

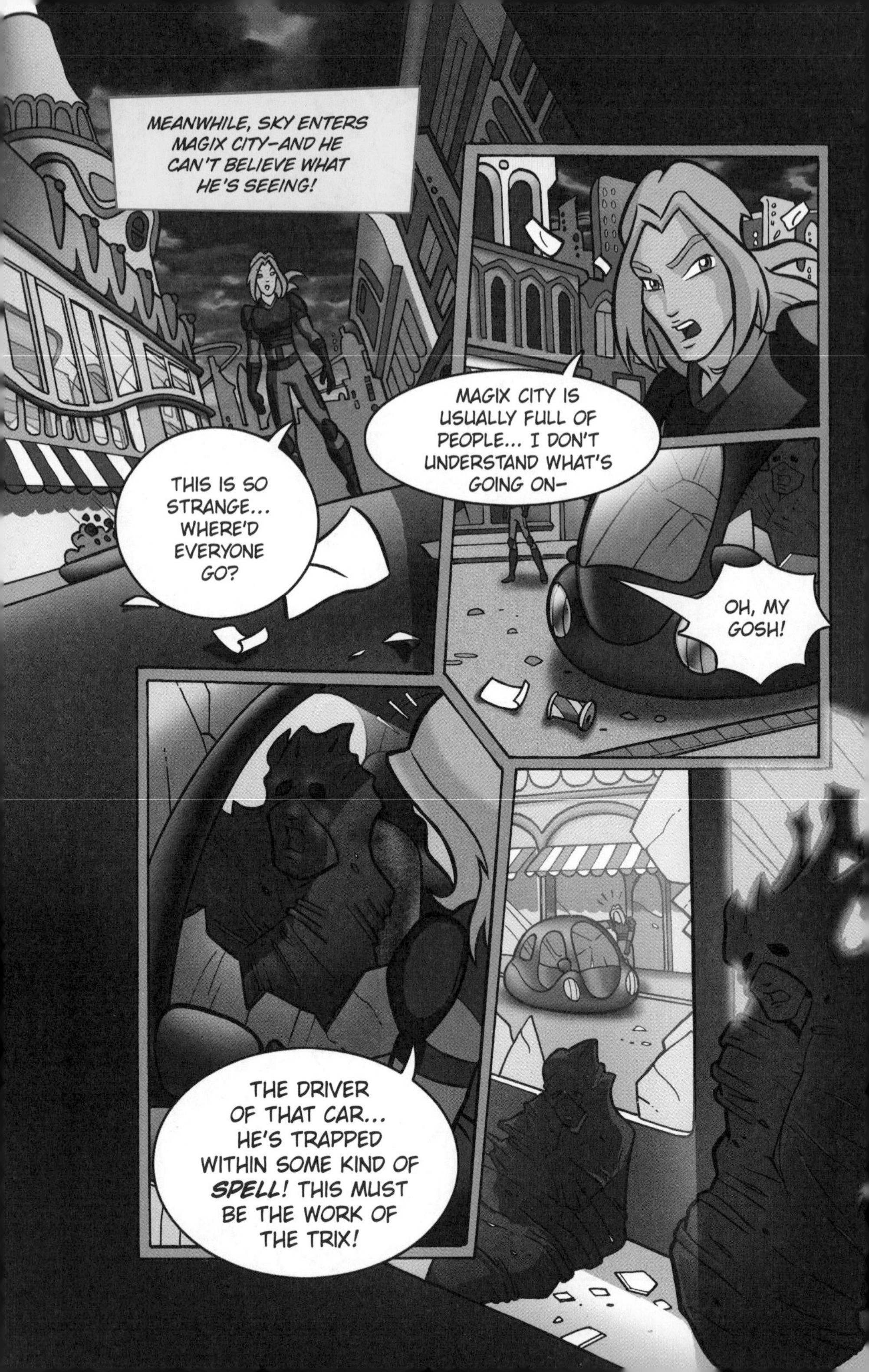
MEANWHILE, SKY ENTERS MAGIX CITY—AND HE CAN'T BELIEVE WHAT HE'S SEEING!
THIS IS SO STRANGE... WHERE'D EVERYONE GO?
MAGIX CITY IS USUALLY FULL OF PEOPLE... I DON'T UNDERSTAND WHAT'S GOING ON—
OH, MY GOSH!
THE DRIVER OF THAT CAR... HE'S TRAPPED WITHIN SOME KIND OF SPELL! THIS MUST BE THE WORK OF THE TRIX!

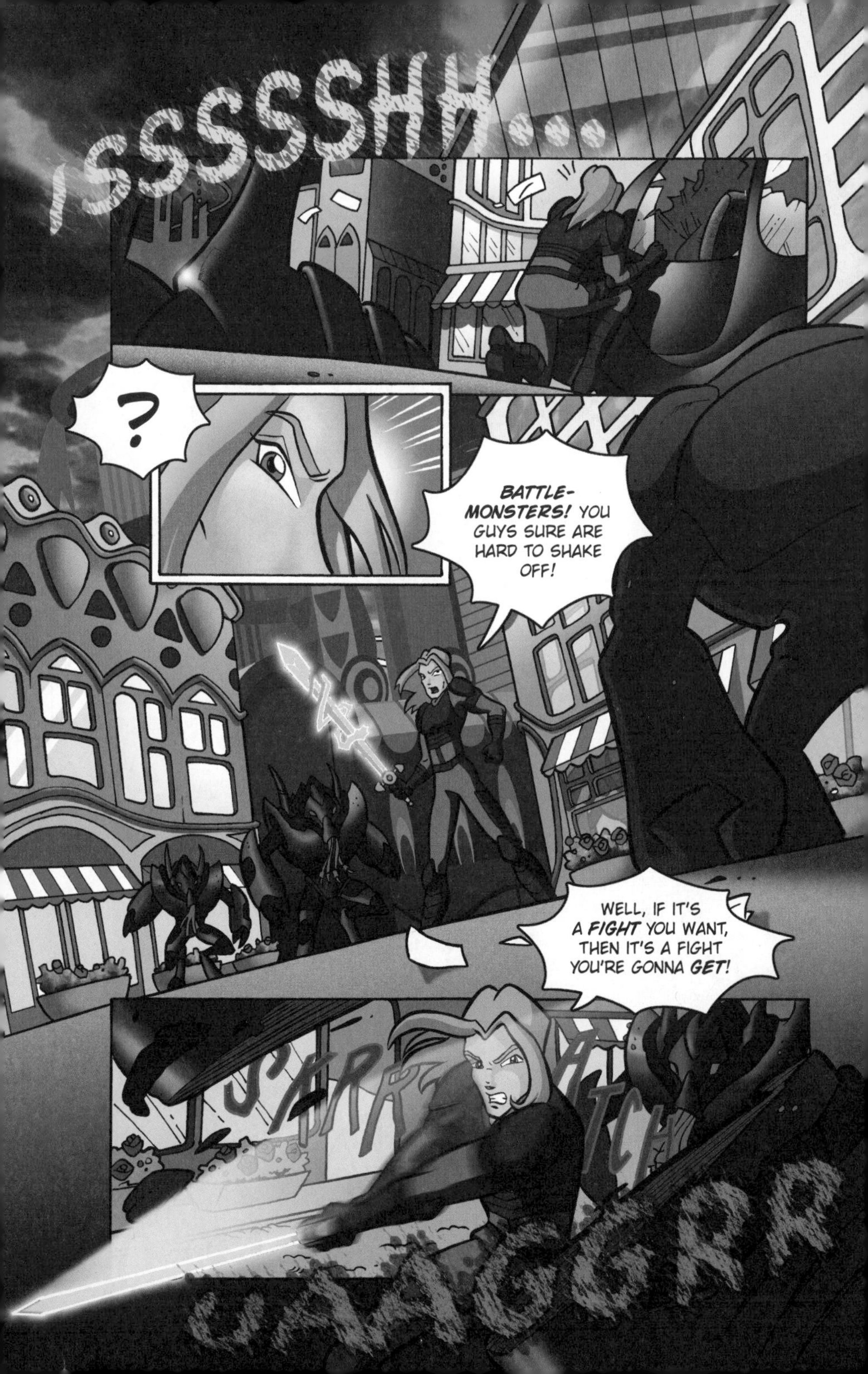
SSSSSHH...
?
BATTLE-MONSTERS! YOU GUYS SURE ARE HARD TO SHAKE OFF!
WELL, IF IT'S A FIGHT YOU WANT, THEN IT'S A FIGHT YOU'RE GONNA GET!
SKRRATCH
GRRR

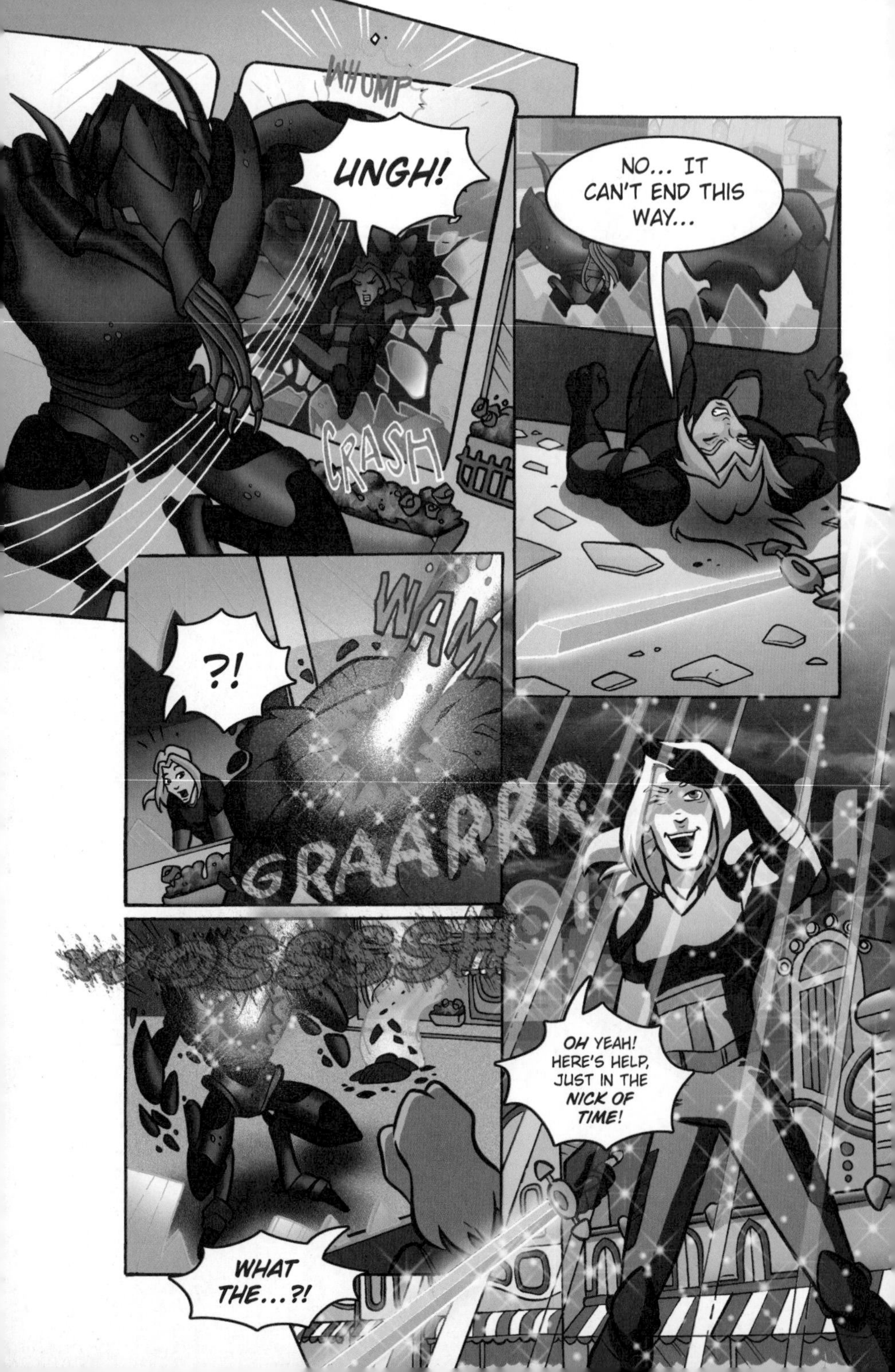
WHUMP
UNGH!
CRASH
NO... IT CAN'T END THIS WAY...
WAM
?!
GRAARRR
OH YEAH! HERE'S HELP, JUST IN THE NICK OF TIME!
WHAT THE...?!

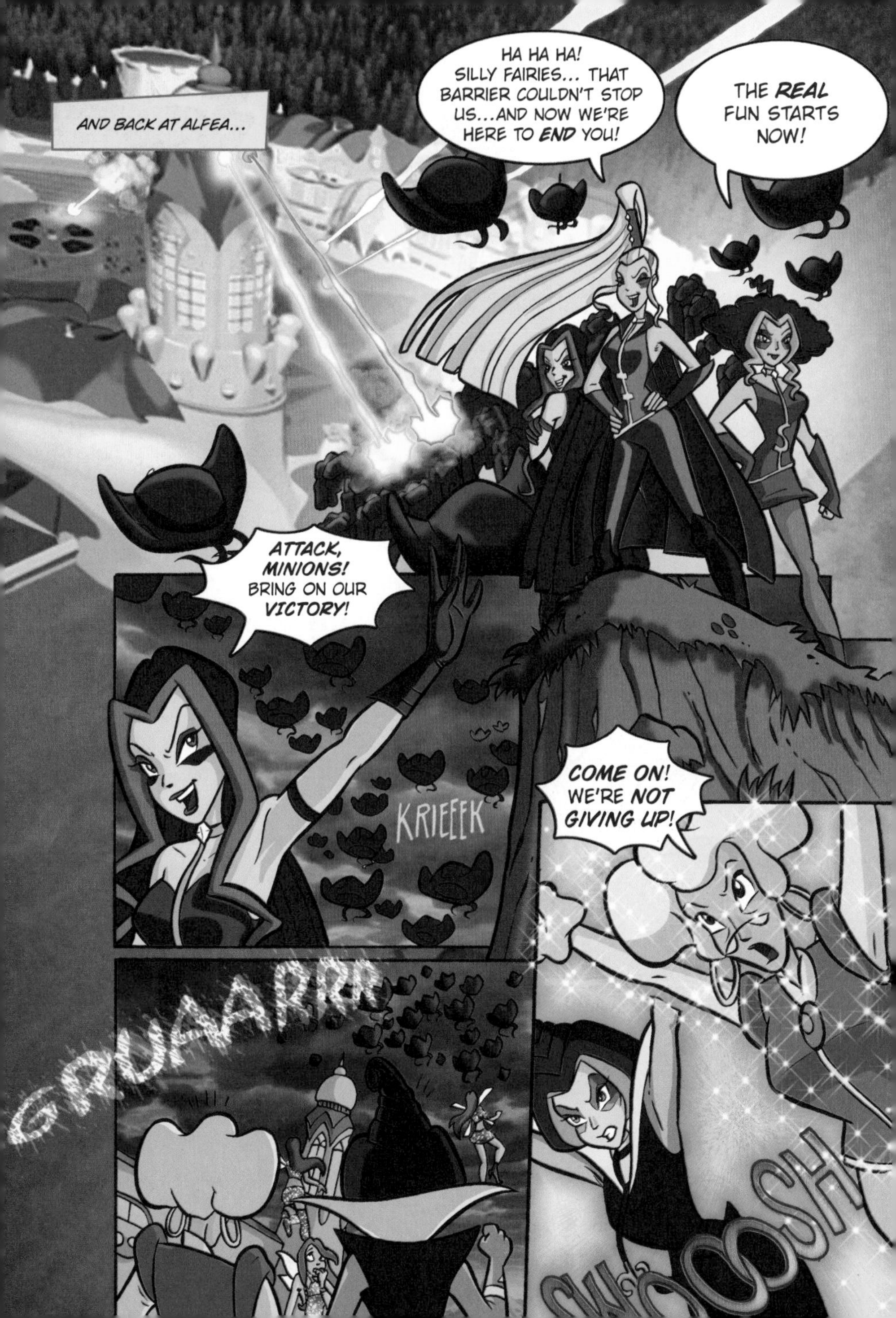
AND BACK AT ALFEA...
HA HA HA! SILLY FAIRIES... THAT BARRIER COULDN'T STOP US...AND NOW WE'RE HERE TO END YOU!
THE REAL FUN STARTS NOW!
ATTACK, MINIONS! BRING ON OUR VICTORY!
KRIEEEK
COME ON! WE'RE NOT GIVING UP!
GRUAARRR
SHOOOSH

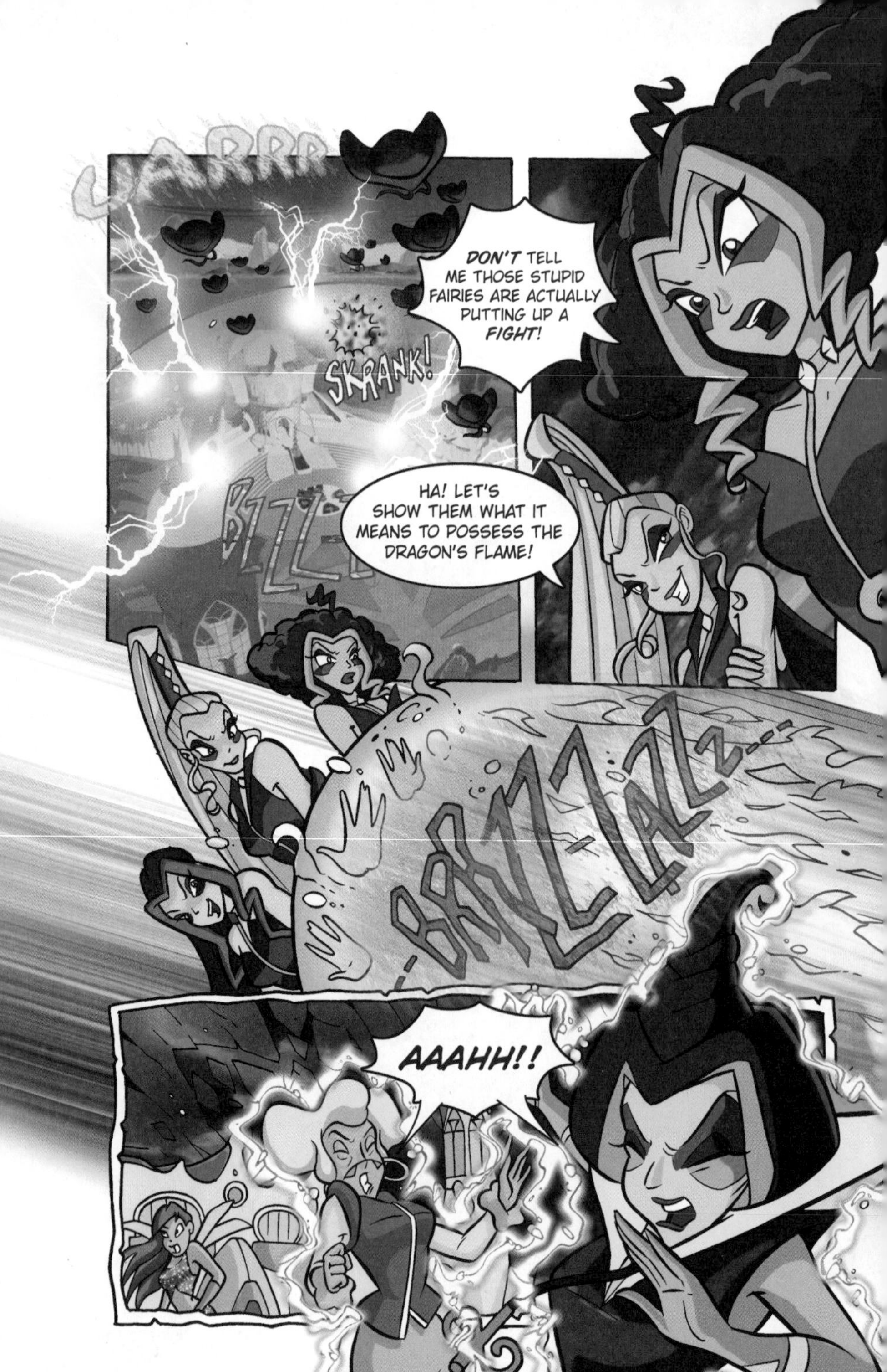
DON'T TELL ME THOSE STUPID FAIRIES ARE ACTUALLY PUTTING UP A FIGHT!
SKRANK!
HA! LET'S SHOW THEM WHAT IT MEANS TO POSSESS THE DRAGON'S FLAME!
AAAHH!!

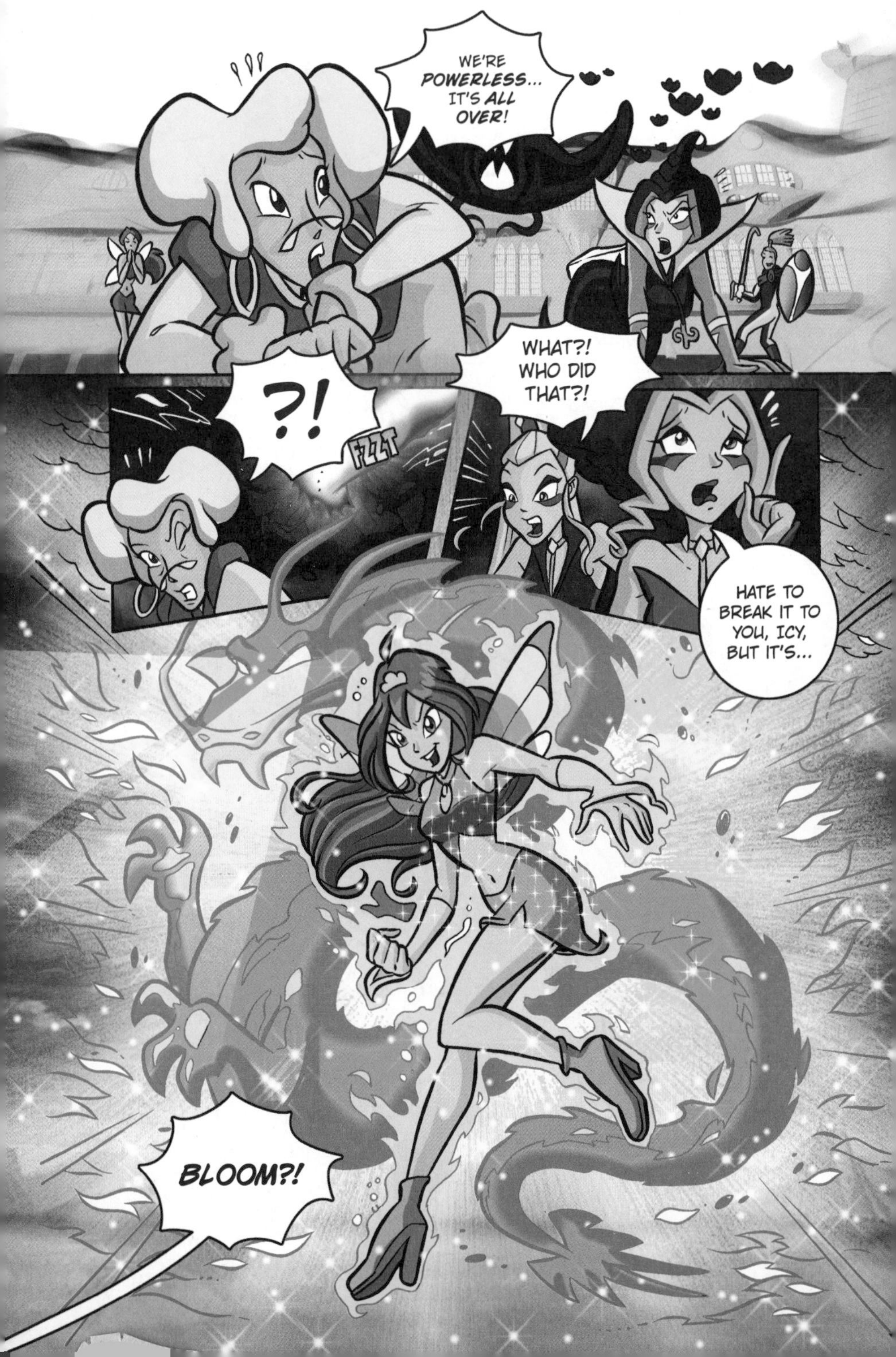
WE'RE POWERLESS... IT'S ALL OVER!
?!
FZZT
WHAT?! WHO DID THAT?!
HATE TO BREAK IT TO YOU, ICY, BUT IT'S...
BLOOM?!

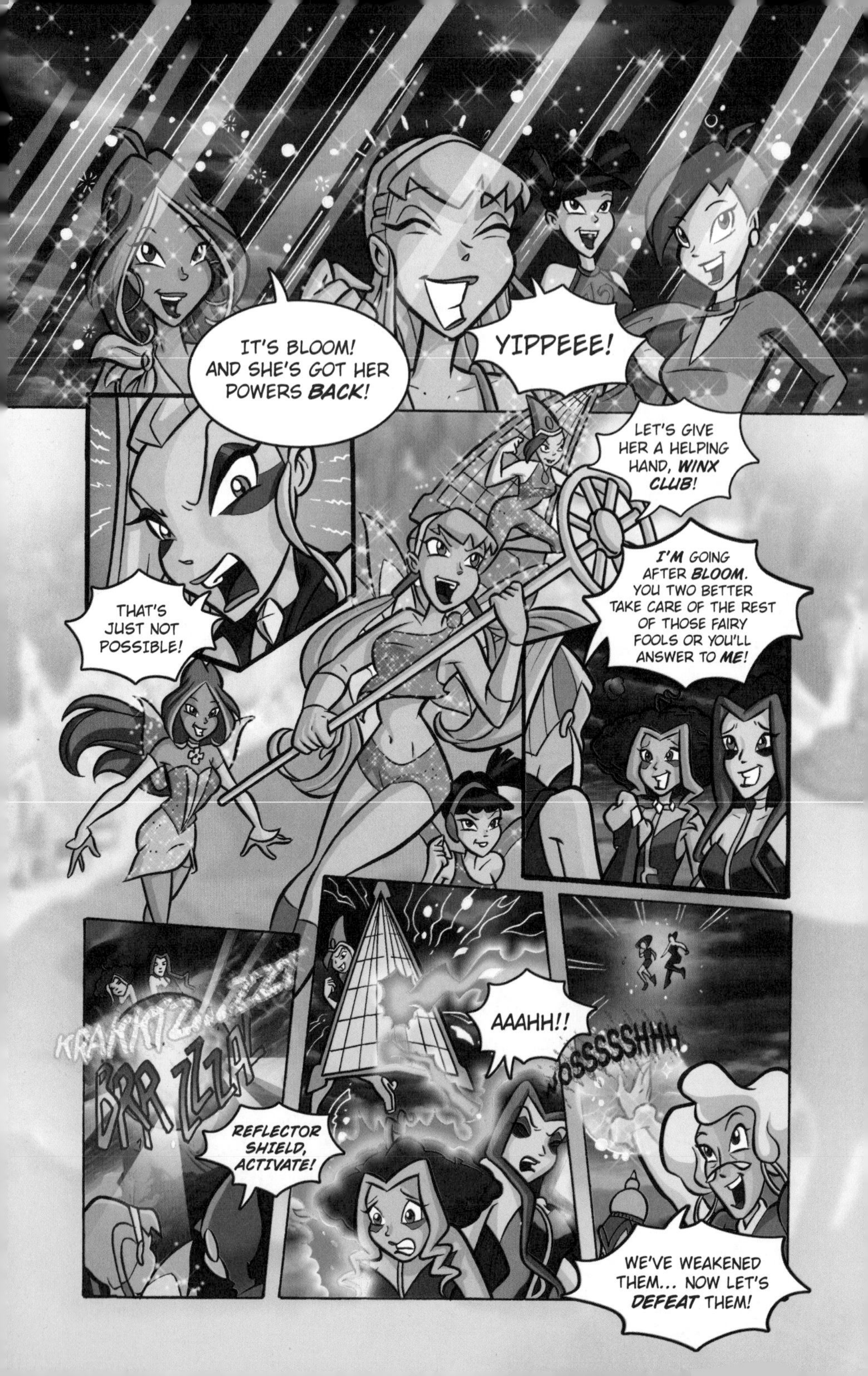

IT'S BLOOM! AND SHE'S GOT HER POWERS *BACK*!
YIPPEEE!
THAT'S JUST NOT POSSIBLE!
LET'S GIVE HER A HELPING HAND, *WINX CLUB*!
I'M GOING AFTER *BLOOM*. YOU TWO BETTER TAKE CARE OF THE REST OF THOSE FAIRY FOOLS OR YOU'LL ANSWER TO *ME*!
KRAKKIZZZZZ
BRR ZZZAK
REFLECTOR SHIELD, ACTIVATE!
AAAHH!!
WOSSSSSHHH
WE'VE WEAKENED THEM... NOW LET'S *DEFEAT* THEM!

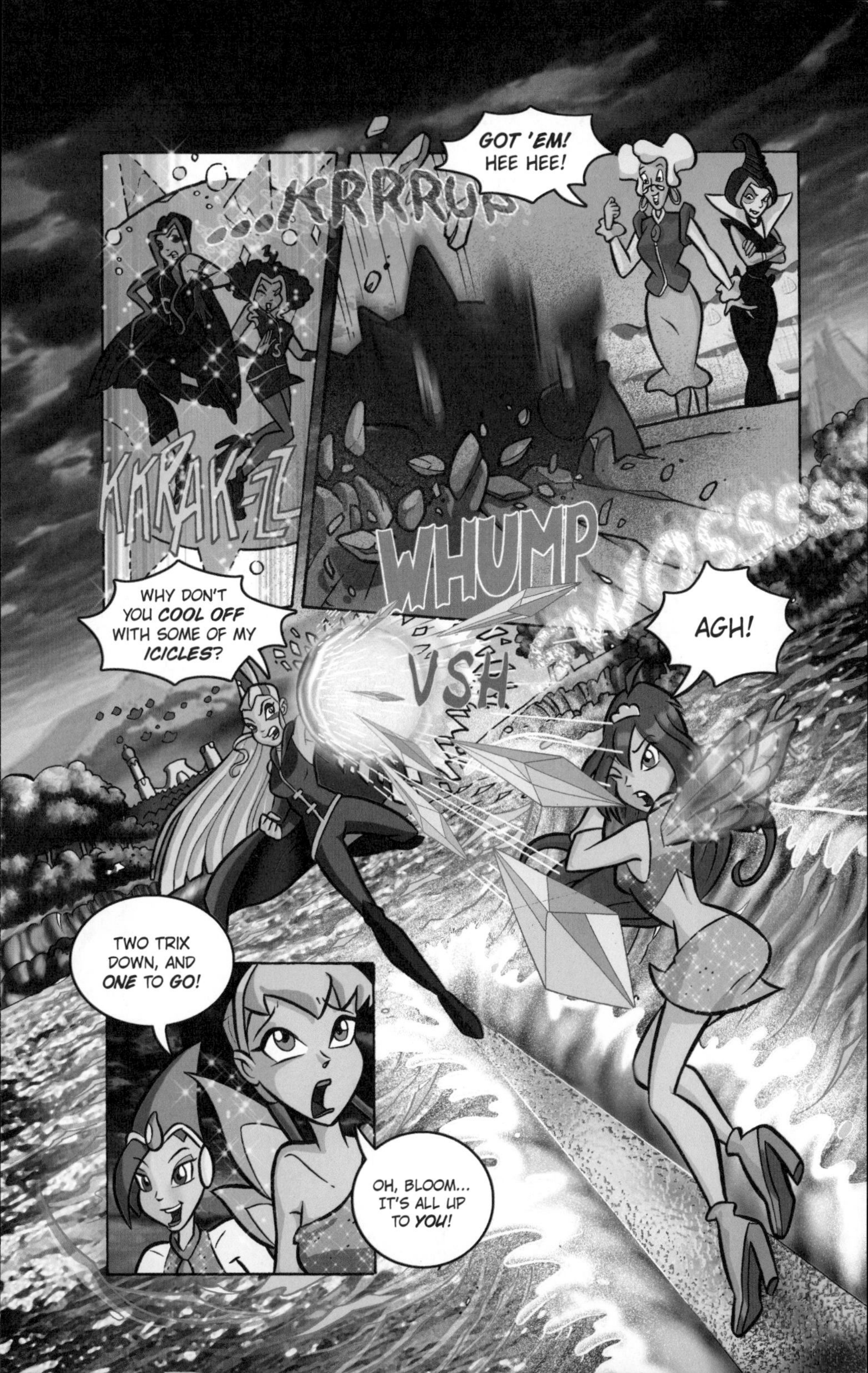
GOT 'EM! HEE HEE!
KRRRRUP
KRRAK-ZZ
WHUMP
WHY DON'T YOU COOL OFF WITH SOME OF MY ICICLES?
VSH
AGH!
TWO TRIX DOWN, AND ONE TO GO!
OH, BLOOM... IT'S ALL UP TO YOU!

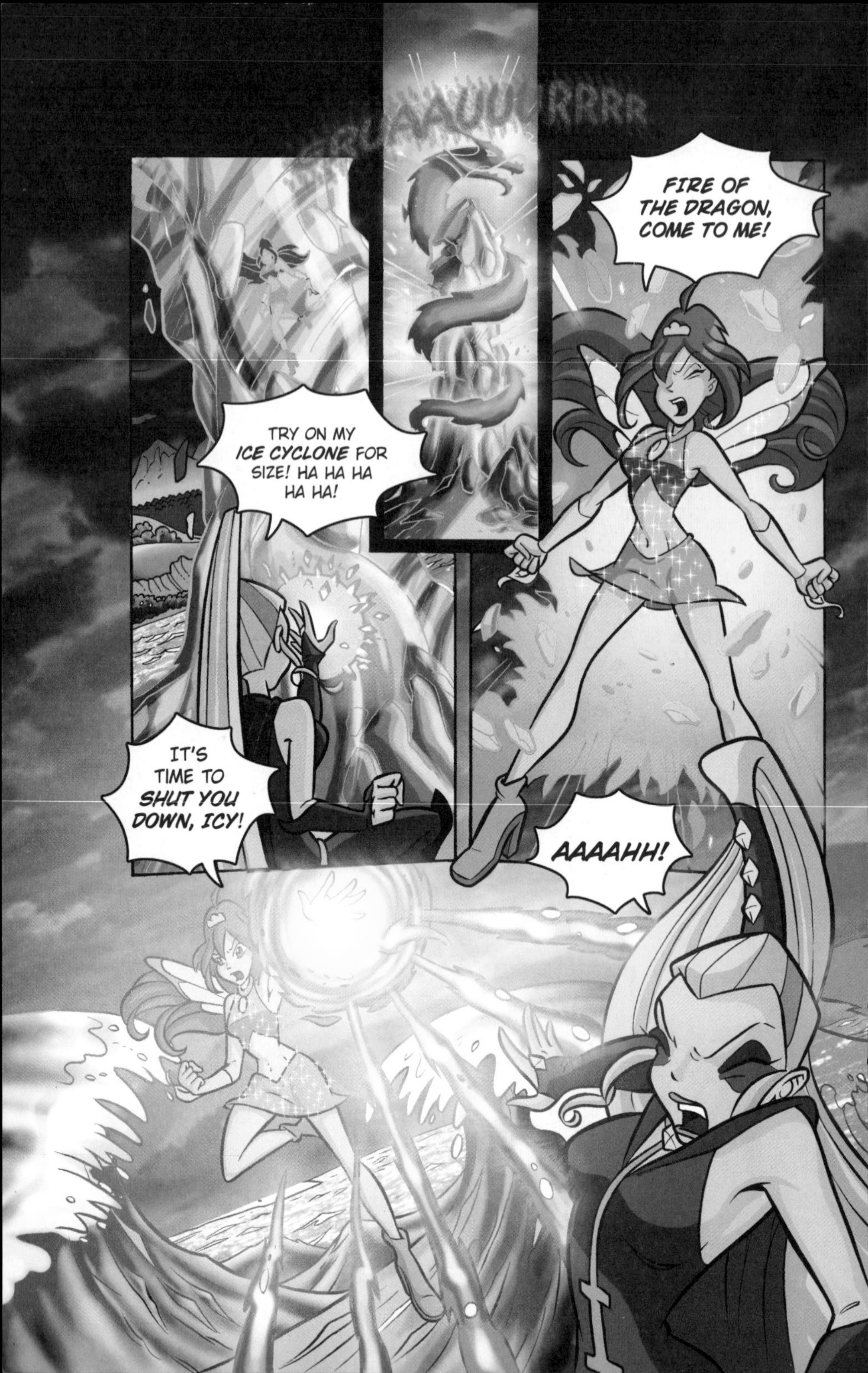
TRY ON MY ICE CYCLONE FOR SIZE! HA HA HA HA HA!
FIRE OF THE DRAGON, COME TO ME!
IT'S TIME TO SHUT YOU DOWN, ICY!
AAAAHH!

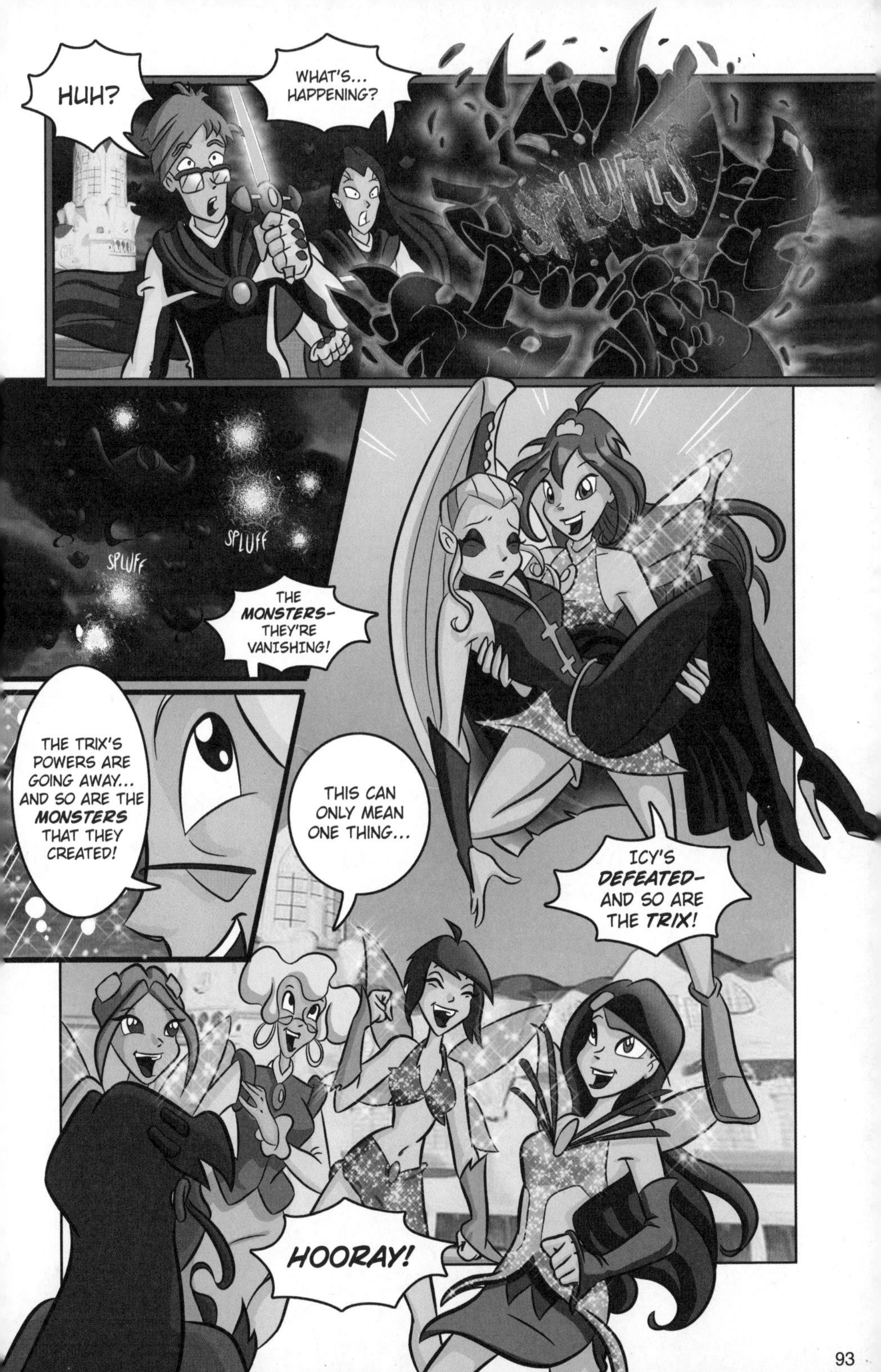
HUH?
WHAT'S... HAPPENING?
SPLUFFS
SPLUFF
SPLUFF
THE MONSTERS- THEY'RE VANISHING!
THE TRIX'S POWERS ARE GOING AWAY... AND SO ARE THE MONSTERS THAT THEY CREATED!
THIS CAN ONLY MEAN ONE THING...
ICY'S DEFEATED- AND SO ARE THE TRIX!
HOORAY!

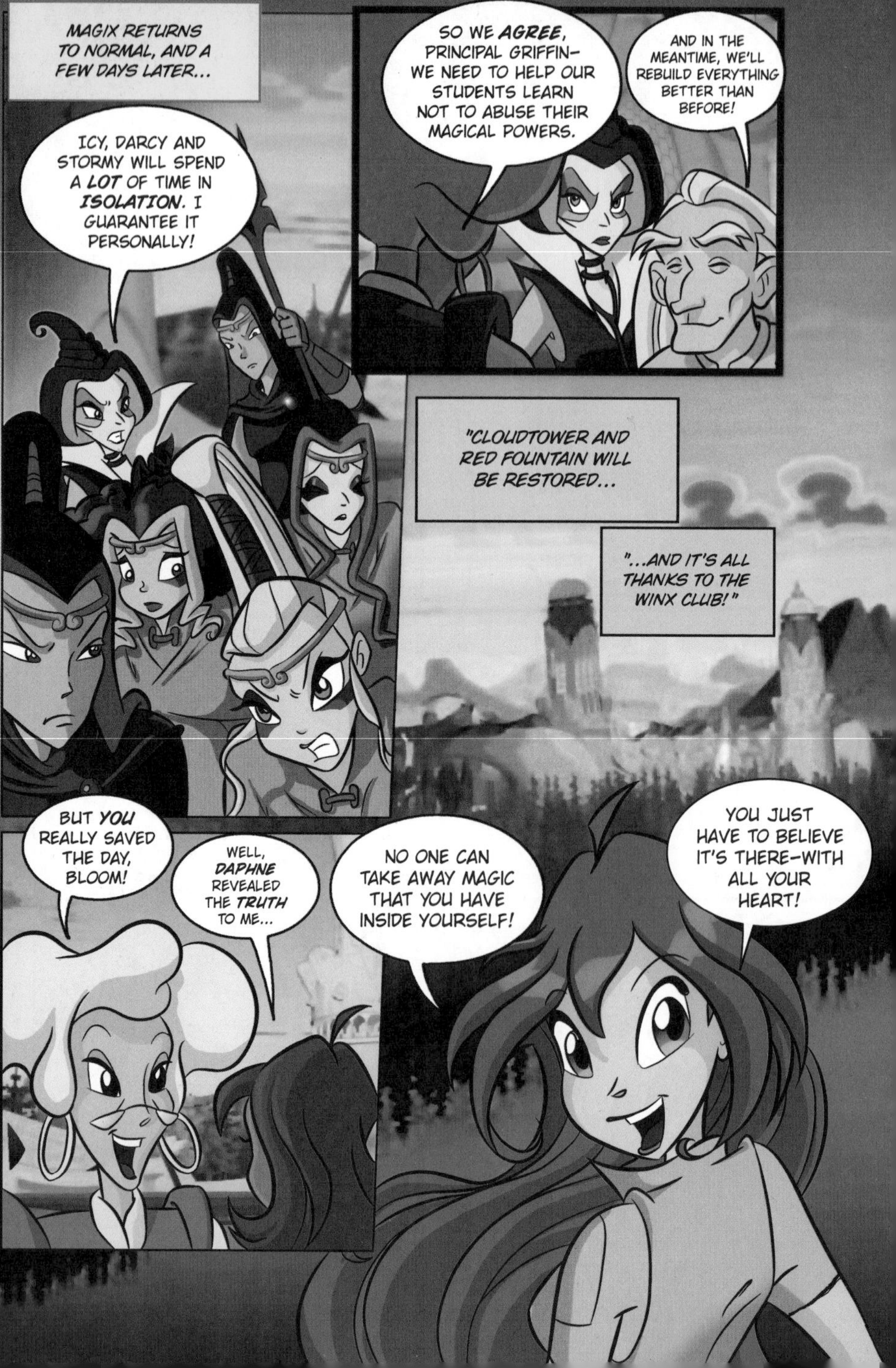
MAGIX RETURNS TO NORMAL, AND A FEW DAYS LATER...
ICY, DARCY AND STORMY WILL SPEND A LOT OF TIME IN ISOLATION. I GUARANTEE IT PERSONALLY!
SO WE AGREE, PRINCIPAL GRIFFIN— WE NEED TO HELP OUR STUDENTS LEARN NOT TO ABUSE THEIR MAGICAL POWERS.
AND IN THE MEANTIME, WE'LL REBUILD EVERYTHING BETTER THAN BEFORE!
"CLOUDTOWER AND RED FOUNTAIN WILL BE RESTORED...
"...AND IT'S ALL THANKS TO THE WINX CLUB!"
BUT YOU REALLY SAVED THE DAY, BLOOM!
WELL, DAPHNE REVEALED THE TRUTH TO ME...
NO ONE CAN TAKE AWAY MAGIC THAT YOU HAVE INSIDE YOURSELF!
YOU JUST HAVE TO BELIEVE IT'S THERE—WITH ALL YOUR HEART!

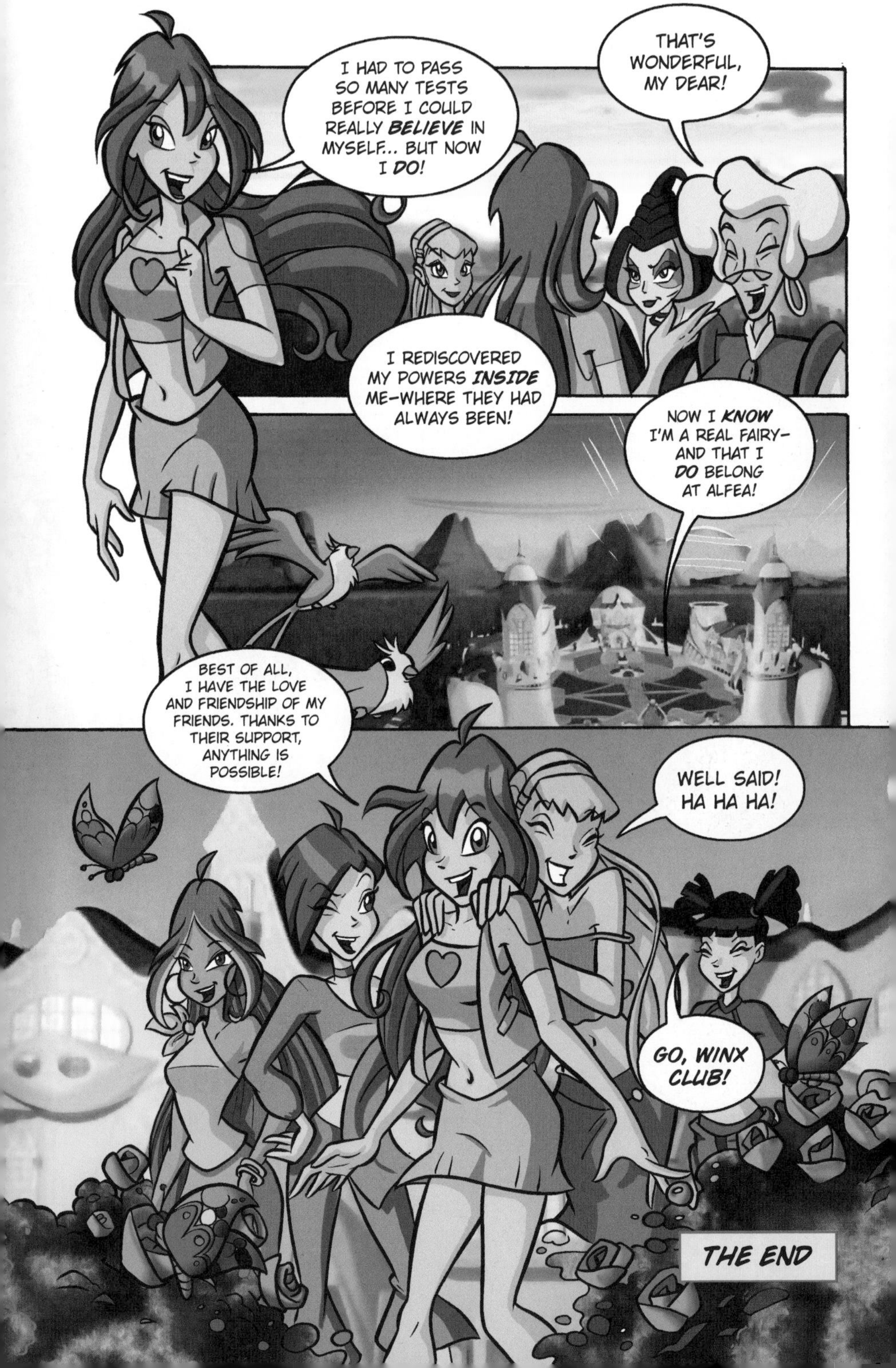
I HAD TO PASS SO MANY TESTS BEFORE I COULD REALLY BELIEVE IN MYSELF... BUT NOW I DO!
THAT'S WONDERFUL, MY DEAR!
I REDISCOVERED MY POWERS INSIDE ME--WHERE THEY HAD ALWAYS BEEN!
NOW I KNOW I'M A REAL FAIRY-- AND THAT I DO BELONG AT ALFEA!
BEST OF ALL, I HAVE THE LOVE AND FRIENDSHIP OF MY FRIENDS. THANKS TO THEIR SUPPORT, ANYTHING IS POSSIBLE!
WELL SAID! HA HA HA!
GO, WINX CLUB!
THE END

Now Available

Winx Club 1
Bloom's Discovery
As seen on nickelodeon
Winx Club 2
Secrets of Alfea
As seen on nickelodeon
Winx Club 3
The Magic of Friendship
As seen on nickelodeon

Look for MORE
Winx Club Adventures
COMING SOON!